Falkirk Council Library Services

This book is due for return on or before the last date noted on the label. Renewals may be obtained on application.

DEATH IN FOUR COURSES

DEATH IN FOUR COURSES

A Key West Food Critic Mystery

Lucy Burdette

CHIVERS

British Library Cataloguing in Publication Data available

This Large Print edition published by AudioGO Ltd, Bath,
2013.
Published by arrangement with NAL, SIGNET, a division of
Penguin Group (USA) Inc.

U.K.   Hardcover   ISBN   978 1 4713 5162 4
U.K.   Softcover   ISBN   978 1 4713 5163 1

This is a work of fiction. Names, characters, places and
incidents are either the product of the author's imagination
or are used fictitiously, and any resemblance to actual
persons, living or dead, business establishments, events or
locales is entirely coincidental

Printed and bound in Great Britain by T J International Limited

For my sister Sue, who never seemed to mind how closely I followed on her heels, and who, like Hayley, is always, always ready for the next meal

ACKNOWLEDGMENTS

Many thanks to Dr. Kiel Christianson for advice on how to think like a food critic, to Mary Kay Hyde for MK's Screw the Roux Stew, Linda Juliani for the fudge pie, and Nikki Bonanni for the gnocchi.

The Key West Literary Seminar provided unlimited inspiration for this book, though any similarities to the seminar staff or the writers who appeared are purely coincidental. Thank you to Arlo Haskell for putting me in touch with Roy Blount Jr. And to Roy Blount Jr. for allowing the use of his perfect little poem "I Like Meat."

Thank you to Steve Torrence, Cory Held, Fritz Ewing, Eric, Bill, and Toby for the use of their names for my utterly fictional characters.

I'm deeply grateful to the usual suspects — Chris Falcone, Ang Pompano, John Brady, Hallie Ephron, Susan Hubbard, Susan Cerulean, and Mike Wiecek — for reading, brainstorming, tweaking, and supporting! Thanks also to Ang for the photo that inspired the book cover of the original edition and last-minute read-through. And a big shout-out to all my mystery writer friends, especially my blog sisters at Jungle Red Writers, Mystery Lovers' Kitchen, and Killer Characters.

Thanks always to Paige Wheeler and the good folks at Folio. Sandy Harding is a terrific editor and advocate — thank you! And thanks to all the other people at NAL/ Penguin, seen and unseen, who've shepherded this book to publication.

A great big thank-you to librarians and booksellers everywhere who put books in the hands of readers, especially Sandy Long, head librarian for forty-one years at the EC Scranton Library in Madison, Connecticut, and Roxanne Coady, founder and owner of RJ Julia Booksellers in Madison.

I lost my father this year. He was an amazing champion of all my dreams. My love and thanks to you, Dad — I miss you every day. . . .

Lucy Burdette
March 2012

Still, his diners are newly accessorizing the table setting: fork on the left, knife on the right, iPhone top center. It's chew and review, toast and post.

— Ike DeLorenzo

1

If you're not at the table, you're on the menu.

— Manuel Rouvelas

My new boss, Wally, slid his glasses down his nose and squinted over the top of the black frames. "Don't even think about coming back with a piece telling us offal is the next big foodie trend," he said. "I don't care what's in style in New York and L.A. We eat grouper and key lime pie in Key West, not entrails." He leaned back in his weathered wicker chair, fronds of faux tropical foliage tickling his hair. "Clear?"

"Aye-aye, Captain." I snapped my heels together and saluted; it wasn't easy to be serious with a man wearing a yellow silk shirt dotted with palm trees. Our company uniform. Which made my complexion look a little sallow, but I would have worn the houseplant and the straw lamp shade that matched the other furniture were those required for the job.

Right before Thanksgiving, I was astonished and grateful to be hired as the food critic for *Key Zest,* the new Key West style magazine. They sure hadn't planned on shelling out big bucks so I could attend the "Key West Loves Literature" seminar barely two months later. But after I explained how most of the top food writers and food critics in the country would be there and we'd look like foodie fools if we missed it, Wally finally caved. With the caveat that I kept up my schedule of local restaurant reviews and wrote a couple of snappy, stylish feature articles about the seminar as well.

At the time, that had all sounded doable. But right now I had big-time nervous jitters about meeting my writing idols and trying to sound smart. And I wished that my Christmas-present brainstorm for my mother had been something other than tuition to this seminar. She was completely thrilled to be visiting here from New Jersey, and who wouldn't feel good about making her mother happy? But for one of my first major (and paid!) journalistic assignments, having my mom tethered to my side felt a little like looking through the oven door at a falling soufflé.

Wally fidgeted with his glasses, opened his mouth once, then closed it again. "Listen. I don't mean to up the ante on this weekend, but I figure you're a grown woman and you should know."

My heart thunked to my gullet and despite the warm, dry air in the office, I felt cold. "Know what?"

"Ava Faulkner has been pressuring me — she's trolling for a reason to let you go."

My eyes bulged. Ava was Kristen Faulkner's sister — the sister of the woman who'd stolen my boyfriend last fall and then gotten herself murdered. "But why? She can't still think I killed Kristen. That's all been settled."

Wally smoothed a hand across his desk blotter. "She's not a rational woman, Hayley. But since she owns more than fifty percent of the magazine, I have to listen to her. It's just — I need your very best work this weekend." He looked up and met my gaze. "If you can come up with something exclusive, like an interview with the keynote, all the better."

"Thanks for the heads-up. Gotta go pick up Mom." I saluted again, but my limbs felt boneless and my smile wouldn't work. I'd e-mailed the main speaker at least four times to request a meeting, with less than

13

stellar results.

I sucked in a big breath and ran downstairs to catch the waiting cab, determined to push Wally's warning out of my brain before it reduced me to gelatin. My mother's parental radar would pick up on the tiniest nick in my facade, and her worries would start seeping into my mind like water into cement sidewalk cracks. And then she'd spend the weekend working on me to move back home. Not going to happen.

Since I didn't own a car, I'd considered picking Mom up on my scooter. But her terror of motorcycles dissuaded me, and besides, she didn't travel light. I'd seen a lot bulkier loads carried on a scooter in this town than two women with an oversized suitcase — like the guy who passed me on White Street with two golden retrievers strapped to the back of his bike and one draped across his lap. But I could still picture my bungee cords snapping and the suitcase bursting, spreading Mom's private essentials through the city streets for the homeless to pick over. Instead I slid into the backseat of a bright pink station wagon that smelled a little funky, even for a taxi. Then I noticed the oversized green parrot riding shotgun in the front, the *Key West Citizen* spread out to contain his droppings.

14

"Where ya headed?" the bird squawked.

"To the airport," I said after a few seconds of stunned silence.

"Got visitors coming?" asked the cabbie as he gunned his engine, swerving around a golf cart full of whooping kids. The parrot lost his footing and tumbled, cursing, into the passenger seat.

"My mother," I said, watching the bird edge sideways across the newspaper on the seat and climb back onto his perch. He pecked at a few feathers that had been dislodged in the fall, then swiveled his neck around to glare at me.

The cabbie's eyes, brimming with sympathy, met mine in the rearview mirror. "Mom came to visit the first year I moved down," he said. "Once she saw my apartment door off its hinges, leaning against the wall in the hallway next to all the empty beer bottles, she turned around and went back home."

The taxi sped up Atlantic Boulevard, the road that hugs the outer edge of the island, lined with swaying palms and the bluest ocean on the whole East Coast. As we drove along parallel to the bike path, we passed the usual parade of outdoor enthusiasts — two well-tanned Rollerbladers in bikinis, a man being pulled on his bike by a large black dog, sunbathers crowding the ice

15

cream and hot dog trucks parked alongside the road.

Like most things in the city, the Key West Airport is easy to maneuver. The taxi driver let me out and pointed to the small parking lot where he and his parrot would be waiting. I went inside and parked myself near the baggage claim, flipping through the displays of tourism pamphlets racked against the back wall. Minutes later, the puddle jumper from Miami skidded to a halt and the passengers poured out and filed across the tarmac, their boots and wool jackets contrasting with the short sleeves and flip-flops of the people waiting. Mom burst through the sliding glass doors, wearing enormous sunglasses and dragging a pink plaid bag.

"Hayley Elizabeth!" she squealed, flinging her arms around me. "I can't believe I'm here! It was so stunning flying over the islands."

"I know, I know," I said, hugging her back.

"My girl." She held me at arm's length to get a good look. "You gorgeous thing." She smiled until the skin crinkled around her eyes, and patted my curls — the same auburn as hers only messier — and then stashed her glasses in her purse. "Which way to the ladies'? Will you keep track of

16

this while I run in?" She passed the carry-on to me. "The big bag looks just like this one. A matching set — like you and me."

She grinned and click-clacked across the room in her smart silver sandals and wrinkle-free pantsuit. Light-years from my palm tree shirt and red sneakers, which I knew she'd noticed.

Once we'd wrestled her enormous bag off the luggage carousel, we rolled it out to the cab, where I introduced her to the driver and his pet bird. He hoisted the bags into the trunk and we set off.

"Excuse me, cabbie," Mom said, once the car was in motion. "I just arrived from New Jersey. Would you mind turning off the air-conditioning and opening the windows?" Once he complied, she leaned out and snapped a succession of photos. "Hayley, can you smell that salt air? Did you tell me how pretty it was here?"

I grinned back at her. "I think I did, Mom."

"So, what's our plan tonight?"

"You have just enough time to say hello to Eric and Bill, unpack your stuff, and get showered and changed. I'm going to nip over to the conference a little early to get my bearings and stake out good seats."

My old friend Eric and his partner, Bill,

had graciously offered to put up my mother for the weekend in their guest room. She never would have let me spring for a motel, but on the other hand, I shared a tiny houseboat with a lovely older woman. Shoehorn my mother into that small space and I would have been diving overboard within twenty-four hours. Maybe twelve, with the extra pressure I was feeling. The taxi pulled up in front of Eric and Bill's house, a cerulean blue one-story with green wicker chairs on the wide front porch and a secret garden in the backyard.

Bill, Eric's partner of seven years — a tall, thin man dressed in black jeans and a white turtleneck — waved at us from a hammock strung across the far end of the porch. Their schedules hadn't allowed for them to sign up for the whole food writing seminar, but they were excited about attending the opening party. And visiting with Mom. Eric had grown up in the same New Jersey town as I had, only seven years ahead and on the shabbier fringe of our neighborhood.

The front door burst open, releasing a yapping ball of gray-and-brown fur — Toby. Eric followed him out, cleaning his tortoiseshell glasses on his white oxford shirt. Mom leaped out of the taxi and dashed up the walk.

"When's the last time I saw you?" Mom asked, squeezing Eric's cheeks between her palms and pulling his head down so she could plant a kiss on his forehead. "Your mother wanted me to remind you to call her this week."

He shook his head and rolled his eyes, draping his arm around her shoulders.

"Mothers," he said to me as I came up the walk with the luggage. "They can never get enough."

"And don't forget that," Mom said with a laugh. "We spend the rest of our lives trying to gather you back in once you kids leave the womb." We all chuckled, but I knew a good fifty percent of her wasn't kidding.

"You remember Bill," Eric said. Bill hugged my mother too and then reached for her suitcase.

"Are you wearing this to the conference?" Mom asked, fingering my yellow shirt and then looking down at my red sneakers as we climbed the stairs to the porch.

"She has no faith in me at all," I said to the men, and then over my shoulder to Mom in the most pleasant voice I could manage: "These are my work clothes. I'm changing too." I held up my backpack as evidence.

"We're so glad you felt comfortable staying with us," said Eric. "I'll show you your room and you can get freshened up. If you're hungry, we made a batch of Bill's special strawberry-rhubarb coffee cake."

"That sounds heavenly," said Mom. "I've never tried it with strawberries."

"I'll take her back to the room," I said, and rolled the monster suitcase down the hall to the guest room.

"He doesn't look well," said my mother in a stage whisper once we got to the bedroom.

"Who doesn't look well?"

"Eric," she said. "He looks tired. Did you notice the lines around his eyes?"

"I think he's fine," I told her, and started out of her room. "We're all getting a little older and it can't help showing on our faces, right? One of the guys will walk you down to Duval Street when you're ready." I retreated to the bathroom, changed quickly, and yelled good-bye to my mother.

"Good luck." Eric came out of the kitchen and tucked a small package into my pack. "I wrapped you up a piece of cake, in case of emergency."

I leaned in to kiss his cheek, looking for signs of the strain my mother thought she'd noticed. A little peaked, maybe the end of a long week. "Thanks for everything."

20

A block down from the white stucco San Carlos Institute Building with its fancy Spanish railings, the usual suspects geared up for a night of Duval Street decadence. A gaggle of teenagers in skimpy clothes a little too cool for the night taunted one another in front of the adjoining empty storefront, looking like they'd started drinking well before happy hour. Two fried-to-a-crisp couples giggled at the gross quotations featuring personal body parts on the T-shirts in the shop next door to that. And the homeless man with his poorly tuned guitar and singing pit bull draped in Mardi Gras beads had set up on a blue blanket on his regular corner, ready to serenade the pass-ersby. A handwritten sign explained that tourists could have their pictures taken with the dog — for five bucks.

Everything is for sale in Key West — for the right price.

I trudged the last hundred feet to the institute, one half of me thrilled about be-ing here and the other half terrified. Three white arches funneled a bejeweled crowd buzzing with excitement into an enormous anteroom tiled in dizzying black and white.

A bookstore had been set up in the alcove off to the left, loaded with stacks of books written by the weekend's presenters. Both of the cash registers *ching*ed merrily.

Just past the marble statue of José Martí at the entrance to the auditorium, I flashed my press ID badge to a seminar volunteer and hurried down the right aisle to grab two places as close to the front as I could manage. Sinking into an upholstered seat, I studied the stage, draped in red velvet like a faded drag queen at the Aqua Nightclub. I would kill to be up there: one of the foodie experts expounding on how to write about the latest trends. But right now I felt more like I belonged on that ratty street corner blanket with the howling dog.

I flipped through the program and found the write-up about the keynote speaker, Jonah Barrows. Could he possibly look as good in person as he had in the *New York Times* style magazine photo shoot last fall? For a guy who'd survived a stint as a restaurant critic for the snooty *Guide Bouchée* and then moved on to take first Los Angeles and then New York City by storm — a tsunami of foodie controversy — he looked thin, young, and unscathed. On the printed page anyway.

Spotting my mother at the entrance to the

auditorium, I waved her down the aisle. She slid into the seat beside me and reached over to pinch closed the V-neckline of my white shirt and then smooth the drape of the pink polka-dotted sweater I'd layered over it. Eyes narrowing, her gaze slid down my khaki stretch pants to the Libby Edelman jeweled sandals she had mailed ahead of time as a thank-you gift for the weekend. I'd never tell her, but I already had blisters on the backs of my heels from the short walk over from Bill and Eric's home.

"Aren't they pretty?" she asked, and then tried to tuck some curls behind my ear.

I grinned and shook my head. She was always dressed for success — in this case a brown suede jacket, narrow tweed trousers, and her own auburn curls gathered into a gold barrette — and ever-hopeful that I'd pick up her sense of style in more than the kitchen. She whipped out a camera from her handbag and snapped three blinding photos of me in succession.

She was about to tap another patron's shoulder to ask that she take a picture of the two of us when the heavyset director of the seminar bustled onto the stage, faced the audience, and threw his arms open.

"I'm Dustin Fredericks! Welcome to the greatest literary house party of the year!"

The crowd roared with enthusiasm, including a loud and embarrassing hip-hip-hooray from my mother. Once the noise died down, Dustin went on to thank the program committee, the volunteers, and the many others who'd worked so hard on organizing the conference.

"The mayor regrets she can't be here tonight to award the seminar the honorary five-parrot seal of approval." More polite clapping. And then he began to read a proclamation from the honorary mayor of Key West, Mayor Gonzo Mays, chock-full of "whereases" and "heretofores."

"Is he ever going to introduce Jonah?" asked the lady in front of us whose silver pompadour partly obscured my view of the podium. "I'm absolutely starving. We should have eaten before we came."

"It'll be worth the wait," said her companion. "When you're trying to impress four hundred foodies and food writers, you can't serve anything that isn't fabulous." She kissed the tips of her fingers and blew that imaginary kiss toward the stage. "I just know they'll have shrimp, piles and piles of Key West pinks . . ."

My mother leaned forward, one hand on the velvet seat back in front of her, the other gently gripping the first woman's shoulder.

"Shhhhh," she said.

I sank lower into my upholstered seat. But it wasn't just those ladies rustling and whispering — the audience was whirring with anticipation, as if they couldn't wait for the real show to start, as if they expected pyrotechnics and hoped to blow past Dustin's preliminaries to get there. Would Mom try to shush them all?

"I know you didn't come all the way to Key West to listen to me," Dustin was saying from the stage. "So I am thrilled to introduce our keynote speaker, a man who truly needs no introduction."

"But you'll give one anyway," I muttered.

My mother took my hand and pulled it onto her lap. "Oh, sweetie. Let him have his moment."

She was right — as usual. But still I rolled my eyes and squeezed her fingers back a little harder than I meant to.

"Jonah Barrows has had four major culinary careers in the time most of us have only managed one. His mother once reported that he had a highly sensitive palate right out of the womb — he would only suckle organic goat's milk."

The audience tittered. How completely embarrassing, the kind of thing a mother might say. Mine, in fact, was chuckling loudly. "Remember when you'd only eat strained carrots and your skin turned yellow from too much carotene?"

"Mom, stop," I hissed.

"Mr. Barrows was a restaurant critic for the highly esteemed *Guide Bouchée* for his first four years out of Columbia. No one — I repeat, no one — lands that job as a twenty-two-year-old. At twenty-six, he co-owned and managed the three-star restaurant *Manger Bien* in Los Angeles before he was lured to the *New York Times* to write their food column for the young at heart, 'See and Be Scene.' And his memoir, *You Must Try the Skate . . . and Other Utterly Foolish Things Foodies Say,* has gone to its third printing, even though it went on sale only today! *People* magazine named him a national culinary treasure, a wunderkind who will shape the way Americans eat for decades. The *Washington Post* called him the most frightening man to scorch the food scene since Michael Pollan. Without further ado, I ask you to welcome Jonah Barrows."

Then the stage curtains swept open, revealing a facsimile of the interior of an old diner — cracked red-and-black leather booths, Formica tabletops balanced on steel posts, fake carnations drooping from cheap cut-glass vases. All we needed was big floppy menus stained with tomato sauce and a worn-faced waitress asking, "What'll it be, hon?"

Jonah strode across the stage, waving a graceful hand at the crowd, grinning broadly, clad in tight black trousers, cowboy boots, and a gorgeous orange linen shirt. The other panelists for the weekend trickled along in his wake, taking seats at the booths and tables of the faux diner. When they were settled, Jonah clasped the director in a bear hug and maneuvered him toward the wings in a fluid two-step. Then he blew a kiss to the audience, who clapped vigorously, finally working itself into a standing ovation.

Jonah waved us down. "I am honored to kick off this weekend. It's hard to know where to begin — it's customary, I believe, to be positive in a speech like this." He flashed a lopsided, regretful grin, teeth eggshell white against his tan. Then he turned to face the food writers seated behind him.

"But I have decided instead to opt for honesty. We have traveled so far from the basics of food and food writing where I feel we belong. We have competitive cooking shows featuring chefs oozing testosterone. We have food critics getting outed by disgruntled restaurateurs using a rush of Twitter posts and Facebook photos." He bounced across the stage to clasp the shoulder of an impish man and ruffle his dark hair.

"I think that's the food critic Frank Bruni," my mother said under her breath.

Jonah moved on to buss the cheek of a heavyset woman in a flowered silk dress who had squeezed into the booth beside Bruni. Mom paged through the head shots in her program. "That has to be the novelist Sigrid Gustafson," Mom whispered, tapping the page. "She must have used 'an early photo.' LOL."

"Mom, behave!" I whispered back.

Jonah continued to wind through the seated panelists, gallantly kissing the hand of a petite Asian woman, massaging the shoulders of a stunning woman in black with a grand sweep of white-gold hair. Finally he returned to the lectern.

"We have message boards brimming with blustering amateurs and unsuspecting diners following them like rats after Pied Pipers into the bowels of dreadful eateries. We have ridiculous modernism overtaking plain good food. Let's face facts." He pounded on the podium, his voice soaring several decibels with each word. "This is one hell of a challenging time to write about food — or even to choose a restaurant meal! We can't afford a fluffy weekend seminar focused on extolling recipes and patting the backs of our illustrious guest writers. They must be held accountable for every word they write."

The audience lurched into a second ragged standing ovation. Several of the panelists seated in the diner whispered to one another. Dustin hovered in the wings, just off stage left, looking as though he might explode into the spotlight and drag Jonah off. Or explode, period.

"Please sit," Jonah begged us. He strode to the center of the stage, his own golden hair glinting in the stage lights. Too perfect to be natural, I thought. "I promise, you'll be exhausted by the end of the night. And you must save some energy for the awesome opening party. And there's so much more coming this weekend."

As we took our seats again, he headed back to the podium and adjusted his notes.

"In my opinion, today's food writers are listing toward endorsing the esoteric and precious and superexpensive. Of course, if we wait long enough, the trends will circle back around. We'll be reading about mountains of creamy mashed potatoes and pot roast that melts into its gravy instead of musk ox sprinkled with elderberries and served on twigs. But while we wait, isn't it our job to call the emperor on his nakedness? Must we endure, or even encourage, the bizarre and the inedible?"

He pivoted to the panelists behind him and opened his arms. The food writers squirmed, their smiles frozen in place.

"He's absolutely right," said the woman in front of us.

Jonah clicked one leather-clad heel against the other and spun back to the audience. "I say no. Which is why I feel I must address the 'best of' restaurant lists. My God, what does it mean when a meal in the number one restaurant in the world costs in the neighborhood of six hundred dollars and is gathered from the woods nearby? *The woods,* people. And can someone spare us from Twitter-driven hyperbole in restaurants' popularity? Since when do untrained palates get to tell us what's good? Since when is everyone a critic?"

He paused, for what seemed like minutes, the auditorium deathly silent. He was asking for trouble — the hoi polloi loved to wax on about what they ate. And many of them were warming the seats of this auditorium. And the writers who produced the reviews he was criticizing sat right on the stage with him. Except for me, of course. I was too new and too green to get invited.

"Here's what I think. Critics must push forward to take their territory back from the amateurs. We professionals cannot abandon this job to the Chowhounds and Yelp boarders."

"What the heck's a Yelp boarder?" asked the lady in front of us.

"It's a restaurant review Web site," Mom said. "Shhhh." The lady turned around and looked dagger death eyes at us as Jonah continued.

"Because A, many of these people have no training. And B, they have all kinds of agendas aside from criticizing food. People are making money by posting reviews. And others are being discouraged from telling the truth by chefs and owners. So we — the professionals in this business — must be excruciatingly honest. If we shy away from criticizing bad or ridiculous food, if we only publish positive reviews, do our words not become worthless?"

Jonah tapped his notes on the podium and frowned.

"From the restaurant perspective — and as Dustin mentioned, I've walked a mile in those moccasins too — when an establishment chooses to open, they must take the

31

chance of negative publicity. It's like publishing a book — reviews ensue. When a meal leaves the kitchen, the chef leaves himself open for criticism."

Onstage behind Jonah, the heavyset woman who had Frank Bruni pinned to a corner of one of the booths harrumphed loudly and muttered something to the lady across the table.

"I can sum the problem up quickly. Honesty is lacking from public figures," said Jonah. "I can't fix national politics." He clapped his hand to his heart and heaved a sigh.

"You can say that again," said the woman in front of Mom.

"But we can start right here in the food world. I've learned this as I've prepared to tour the country with my new book — telling the truth and encouraging my colleagues to do the same has freed me up in ways I never imagined."

He ran a hand over his chin, the blond stubble of a new beard glinting in the spotlight. "You people — our public — deserve the curtains pulled back, not only on the food you eat and the professionals who prepare it, but also on the people who criticize and write about it." He wheeled around again to face the faux diner. "Writers and critics — and you know who you are — you must step up to a higher standard. Food is not just about eating. Food is the very soul of our country."

His voice grew softer. "I am *so* looking forward to the panel discussions and to all my conversations over this fabulous weekend. Caveat emptor — my policy of utter transparency will be in full effect."

I finally took a breath.

2

You do not, of course, want to be responsible for the death of your guests, but sometimes it seems that they will be the death of you.

— Laurie Colwin

Like all of the other four-hundred-plus attendees at the opening, I was dying for a drink by the time Jonah Barrows finished his lecture. I suspected some of them were thirsty for blood as well, and I hated to miss one second of the fireworks. But Mom had other ideas: a leisurely stroll down the busiest blocks of Duval Street with her camera in action on the way over to the reception at the Audubon House. She chattered nonstop the whole way.

Had I seen the woman with the mop of curly hair in the back row of the onstage diner? That had to be Ruth Reichl. And the small adorable man with dimples and dark

34

hair? Definitely Frank Bruni, another former restaurant critic for the *New York Times*. No one seemed to last long in that position. Maybe criticizing restaurants ruined eating for them? What a shame it would be if that same thing happened to me! Anyway, she'd recognize him anywhere — except he was smaller than she'd imagined for a man with such a grand writing voice. She loved him sight unseen for the way he loved his mother. And Billy Collins, former poet laureate, he looked — well, just like a real person. She could not wait to get books signed by each of them. And she could not wait to see how Jonah challenged each of those writers. From the grimacing and rustling on the stage behind him, it sure looked like it was going to be a lively weekend.

And she was thrilled with the weather — maybe seventy degrees with a breeze just strong enough to rattle the palms overhead. And a full moon that would have cast lovely shadows, had we not been walking down brightly lit Duval Street. She stopped to take a photo of the moon centered exactly above the cross that topped the white concrete of St. Paul's Church.

"Did I tell you we're expecting our first snow in New Jersey this weekend?" she asked. "Not just a dusting either."

"You did, Mom," I said.

I listened to her with one ear while trying to formulate a pithy summary of Jonah Barrows's remarks and then a worthy journalistic response. Wally would expect something, if not tonight, certainly by tomorrow morning. And it couldn't be first-draft gibberish either. Not with Ava looking over his shoulder.

Jonah had sacrificed a lot of sacred cows: amateurs on food boards and their Twitter-driven hysteria, endorsement of precious foodie trends, lack of transparency and fortitude from chefs and the writers following them. In forty-five minutes, he'd managed to spurn most of the cutting-edge trends in the food world. And some of them well deserved it. What could I possibly add to his brilliant dissection? And would I have a strong enough stomach anyway? And whom exactly did he plan to wrestle to the mud over the next two days? And how could I summarize it in a way that would beat back the threat of getting canned by Ava Faulkner?

"Do you think we'll get a chance to meet Jonah in person?" Mom asked.

"I e-mailed him and tried to set up an interview, but he's got a very busy weekend," I said. "He told me to look out for him at the party. Fingers and toes crossed he has a spare minute." I held up my crossed digits and laughed.

She crossed her fingers too and smiled, then grabbed my elbow. "Hayley, wait! Isn't this the bar Hemingway used to drink in after he finished writing for the day?"

My mom stopped in front of Sloppy Joe's, where the noise roared out onto the street. Sunburned customers clustered around the tables covered with plastic tankards of beer and baskets of french fries and burgers. My stomach growled and I thought wistfully of Eric's rhubarb crumb cake. More people spilled onto the sidewalk to smoke and drink more beer. A trio of ponytailed men in tropical shirts played aggressive, pulse-pounding rock music on electric guitars at the far end of the bar. I'd never set foot in this place and I doubted that Hemingway would have enjoyed it either.

"Let me get your picture here," Mom said, pushing me toward the painted sign that read "Established in 1933" and sighting through her viewfinder. "Now smile!" She snapped four quick photos.

"Hey, what's that?" She pointed to a camera fastened to the underside of the roof overhanging the sidewalk.

"It's the Duval Street webcam, Mom," I said. "They have it mounted on their Web site so people who aren't in town can see what they're missing. Remember when I first moved here last fall, I wanted you to watch it but it wouldn't load on your computer? Let's get moving. I have a lot people I'd like to meet. And wouldn't it be awful if they ran out of wine?"

"Or food," said my mother, tucking her camera into her handbag and trotting ahead of me up the street.

By the time we reached the Audubon House, a long line of hungry people snaked out of the gated white picket fence onto the Whitehead Street sidewalk. The ladies Mom had chastised in the auditorium — twice — were just ahead of us.

"What is this a line for anyway?" asked the woman with the helmet of silver hair.

"The bar," answered the other. "You would think they could plan better. This is not relaxing."

A waiter in a white shirt passed by with a platter of shrimp toast.

"Smile!" said Mom to the waiter as she took his picture. I managed to snag two pieces just before the plate was snatched clean by the unhappy woman in front of us.

Mom nibbled at hers and pronounced it delicious.

"I think they used fresh dill. And the mayo is definitely homemade. Oh, Hayley" — she learned over to kiss my cheek, her hazel eyes bright with sudden tears — "I'm having so much fun already."

I looked up from the notes on my smartphone and smiled. "I'm glad." I felt a needle of regret that I wasn't enjoying having her as much as she was enjoying being here. I swore to myself that I'd try harder not to allow my nerves or my reactions to her well-intentioned motherly ministrations ruin the visit. As we inched forward toward the bar, the pressure on my bladder grew intense.

"Mom," I said, "I'm going to run to the ladies' room. Will you hold my stuff?"

I handed her the canvas bag containing my phone, notebook, wallet, program, and the press copy of Jonah's book I'd brought in case I ran into him, and dashed down a long brick walkway, passing groups of people chatting at tall cocktail tables with plates of nibbles and glasses of wine. Twenty yards to the right, one serving station was dishing up tiny lamb chops. The smell of roasted meat and garlic called to me like metal filings to a magnet, but I decided it would be rude not to wait for my mother.

At the next station, more waiters were setting up coffee, tea, and enormous trays of chocolate-covered strawberries. Those I could not resist. I veered over and popped one into my mouth, savoring the bright burst of berry coated in a crisp shell of dark chocolate with the smallest hint of orange — no resemblance to the greasy, grainy, overly sweet chocolate I'd had in wedding fountains. I'd pick one up for Mom on the way back.

At the far corner of the property at the end of another long brick walkway, I located the restrooms in a small white clapboard building shaded by dense green foliage — palms, ferns, and bougainvillea vines covered in hot pink blossoms. As a woman climbed the steps ahead of me, I recognized the white-blond hair and slim, black-draped figure of Olivia Nethercut, one of my food writing heroines. Jonah was spectacular and controversial and brilliant, but I could picture myself having a career like Olivia's — food critic, philanthropist, and cookbook writer. My psychologist friend Eric had told me more than once that people who wrote down their goals achieved them more often than those who didn't. So on page one of my notebook, I'd dashed off a list for this weekend. Number one: an exclusive interview with Olivia. Jonah's interview was number two.

"Ms. Nethercut," I said, panting a little as I caught up with her. "I'm Hayley Snow and I just wanted to say how thrilled we are to have you in town. Speaking at the conference."

She nodded blankly. My face flushed as I suddenly realized that accosting her in the ladies' room would probably be considered a journalistic faux pas. On the other hand, it was way too late to pretend I hadn't seen her. I started to hold my hand out, then realized my fingers were covered with melted brown goo.

I began to stammer like a waitress with her first table. "Isn't it a gorgeous night? Never seen such a full moon. They're so lucky that squall blew by to the south. I don't think they had any rain plan at all."

Inside the ladies' room, the novelist Sigrid Gustafson was applying a fresh layer of lipstick at the sink. Hearing me prattle, she caught Olivia's eye and grimaced. Olivia ducked into a stall and I took the one next to her.

"I loved your memoir, *A Marrow Escape,*" I chattered, unable to shut myself up. "And I sent a check off to your foundation at Christmas." So what if it was ten bucks?

That was all I could swing, working only part-time at my friend Connie's cleaning service before starting at *Key Zest.*

"Thanks," she said in a muffled voice. "You're very kind."

Feeling disappointed and slightly brushed off — she hadn't shown one smidgen of curiosity about who I was or what my connection might be to the seminar — I told myself that once we emerged and were busy with the less personal task of hand-washing and away from Sigrid's eye-rolling, I'd announce my credentials and request an interview. But by the time I'd exited the stall, both of the women were gone.

I stumbled back down the stairs, mentally pinching myself for acting like a groupie instead of the professional critic and writer I was supposed to be. Though I was a foodie groupie, like my mother before me. What was wrong with that?

Maybe I'd annoyed Olivia with my gushing. Maybe I'd broken some unwritten rule of courtesy by even speaking to her, even if it was to admire her cutting-edge criticism, gorgeous writing, and generosity. Maybe it was rude to compliment one writer in front of another. Maybe I'd crave the same kind of distance from scruffy fans in the unlikely event I ever got famous. In that case, why the heck attend a food writing conference?

I wandered off to collect myself on one of the black metal benches by the reflecting pool in the corner of the property before rejoining the party. Lush staghorn ferns and mother-in-law tongues shielded the seating area from the restrooms. Two large metal birds — more egret in shape than flamingo — were posed gracefully in the water, and clusters of water lilies floated over most of the surface. I took a seat and tried to slow my whirling thoughts: This weekend could be fun if I would only relax.

A trickle of water burbled out from a pipe in the pool's wall, and I noticed that something was pushing the lily pads up, something surfacing from the dark recesses of the water. The wind gusted, causing the palm fronds overhead to clack like castanets and bringing a whiff of roasted meat that now smelled more rancid than enticing.

I edged a step closer, my heart ratcheting up to uneven thumps like a Kitchen Aide mixer loaded with dough. A third bird statue appeared to have been broken off at the shins and was lying on the bricks next to the pool, the sharp metal beak pointing to a sodden mass of — something.

I squatted at the edge to peer into the water, and was horrified to recognize a swatch of orange linen painfully similar to the shirt Jonah had worn onstage. There must be some reasonable explanation. He didn't own the only orange shirt in the world.

I grabbed the ruined statue and poked at the mass. A pale face bobbed up through the lilies, white flesh and blond hair stained with algae. I tried to scream. The sound caught in my throat, emerging as a strangled squeak.

I kicked aside my mother's expensive sandals, rolled my pants up to my knees, and waded into the water. It was colder and deeper than I'd expected and I skidded on the slick pool bottom and barely caught my balance. Grabbing hold of the orange shirt, I dragged the body to the shallow steps at the end of the pool, propped it up on the edge of the brick walkway, and finally steeled myself to focus. Oh my Lord, it was definitely Jonah.

I pressed my fingers against the clammy skin of his neck, feeling for a pulse — nothing.

What now? My phone was in the bag I'd left with Mom. And the last time I'd practiced CPR was in high school when I'd taken Red Cross training in hopes of working as a summer lifeguard. I'd flunked the water safety portion of the test and dropped out to work for a local caterer.

I screamed for help.

"Breathe, Jonah," I moaned, looking around for someone — anyone — to assist me. In the distance, the loud buzz of a million conversations floated through the trees from the direction of the Audubon House. How could it be that the grounds were mobbed and yet not one person was close enough to hear me?

I squeezed Jonah's nostrils shut and blew two quick puffs of air into his cool lips, noticing an angry red knot on his forehead partially covered by his hair. His mouth tasted of sour coffee and pond water. I pulled away, gagging, and broke off my amateur CPR to try to wrestle him farther up onto the sidewalk. He was too heavy.

I yelled again. "Help! Help!" No one came.

"Help!" I shrieked a third time, then tipped Jonah's head back, leaned my weight onto his chest, and pumped until a stream of greenish water leaked from his mouth. He still didn't seem to be breathing. I couldn't fumble around while his life ebbed away. I leaped up and tore down the sidewalk and around the corner to the dessert and coffee table.

"Call 911," I instructed the woman tending the coffeepot. "I need help right away — a man has hit his head and fallen into the pool! We need a doctor right now. He's not breathing well." Which was the understatement of the decade.

I pounded back to Jonah's limp figure with one of the white-shirted waiters heavy on my tail. "Let's get him onto the walkway," I said.

With the server clutching one arm and me the other, we pulled Jonah completely out of the pool. Rivulets of water ran from his clothing, staining the bricks deep red. His face was ashen underneath the tan. I tucked my pink sweater around his torso, then continued with chest compressions while the waiter blew desperate breaths into his mouth.

"Is anything happening? Do you think he's breathing?" the waiter asked. "Do you think he had a heart attack?"

"He's only in his thirties. I can't imagine he has heart problems. Just keep blowing," I said, sounding more hopeful than what I felt. "His skin tone looks better than when I found him," I said.

"I don't know," said the waiter. "He looks dead to me."

3

Modern recipes were clean and bloodless by comparison, suppressing violence between cook and cooked. Not so here. Truss them . . . lard them, boil them quick and white.

— Allegra Goodman

After what felt like hours, two EMTs arrived, along with Officer Torrence, a policeman I'd met last fall during a murder investigation. He did a double take when he saw me. I'd been the Key West Police Department's favored suspect for the better part of a week. And now here I was again, the first responder at a second disaster that — if I were to be completely honest — also looked like foul play.

Usually the cops in this town arrived at the scene with a "why are you bothering me now?" expression. They've seen too many drunken tourists and panhandling bums

47

weeks away from their last shower to get excited by a man stumbling into a dipping pool. But Officer Torrence's gaze darted from the angry red lump on Jonah's forehead to the lush foliage screening the restrooms to the low brick wall over which anyone might have scrambled.

"Miss Snow, what's going on here?" he asked, which seemed like an odd opening salvo to me. Wasn't it obvious?

"I found Jonah Barrows in the pool and we" — I pointed to the waiter beside me — "pulled him out."

A small crowd of partygoers had followed the cops to the reflecting pool and clustered around us, jostling and craning to see the trauma. Several of the women had begun to blubber at the shock of it all, which made me feel like crying too.

"Move aside, folks," Torrence said, pointing to the approaching EMTs. "These people need room to work."

"Gladly," I said, shuffling away from Jonah's inert form.

The paramedics surged past me, unfolding their portable stretcher, oxygen tank, and defibrillator by the time they reached Jonah. Once two other police officers had arrived to secure the area, Officer Torrence led me to the stairs of the restroom facility.

"You found him in the pool?"

I nodded and felt my pants, looking for a tissue to blot my eyes. No pockets. No bag. I wiped my face on my sleeve. I was starting to shiver and wished I hadn't given away my sweater.

"Tell me exactly what happened," he said. "Right from the beginning."

The beginning — that awful, ominous lily pad bobbing. I sank down to the bottom step, my stomach clamped into a fierce knot. I put my head between my knees and took a couple of deep breaths. When the wooziness passed, I sat up, licked my lips, and began to explain.

"I was waiting in line with my mother for a glass of wine and something to eat. But then nature called and I dashed over here to use the ladies' room. The day has been such a whirlwind, so I went to collect my thoughts at the reflecting pool before rejoining the party." Didn't seem necessary to report that I'd been discouraged because I'd been dissed by one of my favorite food writers.

"When I got here, I noticed that one of the statues had been broken off." I described how I'd come closer, seen the face in the water, and fished out Jonah. "He gave the keynote speech tonight for the food writing

49

conference. We've been trying to get him to breathe on his own for the last fifteen minutes or so." I waved at the waiter, who hovered five feet away, looking as green as the algae that soiled Jonah's shirt. "I couldn't say whether he tripped and fell into the pool or whether someone hit him. Either way, he's got a big lump on his forehead." I fingered the skin under my widow's peak, picturing that angry, swollen knot.

Torrence grimaced, brown eyes narrowing behind his glasses. "Did you see anyone leaving the area around the pool as you entered? Any movement in the bushes surrounding the property?"

"Nothing like that. No one's been around at all. I yelled and yelled for help and not one person came. Finally I had to run out to the dessert table to get help."

"And how about the ladies' room?" Torrence asked. "Did you notice anyone there?"

"Olivia Nethercut used the bathroom the same time I did." I stopped to take a breath and picture the scene. "Another woman — Sigrid Gustafson, I believe is her name — was at the sink when we came in. But there's no way either one would have had time to run out and wallop Jonah — I would definitely have seen them leaving the pool area. Besides, he'd been in that water a few minutes at least before I arrived. He simply wasn't breathing." I shuddered and dabbed my eyes on my shirt again.

"Who's in charge of this conference?" he asked.

"Dustin Fredericks. I'll find him and bring him over." I couldn't wait to get away from the scene of Jonah's accident. I snugged the sandals back on my feet and bolted before Officer Torrence could insist I remain in the area.

I pushed through the crowds around the bar and the hors d'oeuvres tables and found Dustin at the far side of the grounds. He was talking with Julia Child's longtime publicist, a man known for his spot-on imitations of his former client, and a food critic from the *Washington Post*. I grabbed Dustin's wrist and tugged, ignoring his companions' stares and his outrage.

"Listen, you have to come with me," I said quietly. "I'm Hayley Snow. With *Key Zest*. Someone's fallen into the pool and hit his head." How could he not have heard the sirens?

Dustin shook me off. "Find security and have them handle this. I'll get there shortly."

"It's urgent," I added. "It's Jonah."

Shoulders tightening, he whistled out an irritated sigh. "Opening night of the biggest show in town, my career's on the line, and that buffoon goes swimming?" Dustin turned to the two men he'd been chatting with. "Excuse me, please. Something's come up." He lumbered off ahead of me, grumbling. "He needs to get over it — put a Band-Aid on his boo-boo and get out here and do some patch-up work with our sponsors. He didn't give a keynote address. He whacked our seminar like it was a cheap piñata. I should have known better than to tap him. When has he ever done what I asked him? He thinks he's like one of those banks, too big to fail. We'll see about that. . . ."

I followed him to the reflecting pool, which was now roped off, to the dismay of partygoers with pressing bladders who were being turned away from the restrooms. And others who wanted to rubberneck the emergency.

"What's going on here?" Dustin asked Office Torrence. "You're ruining our party. Where the hell is Jonah?"

"Mr. Barrows has been removed to the emergency room," said Officer Torrence, raising his voice to match Dustin's intensity. "And to your first question, as a precaution, we're treating this area as a crime scene. Mr. Barrows may have been the victim of an attack."

Dustin jutted his chin toward me. "You told me he'd fallen and hit his head," he said fiercely.

I swallowed and shrugged. "I just found him in the pool. I have no idea how he actually got there." I turned to the cop. "Can I go to let my mom know I'm okay?"

He nodded curtly. "Then I'll need you back here. Did Mr. Barrows have any detractors that you were aware of?" the cop asked Dustin.

"Detractors? You mean enemies? You mean people he had insulted recently, or planned to attack later this weekend?" asked Dustin, his reddening face now damp with sweat. "You'd have to line up to join that party," he added as I walked away.

By the time I located my mother to inform her that the evening was over, she had moved to a tall cocktail table in the garden and was busy chatting like old friends with the women who'd been seated in front of us in the auditorium. "Oh, look, here's my daughter who I was telling you about," she exclaimed to the women. "Hayley's a food critic — she really should be lecturing up onstage this weekend."

She handed me one of the glasses of white

wine in front of her and drained the last half inch in the other. I noticed the remnants of a plate of hors d'oeuvres on the table next to her camera. Three tiny lamb chop bones without a shred of meat on them rested on the plate's rim.

Mom saw my dismay. "This was all I could manage — this crowd is like starving wolves falling on a carcass. And I was ravenous too. And then it took you so long — I must have texted you five times. . . . If it helps at all, I got two of those lamb chops for you." She smiled sheepishly.

I dug through the bag she'd been carrying for me and pulled out my phone, and yes, there were multiple messages.

"I left my phone with you — remember?" I tapped my khaki-clad thighs. "These pants don't have any pockets."

"But where in the world —" Mom stopped talking and finally looked at me: the rolled-up pant legs wet to the knees, the wilder hair than even usual, the shirt stained with greenish splotches and a bit of Jonah's regurgitated spittle. "My God, Hayley, what happened?"

I took a big sip of wine and pulled her away from the other women. "There's been an accident," I murmured. "Jonah Barrows fell and hit his head and nearly drowned.

I'm sorry about cutting the evening short, but I have to go. The cops have some more questions."

"Is he all right?" She scrunched her face up. "Wait a minute. What do you mean, more questions? Why are you involved?"

"I found him, that's all." I folded my arms over my stomach and tried to radiate firmness: end of conversation. Sometimes it worked.

"Why are you wet? And where's your sweater?"

"I found him in the dipping pool and had to drag him out. I'll tell you the gory details later, okay?"

Mom looked at her watch. "I'm supposed to meet Eric and Bill about now anyway and walk back to their place." She narrowed her eyes and scanned my body again, every rumpled, anxious inch of it. "You look awful. What aren't you saying?"

I almost started to sniffle but pulled myself together and whispered, "I think he's dead, Mom." No need to have half the party guests leaning in to listen.

"He's dead?" she bellowed.

"Shhhh . . . I'll walk you out to the gate." I gulped another big swallow of white wine, downed a piece of cheese, and herded her off to the entrance of the grounds.

"Over here!" called a familiar voice. Eric's partner, Bill.

"Where's Eric?" I asked. "Did you get something to eat?"

"He developed a sudden migraine," Bill said. "I tried to get him to stay for a few minutes, but he really felt sick. I've never seen him so pale."

"Oh, poor guy," Mom said. "We'll get him an ice pack. Does he carry migraine medicine? I can loan him a tablet of Imitrex. That never fails for me."

Bill squeezed her hand. "You're such a doll. Hope you don't mind walking," he added, "because I told him to take the car. We can certainly call a cab."

"Don't be silly," my mother said. "I'm perfectly capable of walking. I wore my sensible shoes." She leaned over to kiss my cheek. "Hayley's the glamorous one in this family." She started to follow Bill out but then turned to look at me one last time.

"Are you sure you'll be okay? I can stay if you need me. When I spoke to Miss Gloria on the phone last week, she said she'd be happy to have me camp out on the sofa."

All I needed was my mother on Miss Gloria's lumpy settee — only she wouldn't be on the couch, because I'd feel too guilty about letting her sleep there. "I'll be fine," I said, flashing a bogus smile.

"See you tomorrow," Mom said, and returned to hug me again. "Get a good night's sleep — I'm sure everything will turn out just fine."

She wouldn't have said that if she'd seen Jonah, but I patted her arm and tried to radiate reassurance through what felt like a very weak grin. Then I turned and trudged back to the pool as instructed. Officer Torrence and a young policewoman with a blond ponytail and a torso as thick as a tree trunk were still talking to Dustin. Torrence beckoned me over.

"Miss Snow, had you encountered Mr. Barrows earlier in the evening?"

"I saw his lecture, of course," I said. "I'd hoped to meet him and ask him to sign my book, but my mother insisted on sightseeing, so we were late to the party."

"Did you have an existing relationship with Mr. Barrows? How were you certain it was him in the pool?" Torrence asked.

I took the easier question first. "The color of his shirt was so distinctive. And we'd just watched him onstage for forty-five minutes. He was very much on my mind."

"So you weren't acquainted before to-night?"

I felt my face pink up with embarrassment. "I'm a fan," I admitted. "I've written to him. And I'd hoped to interview him for my magazine."

"Written to him?" asked Torrence, his forehead creasing. "How many times?"

"Three. Possibly four. Though I never got more than a perfunctory acknowledgment. 'Thanks for your kind words' or something to that effect."

"Wrote him about what?" asked the lady cop.

I cleared my throat, looking down at the policewoman's sturdy black brogans. "Career advice," I muttered. "Tips on how to become a food critic. And then requests for an interview."

"Did you make arrangements to meet with him tonight?" Torrence asked.

My heart was hammering so fiercely, I was sure they could hear it. And my palms were slick with sweat. Why did I feel so guilty when I hadn't done anything but admire his work and try to save him?

"He said to look for him at the party. I knew he would be busy, and a million people would want a piece of him. But it was the chance of a lifetime. I also brought a book, hoping to have him sign it."

"Was he angry about the way you pressed him? Or frightened?" asked Torrence.

"Of course not! I was completely professional. Not a fan freak."

Dustin listened to this conversation unfold, a look of horror creeping onto his face that caused his jowls to quiver. "Maybe he was giving you career advice when he, uh, *slipped* into the pool?"

"That's not how it went!" I yelped.

At the same time, Officer Torrence said sternly, "We'll handle the questioning here, Mr. Fredericks." And back to me: "Earlier you said that you used a bird statue to try to fish him out of the water. Can you show us that, please?"

I led them over to the brick patio surrounding the pool. Two of the metal birds wading in the pond were still there, high-stepping through the water lilies. But the broken egret statue had disappeared.

"The other bird is gone," I said. "Maybe one of your guys picked it up?"

"What other bird?" asked Torrence.

4

When a camera flash goes off in a restaurant, I no longer look around for the birthday party — I look for the food blogger.
— Nick Fauchald

Half an hour later, I was back on my scooter, heading up the island to the Tarpon Pier Marina where I lived in a tiny second bedroom on my friend Miss Gloria's houseboat. The moon laid a silvery path across the water of the bight, which slapped gently against the dock. A whiff of fish floated from the cleaning table on the other side of the walk as I locked up my bike.

Miss Gloria's snores were rattling through the living room by the time I reached our home. Seventy-eight and an early riser, she was often lulled to sleep by her boat's motion before the ten o'clock news. My nerves tightly wound by the disaster with Jonah, I'd be lucky to get any sleep at all. I considered popping down to have a nightcap with my former roommate Connie, a couple of boats up the finger. She'd suffered with me through the aftermath of the first murder I'd witnessed, and our friendship had only improved since I'd moved out of her place and into Miss Gloria's. Just as I decided to go, her lights winked off. So I settled down in my bunk, my gray tiger, Evinrude, beside me. I ran my hands over the curves of his head and neck and buried my face into his dense fur. His motor sputtered and caught.

Maybe I should have called Detective Nate Bransford instead. He'd led the investigation of a murder late last fall in which I'd been one of his "people of interest." Once the case was settled, it was clear we were both interested — in each other. In fact, we had a date for dinner tomorrow night. I hit his number on redial before I could start obsessing whether it was too late for a social call or inappropriate to discuss business after hours.

"It's Hayley," I said. "I figured you were up — they say crime doesn't sleep. So I guess the cops aren't allowed to either?" I snorted with nervous laughter. "I suppose you heard what went on at the literary conference?"

"I heard," he said. "Why was I not surprised to see your name in the report?"

Which hit me in an entirely bad way — if there was a good way — because it had been a long, stressful day and I was hoping for some empathy. I had a choice of getting mad or starting to cry. And one of my New Year's resolutions was to cry less and speak up more. I hated to ruin a perfectly good resolution this early in January.

"And why was I not surprised to be treated like public enemy number one when all I did was find the guy and try to save him?" My voice trembled in spite of the resolution.

"Look, Hayley," said Bransford in his most soothing way — which wasn't all that soothing once you had been under the microscope in one of his cases — "they're only trying to figure out what happened. And you found the body. It's quite possible that you noticed things you weren't even aware of seeing — and it's their job to dig for these details. My guys were trying to cover all of the bases."

"One was a woman, not a guy. And she was a bigger jerk than Officer Torrence."

Bransford heaved an impatient sigh. "Torrence is the best investigator we have on the force. Besides, your information was not particularly reliable. The alleged murder weapon was not where you said it would be."

"That stupid bird," I said. "I knew your cops didn't believe me."

"You said you left it next to the pool, but it wasn't there," said Bransford.

"So you're suggesting that I'm lying?"

"I'm suggesting that perhaps you mis-remembered where you saw it." He paused, his voice carefully emptied of expression. "If in fact it was actually there."

"It was there all right," I said. "How should I know what happened to it? Maybe someone kicked it into the bushes? Or the staff saw it was broken and threw it in the trash? Or maybe the guy who really hit Jonah carried it off. And I can assure you that it wasn't me."

"Come on, Hayley. Don't get your hackles up. My guys have to do their jobs. They have to consider all the possibilities. They owe it to the man down."

The man down? First of all, why would he defend his cops, who made me feel like a suspect when the worst I'd done was send Jonah a few e-mails asking for an interview? And then try to save him. And second, I was starting to have flashbacks of me and my ex-boyfriend Chad as our relationship tanked. I'd followed Chad to Key West and then discovered he was far more dedicated to his divorce law practice than he'd ever be to me. Never mind discovering the other women in his life about whom I'd had no clue.

Here was another man whose work — whose everything but me — would come first. Better to cut him loose now before I got attached. Better to cancel the dinner date we'd finally scheduled before we both wasted a rotten evening.

"Let's forget about tomorrow night," I said. "I have a job to do too, and you're not helping. Besides," I added, not wanting to sound completely shrewish, "I should never have agreed to schedule that dinner. Not only do I need to review the restaurant, but my mother's in town for a couple of days and it's rude to go off on a date and leave her alone. Some other time. Or not," I muttered under my breath.

"Have her join us," he said gallantly, ignoring my dismissal. "I'd like to meet her. You said seven o'clock? And I'll speak to the officers about their interviewing technique."

I waffled, somewhat mollified. I wanted to go out with him, but I didn't want to be a pushover. Was he really another Chad or was I being too sensitive because of my history? Too early to tell. "It wasn't only what they said. It was their tone — all condescending and accusatory, as if they thought I was hiding something and if they pushed me a little harder, it would all spill out."

"Their tone," he said flatly. And after a pause: "We'll work on that."

Miss Gloria's cheerful clattering in the galley woke me early after a restless night. "Are you up, Hayley? Stay there. I'll bring you some coffee."

I was up now. But I couldn't get mad at her. Her son had offered me a perfectly sweet place to live in exchange for keeping an eye on his mother. And she was so obviously thrilled to have my company. And she was adorable.

Minutes later, she arrived in my room, wearing her pink sweatshirt with the Florida Keys outlined in rhinestones. Both of the cats, her black Sparky and my striped Evinrude, trotted in her wake.

"One coffee, heavy on milk and light on sugar, comin' right up," Miss Gloria sang out. Evinrude hopped onto the bed, butted my hand with his head, and began to purr. Miss Gloria settled the steaming cup on my bedside table. "How was the conference?"

"Anybody up?" called a voice from the

65

dock before I could tell her the story.

"I'll let her in," said Miss Gloria, bustling out to the living room to greet our neighbor Connie.

"Could have been better," I muttered, pulling myself to a seated position and reaching under the bed for my laptop. Sipping the coffee, I turned on the computer and flipped to my e-mail. At the top of the queue was a message from Dustin Fredericks to all the attendees of the food writing seminar. The subject line read *Urgent communication from the director!* I opened it up.

"I write to inform you that Jonah Barrows slipped and fell last night and accidentally drowned. We deeply regret his passing but know he would want the conference to continue as planned. We have made the decision to dedicate the weekend to Jonah and his legacy. So in addition to the events already in place, we are planning a final session on Sunday honoring his life and his work."

The confirmation of his death went down like a mouthful of sour milk. Though I shouldn't really be surprised, considering what Jonah had looked like — limp and sodden and pastry white — as we extricated him from the pool.

Miss Gloria and Connie came into my

room carrying their own cups of coffee. Their smiles faded when they saw my face.

"The keynote speaker died last night. But I can't really talk about it," I said, holding up a hand. "I can't afford to get upset. Too much work to do."

"Died of what?" Connie asked. She ran her fingers through her short hair, still damp from the shower, until it stood up like a hedgehog's.

"Drowned." I grimaced, flashing on the peculiar texture of his skin and his fishy lips and eyes. "I found him. I swear I'll fill you in about everything tonight."

I slid out from under my comforter, hugged Connie, kissed Miss Gloria on the top of her head where the pink skin showed through her thinning white hair, and hurried into the shower. While soaping and rinsing, I worked to push last night's events out of mind and instead focus on the opening paragraph of my piece on Jonah's lecture. He'd made a lot of interesting points and I hated to think they'd be lost in the brouhaha over his death. And if I lost my focus, my job would be next.

I worked a teaspoon of hair product through my curls and dressed in jeans, a peach-colored swing top, and my mother's sandals, which rubbed painfully on yesterday's blisters. I applied a couple of Band-Aids to the backs of my heels and tucked some extras into my pockets. While packing the conference program, Jonah's book, and two notebooks into my backpack, I found the chunk of the strawberry-rhubarb coffee cake Eric had given me yesterday. I packed this on top so it wouldn't get more crushed, then hopped on my scooter and drove down Southard to the office.

Early last fall, Wally had rented a small attic space for the magazine above Preferred Properties Real Estate. Two enormous palm trees outside the only window blocked most of the light, but our receptionist, Danielle, decorated so it felt like a cozy tropical haven instead of a cave.

Both Wally and Danielle were at their desks by the time I arrived. And both were wearing their *Key Zest* company yellow shirts.

"Good Lord, Hayley. Jonah Barrows died last night?" asked Danielle before I'd even struggled out of my helmet and sweater. "Is that coffee cake?" She pointed at the plastic-wrapped package I pulled out of my pack.

"I'll share," I said, and cut it into three equal sections. I nibbled on mine — the strawberries made it moist and sweet; the rhubarb lent it tang.

"How did this happen?" asked Wally, reaching for his piece. "The e-mail said it was an accidental drowning, but there's no water near the Audubon House. Did you get the real story?"

"Every time I walk along the dock by the old harbor, I imagine how easy it would be for someone to push me over." Danielle shivered. "I can't swim a lick — I'd be a goner. Like that poor woman who was shoved into the path of a subway train in New York City."

"Down, girl. Your neuroses are showing," said Wally. "We're in Key West. Let Hayley tell us."

So I explained everything — Jonah's provocative lecture, the squirming panelists, my discovery of the body in the dipping pool, the missing statue. "How am I supposed to write about foodie trends with all that happening?" I asked in a wobbly voice. Because it was hitting me that Jonah might well have died exactly during the moments that I was trying to save him.

"You take the day off," Wally said. "I'll come up with something. I can use your press pass. It's going to be super important to get a piece written up on Jonah and his life work. What he meant to people . . . his major contributions . . . and of course any hints about personal issues that might be behind the death. We're the hometown news — *Key Zest* can't be late to the party." He popped the last chunk of the coffee cake into his mouth and gave me a thumbs-up. "I can try to explain to Ava that you had a personal emergency."

And she'd take that as exactly the kind of evidence she was trolling for to fire me. I'd worked too hard to land this job to fold up like a paper napkin. "Absolutely not. I'm up for it. I'm going over to talk to folks now." I gathered my things and started for the door.

"Don't forget your restaurant review," Wally called after me. "We still need that."

I turned back to look at him — he was smiling. A month on the job and he already had my number. Ambitious even if it killed me. "Got it covered," I said with a smart salute.

I left my scooter in the office parking lot and walked the few blocks down Southard to Duval. Early morning was actually a good time to see the city — street-cleaning crews had swept away the detritus of the parties from the previous night — the Mardi Gras beads, the broken beer bottles, the pizza crusts — along with its accompanying odors. The streets were peopled by roosters and joggers and a few of the homeless folks who'd spent the night in places not conducive to sleeping in, but none of the evening crowds of revelers were up this early.

I crossed the street to avoid the powerful smell of a deep-fat fryer from a fast food grill serving greasy breakfasts and headed east on Duval Street to the San Carlos Institute. I spotted Dustin on the sidewalk outside the building, talking with a cluster of the conference organizers and Officer Torrence — fully recognizable because of the mustache and the wide shoulders in spite of his street clothes. I ducked my head and scuttled by, not wishing to rehash my discovery of Jonah's body. Or get sucked into more questions on the unfortunate death. Besides, I had a lot to do before Mom arrived and distracted me from my *Key Zest* business.

Having my mother here with me cemented the connection I felt between food and love. Between food and taking care of someone you loved. Or might want to love. Between food and guilt. I appreciated her enthusiasm and confidence in me, but I wasn't convinced she understood how important this weekend was for my career. She'd understand if I explained that I was in danger of getting fired if I didn't produce something brilliant, but she'd also worry. And hover, motherly rotors a-whapping.

I climbed the white marble steps circling to the second floor above the lobby. In the large room across from the stairway, a sumptuous continental breakfast had been laid out for the conference speakers and attendees — pastries, fruit, an egg casserole with onions and sausage, three kinds of juice, and coffee. I imagined that anyone providing food for this seminar would be hypervigilant about its quality. Who'd want a roomful of restaurant critics and food writers wrinkling their collective noses at your offerings? Or worse still, suffering a wave of food poisoning?

I loaded a plate with a little of everything and looked around for someone to chat with. A group huddled in the far corner of the room included three of the conference speakers and several others. Their body language was not welcoming, but if I let that stop me I'd gather nothing but uninformed suppositions from the home cooks and fringe writers attending the conference. I pictured Ava Faulker poised to can me, and then wedged into the space between a well-known Asian cookbook author and Sigrid Gustafson, the author of three novels centering on Scandinavian food, whom I'd seen in the bathroom at the reception the night before.

I surfed into the first silence. "Good morning," I said brightly. "I'm Hayley Snow with *Key Zest* magazine, headquartered right here in town. We're so happy to have you visiting."

There was the smallest pause and then they continued to talk as if I hadn't appeared — about the pitiful state of advances in book contracts and whether e-books were truly the way of the future.

"Surely not for cookbooks," said Yoshe King, a small dark-haired woman in a sequined tunic and black leggings. "Who wants to look at a recipe on an iPhone?"

The novelist scowled. "Haven't you heard of Epicurious, darling? And the apps that are being developed are nothing short of miraculous."

I ate a little of my breakfast, waiting for another break in the conversation, and telling myself not to take the cold shoulders personally.

"I adored your most recent cookbook," I said to Yoshe when I got the opportunity. "It read like a novel. Sheer pleasure! I tried the Asian noodle salad with sticky ginger tofu cubes — I swear it's the only time my guy hasn't refused tofu outright."

In fact, I didn't have a guy and if I did, I wouldn't force tofu on him, but she wouldn't know that. "We're running features on conference panelists in our magazine for the rest of January and I'd love to do one on you and your work. Believe it or not, most of our articles are starting to get picked up by the Associated Press."

Finally she beamed, slid a business card out of her pocket, and handed it over. "Thanks. It would be my pleasure."

I turned to the rotund woman next to her, Sigrid the novelist. "Your latest novel," I said, "was like eating a great meal. I savored every word."

She simpered. "Why, thank you."

Though I had admired her novel for its meticulous wordsmithing, it read more like the prickly Scandinavian top chef Jonah had scorned in his opening remarks than the romance-laden comfort food I preferred when I wasn't working. My ability to manufacture bologna seemed to be expanding with each minute on the job.

On the other hand, yes, I was feeding them lines, but at the same time, I wasn't. Every overwrought word was true. Because underneath the writers' posturing and jostling for position, in each of their books, I recognized their true love for food. This was my tribe. If they'd only let me join them.

"I was so sad when I came to the end," I added to Sigrid. "Any chance I could talk with you later about your creative process and how you manage to make food such a vibrant character in your fiction?" This woman perked up too, her multiple chins wobbling as she thanked me. She took her colleague's card from my hand and jotted her cell phone number on the back.

"Perhaps I could take you to lunch?" I asked. Both of the women nodded.

The conversation veered to Jonah and his unfortunate demise. "Someone said a local writer had to dive into the swimming pool and pull him out," Sigrid reported breathlessly.

"I was the one who found Jonah," I said in a quiet voice. "It was really more a decorative pool than anything. I only got wet up to my knees. He got unlucky drowning in water that shallow."

Yoshe nibbled on her lower lip. "Is it possible that he had a heart attack or an embolism, fell into the pool, and was in too much distress to save himself?"

"Anything's possible," I said, thinking Bransford would kill me if I started to blab about the missing broken bird statue or the

75

blow to Jonah's forehead.

"He looked — so pale he was almost blue." I sighed. "Other than that, I don't know what really happened."

"Awful," said Sigrid. "I'm not saying this has anything to do with it, but Jonah was chugging those little cans of caffeinated drinks all evening. While we were waiting to go on with him backstage, I'm certain he had two of them."

"He could just as well have been drinking alcohol," said the man who'd been standing by silently. I thought I recognized his face from the conference program — he called himself a culinary poet.

"Have you glanced through *You Must Try the Skate*?" he asked. "That book is positively riddled with allusions to impulse control. And who chose that ridiculous book title?" he added. "He practically had to have been drinking to go on about bringing up the curtains on the rest of us, the way he did last night. All of us have skeletons we'd rather not rattle — he simply chose to dump his on the unsuspecting public. If I had known this was an invitation to a public encounter group, I would have declined."

Note to self: Interview this fellow alone later. I dug in my pocket for a business card, but found I'd given out the last one. Then before I spotted her and could head her off, my mother bounced into the middle of the group.

"Oh, Hayley, here you are! I've been looking for you —" She stopped and stared at the women next to me, her mouth dropping open. "Yoshe King! Hayley, you never mentioned you knew her. Oh, Miss King, I have your book right here. I've been preparing your recipes since Hayley here was a little girl. You should see the pages — absolutely paper-thin and covered with stains from your sauces. In fact, I bought a brand-new copy at the bookstore downstairs." She rustled through her enormous straw bag and pulled out a cookbook the size of a dictionary. "Would it be too much of an imposition to ask you to sign it?"

She handed the book over and then pinned me in a hug. "It's so much fun to be attending this conference with my daughter. Do any of you have children? What a treasure to have been able to hand down my passion for food to Hayley. You'll be hearing about her — mark my words. Soon she'll be up on the stage with you, rather than in the audience." She took her signed book back and thanked Yoshe.

"Darling, let's get our seats. The day's about to begin," she said, pulling me away as if I were still five and balking on the way to my kindergarten classroom.

5

As for greed and envy, no one can accuse a man who serves such copious portions, who relishes the company of others, who gets hurt if you don't drink with him and who gives such enveloping drunken bear hugs . . . of hoarding and withholding.

— Julian Sancton

After Dustin had taken a solid half hour on center stage to express his grief over Jonah's death and to assure the audience that the conference would continue with more energy than ever, the first panelists trooped onto the stage. The moderator turned out to be the narrow-faced unfriendly man we'd seen at breakfast, and his panelists were the women who'd been clustered around him — Yoshe King and Sigrid Gustafson, joined by Olivia Nethercut in a last-minute swish of midnight blue silk. They settled into a semi-circle of chairs that had been set up in

79

front of the faux diner, all three women tilting forward like racers at the start line.

I tried to judge how the audience was feeling in the wake of last night's tragedy. "Deflated" and "anxious" seemed the most accurate words to describe them. I'd overheard multiple horrified versions of Jonah's death being discussed. And Mom hadn't had to shush the ladies in front of us even once.

"Food writing as a fun-house mirror — Marcel Proust meets Bobby Flay," said the moderator. "That is the title of this morning's panel. I have to say, only Jonah Barrows would have understood what that means." A wave of subdued chuckles rolled through the theater.

"I join Dustin in saying that we shall all miss him terribly, both this weekend and going forward. But never fear. We shall do the best we can to decipher and translate the organizers' intentions for our panels, as Jonah would have done brilliantly. My name is Fritz Ewing and I'm the author of nine nonfiction and poetry books, most recently *Out of the Frying Pan,* a collaboratory memoir with chef Michael Bozeman. A *foodoir,* as it were. *Into the Fire,* a collection of poems about meat, is scheduled for publication next year." He grinned and bowed at his panelists. "As you can quite imagine, those are not the titles I sent in with my manuscripts.

"Mr. Fredericks asked me to channel Jonah Barrows." He touched his balding head and held out one sneaker-clad foot. "I'm afraid I have neither the hair nor the boots to make such a statement. So I've decided to lead off by asking our panelists to offer an opening remark that best reflects the essence of their relationship to food writing. One sentence only, please, ladies."

"That's easy," said Yoshe, the Asian cookbook author, jumping in before the other two women could speak. "Good cooking has a point of view."

"A point of view," said Fritz, tugging on one pink earlobe and grimacing. "Meaning the pot stickers talk back?" The audience tittered. "I'm going to get back to you on that. Anyone else?"

"A writer's personality is revealed by her connection to food," said Olivia. "Some people are feeders and some are withholders."

I wrote that down and underlined the words twice. Feeders. Withholders. I knew which I wanted to be. Mom reached over to squeeze my hand.

"I see why you admire her," she whispered. "And isn't her outfit gorgeous?"

"I use food as a vehicle for my characters' turning points," said Sigrid. "In *Dark Sweden,* for example . . ." She paused, resting her pointer finger on her chin and looking out at the audience. "Dare I mention something that might be a spoiler in the denouement? I imagine you are more interested in food than mystery — am I right?" She nodded, hearing murmurs of agreement. "So, as I was saying, in *Dark Sweden,* the murderer reveals himself over a platter of raw oysters. Only the detective doesn't realize it until much later because he's so distracted by the distasteful act of swallowing something slick and slimy. He's picturing how difficult it is to get inside the shell, and then how disgusting this creature is. In fact, he's wondering who in the world ever thought of eating an oyster, rather than paying attention to the conversation. At the moment he realizes how he'd missed this opportunity to clinch his case, he also understands that his finicky palate will continue to interfere with his job unless he opens himself up. Sort of like a reluctant mollusk," she added.

The audience tittered.

"That's at least three sentences," said Fritz. "Maybe four? Or five? But we'll allow it because you made us laugh. So basically all of you people are saying in one way or another that writers pretend to write about food but it's really about something else?"

"It's not a pretense," said Olivia as she waggled a forefinger. "We write about food because not only is it necessary to our human condition, but we love and appreciate it dearly. The underlying messages betray themselves whether we intend to reveal them or whether we'd prefer that they remain concealed. And it's not only food writers, by the way. It's all writing. All good writing."

Fifteen minutes later, I could imagine how sharply Jonah would be missed this weekend. Like Fritz, he'd have preened a bit like a bantam rooster. But I thought he would have pushed these writers harder to bare the embarrassing truths in their histories. He'd have insisted that Yoshe describe her point of view and then challenged her consistency over the range of her cookbooks. He'd have egged on each of them to say whether she was a feeder or a withholder, perhaps implying that Sigrid, whether or not she cooked for others, certainly knew how to feed herself. He would have coaxed out the underlying competitiveness of these women and watched them nip tiny bites from one another's flesh like birds tasting ripe tomatoes. It would not have been boring, as this first half hour threatened to be after those titillating introductions.

My mind pinged to this question: Was it possible that Jonah's killer was on the stage? What kind of person would have the nerve to kill a prominent food critic, writer, and chef, and then sit before four hundred people and pontificate about recipes or the way food was woven into her fiction like a character? I couldn't imagine doing this myself — wouldn't a killer's hands and eyes and words betray him or her? But I didn't know any of these people well enough to rule them out.

Although tempted to return to the lobby to see if I could catch one of the women fresh off their panel for an interview, I didn't want to miss one second of the second panel of the morning — a roundtable of three of the food critics I'd admired for years: Ruth Reichl, Frank Bruni, and Jonathan Gold. They marched onto the stage, Ruth tall and thin with a wedge of curls, Frank small and adorable with dimples that rivaled Detective Bransford's, and Jonathan massive, with the tan and light hair of a Californian. Jonah Barrows had been set to moderate this panel too, but this morning the organizers had opted to let the three veterans go it alone.

"You have to have a certain bloodlust to be in this business," said Ruth, "because a bad review is an arrow in the chef's side. If you write a negative review, the restaurant may actually have to close. Or at the least, the chef is fired."

"Bloodlust," I wrote in my notebook, and then circled the word as if it might bolt off the page. I'd discussed similar concerns with Eric over the past few months — would I have the necessary taste for blood that a critic seemed to need? And he'd reminded me to think about why I was drawn to the profession and focus on that: People deserved well-informed opinions about spending their money. As Jonah would have said, they deserved *truth*.

As this discussion wound down, I tapped Mom on the leg. "I have to get out," I said. "I'm taking Yoshe and Sigrid to lunch."

"That sounds wonderful," she said. "What a terrific idea. Where are we eating?"

I didn't have the heart to suggest that I'd feel less self-conscious talking with them by myself. And besides, maybe having her along would keep them off balance. Because what kind of investigative reporter brings her mother along to an important interview?

"I was thinking of *La Crêperie*," I said. "I've never had a bad meal there. Wouldn't that be awful, taking a food writer out for a lousy lunch? They'd think I didn't have a clue."

Mom and I hustled out to the lobby, where Sigrid and Yoshe waited. I hailed two pedicabs on Duval Street — bicyclists pulling rolling benches for tourists. No Key West native would be caught dead in one of these, but they'd be perfect for transporting the ladies to lunch. I settled Mom and Yoshe in the first cab, behind a young Rumanian man with huge, muscular thighs.

"We're headed to *La Crêperie,*" I said to him, and then climbed into the second cab next to Sigrid. Our bicyclist/driver pumped his legs hard to get the cab moving. "Considering how badly we feel about Jonah, I think it's going well so far," I said to Sigrid. "Don't you?"

"It would have been nice if he'd asked us about our most recent work," she said, sliding on a pair of large black sunglasses. "It's so awkward to have to cram your own material into the discussion without being invited."

An issue I hadn't noticed her having any trouble with at all.

Our cabdriver dodged expertly between a turquoise golf cart loaded with drunken college students and two wobbly scooters and

86

turned left on Petronia Street into the Bahama Village, where a large wrought-iron arch was the only vestige of the formerly bustling Bahama Village market. After a few more minutes of vigorous pedaling, he deposited us at the café across from the more famous — and more touristy — Blue Heaven. His forehead was dotted with beads of sweat and he was breathing hard. I paid the tab and added a generous tip for the load he'd carried. Mom and Yoshe descended from their cab and I paid that driver too, wondering how much of this might have to come out of my own small paycheck. Wally hadn't said anything much about expenses, other than "keep them down."

"This little restaurant used to be located on Duval, but it burned to the studs a few years ago," I told the women. "Both of the chef-owners are from Brittany, France. They rebuilt, and from what I've experienced, it's better than ever."

After a short wait, we were escorted to a small metal café table on the sidewalk, where we took a minute to study the menus.

"I can't believe we are actually eating outdoors!" said my mother, tucking a white napkin over her lap. "Everything's gray and frigid back home."

"Have you tried the Croque Madame?" Sigrid asked me, and then read aloud the description of a grilled ham and cheese sandwich finished with a fried egg.

"That's loaded with fat and cholesterol," said Yoshe. "Don't the salads look fantastic?" She pointed to the woman at the next table, who was eating a spring mix topped with avocado, strawberries, and pears.

Sigrid glared at her.

"I have eaten their Croque Monsieur. It's delicious and comes with a nice green side salad," I said, hoping that compromise would be oil on the rough waters between them.

The waitress, a blond woman with a French accent, swung by to take our orders — one sandwich with a side order of *frites,* two salads, one omelet. She spun away to the kitchen.

Before Yoshe could weigh in on the fat grams in Sigrid's french fries, I said, "I'm curious about how you think the panel might have gone differently with Jonah at the helm. After all, he promised us full disclosure."

"Threatened us is more like it," said Sigrid.

"He wouldn't have been satisfied with Olivia Nethercut alluding to what's hidden behind her writing," said Yoshe. "He would have asked her straight out what she didn't have the nerve to say."

"Really?" Mom's eyes widened. "I thought that was so interesting. Did you agree with her comment that all writers show more than they intend?"

Sigrid snorted and smoothed her flowered dress over her belly. "I didn't appreciate that — if I have something to say about a subject, I say it right out," she said. "She made it sound like we're all hiding things or too dumb to know what we've written."

"I think the more interesting fireworks would have come outside of the panels," Yoshe added. "Of course, you knew that Jonah and Dustin were an item?"

"They were?" Mom and I asked simultaneously.

"Was that recent?" I asked. "Dustin didn't mention anything about a personal relationship with Jonah last night when we were talking to the cops. He didn't act like a guy who'd just lost his boyfriend. In fact, he seemed most annoyed that Jonah might have irritated the conference sponsors."

"Jonah dumped him in record time," Yoshe said. "He isn't going to brag about that."

The waitress delivered our meals: Greek

salads thick with feta cheese and Niçoise olives folded into buckwheat pancakes for Yoshe and me, a spinach and mushroom omelet for Mom, and the ham and cheese sandwich crowned with an egg over easy and an order of french fries on the side for Sigrid.

"Besides, if the conference sponsors aren't happy," Sigrid said, plunging her knife into the sandwich so that yolk flowed like yellow lava over the ham onto the crunchy stalks of potato, "Dustin's out of a job." She carved off a large corner of her sandwich, mopped it through the pool of egg yolk, and wolfed it down. "And I don't believe it was serious between them. For Jonah, nothing was ever serious outside of his work."

As we ate, the conversation turned toward admiration of the food — the crispy tang of the buckwheat pancakes, the creamy feta, the fresh tomatoes. A vinaigrette with a secret ingredient. Extra garlic? Tarragon? Mustard? No one agreed.

"Tell us about your new project," Mom said to Yoshe. "You didn't get a chance to expand on its 'point of view.'"

Yoshe blushed furiously and looked hard at Mom, like maybe she'd underestimated her. "What I meant by that is that no cooking occurs in a vacuum. In fact, the best

90

recipes sprouted in some grandmother's kitchen somewhere. Doesn't matter whether she was Polish or Italian or a pioneer woman from Iowa. We need to learn from the women who came before us."

Mom leaned forward eagerly. "When Hayley graduated from college, I gave her a box of my mother's recipes — written in her own hand. And a few from my mother's mother and my mother-in-law. Some of them are delicious and some simple and several just awful, but the point is, they demonstrate the history of these women in such a tangible, personal way. And it's our history too — we're all connected."

I didn't dare mention how close I'd come to losing every last recipe card in the box during the breakup with Chad Lutz last fall.

"Exactly!" said Yoshe. "I should have hired you to write the preface."

Now Mom blushed and ducked her head.

"The food of my ancestors sucked," said Sigrid with a big belly laugh. "That's why I write fiction."

The alarm on my phone beeped — almost two o'clock. "I hate to cut this short, but I need to get back for the afternoon sessions," I said.

"I'm skipping the panels this afternoon," said Sigrid. "We have a long night ahead.

And there won't be anything said that I haven't already heard."

Yoshe nodded in agreement.

"You go on," Mom suggested to me. "I'll make sure the ladies get dessert and help them find a cab to take them to their hotels. I can cover the bill and bring the receipt to you later."

I flashed a grateful smile. As much as my mother had looked forward to every moment of this conference, precious private time with her cooking idol, Yoshe, would be even better. And Sigrid added to the raw entertainment value of the afternoon. I left them arguing over Nutella dessert crepes with bananas versus the more extravagant raspberry chocolate ganache red velvet, with Yoshe proposing maybe they should stick with herbal tea. Did she realize that her weight-conscious barbs hit home every time for Sigrid? I wondered as I walked away. Only the result seemed to be that Sigrid ordered more, not less, each time Yoshe mentioned calories. To give Yoshe the benefit of the doubt, maybe they were a running commentary in her own head and she was merely giving them voice.

I jogged the few blocks to the San Carlos Institute, arriving slightly sweaty and a couple of minutes late. As the lights of the theater were already dimmed and the audience quiet, I slid into a seat in the back row. Floor-to-ceiling velvet curtains covered the diner set onstage. Dustin fought through them and announced the next speaker, Fritz Ewing, the culinary poet who had moderated the morning panel. Based on his earlier introduction, Fritz seemed to be best known for using food as metaphor for strong emotion. Most recently his focus had become protein. He approached the podium, shook Dustin's hand, and launched into a monotone reading.

"Mutton, gray strands, like tough sinews of conversation with my ex," he began. "Beefsteak, raw and tender flesh, calling a lover home. One I shall spit to the side of the plate, never to taste again. The other swallowed, joining enzymes in my belly . . ."

Feeling a little queasy, I sank lower in my chair and tried to block out the meat metaphors by reviewing the conversation we'd had over lunch. Neither of the women had seemed all that fond of Jonah, though there was a general admiration of his competence. The news of a failed relationship between Jonah and Dustin surprised me. As I'd learned the hard way last year when Kristen Faulkner was murdered and I landed on the hot seat, this derailed romantic connection would certainly make Dustin a person of interest in the eyes of the cops.

A few rows in front of me, Dustin stood, looking at the vibrating phone in his hand with some annoyance. He strode up the aisle toward the lobby. I slipped out behind him, trying madly to think of a way to ask about his relationship with Jonah. Before I could get his attention, two uniformed cops met him in the lobby and led him to the side of the room. I ducked into the cubby that served as the conference bookstore and pretended to browse the books nearest the door, trying to eavesdrop on their conversation.

"I understand that you need to do your jobs," Dustin was saying, his pleasant tone not quite covering the irritation underneath. "Could we possibly talk after the day's panels are completed?"

I thumbed through a paperback copy of Sigrid's latest novel, not able to make out the policeman's reply.

"I have no idea what happened to the damn bird," Dustin replied. "I can only tell you I had nothing to do with either hefting it or causing it to vanish." Then he stalked back across the foyer and disappeared into the auditorium.

I returned Sigrid's novel to the stack and

headed out, exhausted by the day and anxious about the night to come.

6

When I write about a line cook's bad night, it's not just about a bad night, it's about not being good enough, period, about personal shame and failure.

— Michael Ruhlman

If Key West can be said to have a ghetto, the walk down the blocks of Petronia Street from Duval Street to Santiago's Bodega led us right through it. It was one thing to ride along this path in full daylight, in the back of a pedicab, as we had done this afternoon, another to march the same distance in the darkness.

Mom did her best to keep up a chipper smile as we passed along the drab blocks of small homes, yards littered with odd bits of trash and dour dark-skinned residents who looked as though they'd just as soon not have pale strangers tromping through their neighborhood.

"Maybe we should have had the detective pick us up," she said in a soft voice that let me know she was a little nervous even though she didn't want to be.

I linked my arm through hers. "We're perfectly safe and we're almost there. And he was coming straight from work."

Which was a tiny stretcher. In truth, I preferred to meet him at the restaurant on my own terms. I'd been looking forward to a date with Bransford for weeks, though after last night's conversation I was filled with a greater percentage of dread than anticipation. And besides, having Mom along ensured that we wouldn't be indulging in anything more thrilling than dinner.

Sparks had flown like the worst romantic cliché right from the first minute I laid eyes on Detective Bransford, despite inauspicious circumstances (me as his murder suspect). He asked me out the same day the real killer was arrested. But it took almost five weeks to find an evening that worked for both of us. I'd spent ten days visiting both my families in New Jersey before Christmas — ten days can start to feel like a life sentence under those conditions. But I'd figured one thing out for certain since my parents' divorce: My time had to be divided equally between Mom's house and

Dad's. On top of my family issues, the holidays, especially New Year's Eve when Key West goes party-in-the-streets crazy, were stressful times for the police department.

All that to say anticipation made my heart race and my decision-making difficult — it took me a solid hour to figure out what to wear to this dinner. First I tried on the black swing dress that made me feel sexy but in just the right girlish kind of way. Until I remembered he'd already seen me wear it to a funeral. Bad dating Karma. So I switched the dress out for my black jeans — a little snug at the current payload — and a light blue sweater that made more of my cleavage than actually existed. Mom's and Eric's enthusiastic responses had left me feeling that I'd made the right selection, even though my feet felt like I'd been walking on a bed of bamboo skewers in Connie's borrowed patent leather stilettos. And the heel-strap rubbed exactly on the spot where my mother's gift sandals had created a tender blister. All in all, a fashion-for-comfort blunder I would not repeat. Ever.

Detective Bransford was pacing outside Santiago's. He stopped still when he saw us. "I would have been happy to pick you up," he said, looking worried, glancing from

Mom's sandals to my heels and then into the darkness of the Petronia Street approach.

"I told you we should have asked him," said Mom, reaching for his hand. "Oh my, he's just as handsome as you said he was."

He grinned foolishly and I felt myself turn the color of a roasted beet. "Detective Bransford, this is my mother, Janet Snow. Mom, Detective Bransford."

"Nate, please." He smiled again, flashing the killer cheek dimples that matched the cleft in his chin. "It's an honor to meet you. And you're just as lovely and youthful as Hayley described. You two could be sisters."

I rolled my eyes, but Mom beamed, and he ushered us past the narrow porch with its handful of tables, inside to the hostess station, a hand on each of our backs. The warmth of his touch sizzled like a blazing brand on mutton, as Fritz the meat poet might say. To keep my knees from buckling, I forced myself to focus on the restaurant decor — simple wooden chairs, white tablecloths, sponge-painted walls with a few big paintings for accents, and an orange ceiling for color.

"Where would you like to sit?" asked a tall woman in a tight dress.

"Inside, please," I said, just as Nate said,

"Outside."

"Whatever the lady wants is fine with me," said the detective to the hostess. He grinned at me. "Inside."

She gathered a stack of menus and led us to the corner of the back room, which had a lively bar and marginal acoustics. I minced along after her and took the seat at the table against the wall so I could make mental notes about the restaurant's ambience and clientele. I shucked off the offending high heels and rubbed one aching foot and then the other. Our drink orders — white wine sangria for me and Mom and a Key West Sunset Ale for Nate — were finally taken by a waiter so goofy and smiley I wondered if he'd been tippling something out in the back alley.

I glanced at the menu. "And could you put in orders for the trio of hummus, a spinach salad with strawberries, and the *bocconcini di* mozzarella while we're waiting?" I asked. As soon as the waiter left, I listed off a few more of the tapas that I wanted to be sure we tried — including asparagus, spanakopita, seviche, saganaki, and grouper.

Nate looked down at his menu and then back up at me. His eyes were the color of moss, only nothing soft and fuzzy about them right now. "I'm going to have the Roman meatballs, the potato croquettes, and the lamb patties," he said. "Seems like you've already got the vegetable department covered."

"Those are wonderful choices — I tried them the last time I was here," I said, lowering my voice and smiling sweetly. "If it's possible, I really do need you to branch out." I'd warned both my mother and the detective ahead of time that I had a review agenda for this meal — apparently I should have been more clear because he didn't look happy. Note to Hayley: Don't expect a police detective to be the kind of man who enjoys ceding the lead. On anything. When the waiter returned, I made a big show of ordering the three dishes he'd mentioned and then added my choices.

"Oh, wow, man, you guys must really be hungry!" the waiter said.

"That we are." I closed my menu and passed it to him. If Wally had a fit about the bill, I'd cover the excess. Somehow. Considering the unexpected lunches and the double pedicab bills I'd piled up earlier, I was already way over budget. How much madder could he get?

Soon after, the trio of hummus, the spinach pie, and the spinach salad with strawberries arrived. Mom served us each some salad and then picked up a triangle of pita bread that came with the hummus and sniffed it.

"Remember what Ruth Reichl said this afternoon? She can tell right away about a restaurant from trying their bread." She spread her corner of pita with a teaspoon of black olive tapenade, and nibbled. "Oh, Hayley, you have to taste this. It's heaven," she said, spearing another piece of pita and spreading it with the plain hummus. "This one has lots of lemon, I think. And I have a feeling they brush the bread with butter or olive oil and toast it — if it isn't homemade. If I was reviewing this place, I'd be tempted to write that they have the best chickpea dip outside of Athens."

I couldn't help feeling the tiniest prick of annoyance. She'd said it better than I would have — and faster too.

"You'd be really good at this job," I said, trying to cover my negative reaction with a wide grin. "But no offense, Mom, I have to figure out how to say things myself or I'll be lost once you've gone back home."

"Just trying to be helpful, dear," she chirped. "Remember, I was a cook before you ate anything other than strained carrots." I flashed her another tight smile as the waiter delivered the detective's Roman meatballs and lamb patties.

"So you're a food expert, just like your daughter," Nathan said. "Me, I'm strictly meat, potatoes, and pasta." He poked at the nest of angel hair holding the meatballs. "Though it tastes better if you just call it spaghetti. Want to try it?" he asked Mom.

"Definitely," Mom said. "If you'll try this lovely spinach pastry in exchange. That's how I used to get Hayley to try new things — wrap them in dough or phyllo pastry. And it's all paid off, hasn't it?"

"Yes, Mom." I cut off a corner of the spanakopita before she passed it across the table to him. Delicious layers of buttery, crispy phyllo with a spinach-feta filling and a drizzle of white sauce zigzagging across the top. "Any developments with Jonah Barrows?" I asked the detective once I'd finished chewing. Anything to change the subject.

"Not worth mentioning," he said, and then rubbed a hand across his chin, leaving a small streak of grease.

Mom touched her chin and raised her eyebrows at him. "Grease spot," she said.

He wiped his face with his napkin. "You're absolutely certain you saw no one leaving the area of the dipping pool last night after you found the victim?"

"Honestly, I told you everything I could think of, but I'll try again." I closed my eyes and pictured the sequence of events. "I went to the bathroom. That's where I spoke with Olivia Nethercut. And I'm sure I told Officer Torrence that Sigrid Gustafson was there too. But they were both gone by the time I came out — I guess it might be worth talking to them if you haven't already." I opened my eyes and he nodded.

"We have."

"Then I walked over to sit by the pool. Almost right away, I noticed something off." I tried to keep the gruesome slide show from flashing through my head: Jonah's sodden body bobbing in the lily pads, my feeble attempts at resuscitation, and all that followed after. Should I mention to him that I'd overheard a couple of his men grilling Dustin Fredericks about the bird statue at the conference this afternoon, in hopes that he'd tell me whether and where they'd found it? A waste of breath — he wouldn't tell me any more than he had to. And he'd be annoyed about my eavesdropping. I speared his remaining meatball and twirled a bit of pasta on the fork.

"I wonder who else at the party might have used the restroom about then?" Mom asked. "Of course Hayley wouldn't have known if anyone was in the men's room. Have you thought of that?" she asked the detective, then added quickly, "Of course you've probably thought of everything." She smiled and touched the back of his hand. "None of the ladies that I was talking with while I waited for Hayley left the table. We were too busy drinking and gabbing and taking pictures of everything. I bet I got mug shots of everyone at that party!" She turned to look at me, serious again. "But didn't Bill say something about Eric going over to get one of the fancy drinks they were making near that end of the property? Maybe he saw something that would be helpful."

"I wasn't there, remember? But I'm sure he would have mentioned it," I said. "I thought he had a migraine anyway — would he have been drinking alcohol with a headache?" The waiter reappeared and added the croquettes and two more dishes to the array on our table.

"Rock 'n' roll," said the waiter. "How's everyone doing?"

"Fine," said Nate gruffly. The waiter backed away.

"We had lunch with two of the conference panelists," my mother told Nate. "One of them happened to be Sigrid Gustafson.

105

Hayley asked them all about Jonah Barrows — what people thought of him and how the conference might have been different if he was alive."

"He didn't suffer fools," I said. "And you're bound to get some when you put people onstage and encourage them to hawk their work in front of a big audience."

"Hayley thinks maybe one of the writers had a secret — something they were afraid Jonah might have revealed."

Nathan frowned and took a sip of beer.

"I'm sure he's thought of that," I said. "Mind if I try your potatoes?"

He pushed the plate closer to me. "Go ahead."

I sawed off half of a fried potato patty, dropped a dollop of sour cream and green onions on top, and bit into it. Creamy, crunchy, with the right jolt of heat.

"But I'd prefer that you leave the interviews to my department," he added.

I finished swallowing the bite of potato and laid the empty fork on my plate. "I'm assigned to the conference as a writer. *Key Zest* is paying me to be there and they paid my registration fee, which was hefty. I've been told to write a piece on the life and work of Jonah Barrows. Which would be difficult to do without talking to the people

106

who knew him." I didn't add that I'd be fired if I didn't produce something brilliant, because I was afraid I'd cry.

"He didn't mean it like that, honey," said Mom. "Did you, Nathan?"

Bransford and I glared slitted dagger eyes at each other — as close to fighting as we could have gotten in a nice restaurant when we didn't know each other well to begin with. And didn't want to draw attention to ourselves and had my mother poised to meddle. This was the first night that suited both of our calendars and it looked like Jonah Barrows's corpse — and my mother, still very much alive — would spoil the whole thing.

After we'd plowed through most of the dishes, the waiter stopped by again and cleared some of the plates onto a tray. "How about dessert, folks? We have some utterly amazing choices!"

"No, thank you," said Bransford.

"Of course," I said at the same time.

The spacey waiter's hand froze above his pad.

"Suppose we order something for the table?" my mother suggested, her head buried in the menu. "How about the choco-late crepes and the bread pudding?" She flashed a dazzling smile, closed the menu, and handed it back.

As the waiter left, Nate's phone buzzed. He pulled it out of his pocket and looked at it, frowning again. "I hate to do this, but I have to get to the station. I'll call you a cab. Say half an hour from now? I don't like to have you walking home this time of night in this neighborhood."

"We'll be fine," I said firmly. "We need the exercise after all this dinner — and finishing your part of the dessert too."

Nate got to his feet, grumbling and pulling his wallet from his back pocket. He threw three fifty-dollar bills and a twenty on the table. "I think that will cover it. You'll let me know if it doesn't?"

I couldn't let him pay; Wally would have heart failure. But Nate would never accept the money later — it could only get more awkward.

"Thanks, but I'll put it on my credit card," I said, beaming foolishly and pushing the money back in his direction. "I have an expense account that I'm required to use to keep the reviews on the up-and-up."

"I thought I asked you to dinner," he said.

"You did and thanks so much anyway, but the magazine really needs to keep the boundaries clean. If it appears in any way that the reviews were skewed, we lose all our credibility. And quite possibly our advertisers as well." I squinted and shrugged. "I'm sorry if I wasn't clear. You can get it next time? When I'm not on the clock?" I doubted there would be a next time, the way this evening had gone.

"Fine," he said, shuffling the bills back into his wallet. He ducked his head in my mother's direction. "Janet, it was a pleasure to meet you. I'll call you," he added to me. But not, I thought, like he meant it. I watched him leave, wondering how something that had seemed so full of promise could have ended up falling so flat.

Mom gripped my wrist, her eyes wide with excitement. "Hayley, isn't that Olivia Nethercut who just came in? I know you were disappointed about your conversation getting cut off the other night. Here's your chance to talk with her. I'm sure she hasn't eaten here before. You could tell her what we enjoyed."

"We enjoyed all of it," I said, looking at the silverware and napkins and crumbs littering the table. "Besides, she doesn't want random people bothering her while she eats. And dessert will be here any minute."

"Well, I'm going over, then," said Mom as she pushed her chair away from the table. "It's only polite to say hello. And it's not like she's some kind of rock star or top-level politician who needs to guard her privacy."

What choice did I have but to follow?

"Ms. Nethercut," Mom gushed when she reached her table. "I'm Janet Snow and this is my daughter, Hayley." She pulled me forward. "We're both attending the food writing seminar and we just loved your panel discussion today."

"Thank you. I'm delighted to be part of the conference," said Olivia. Her polite smile, I thought, did not invite further conversation. And she did not introduce us to the woman sharing her table, who was busy thumbing through messages on her smartphone.

"I arrived just in the nick of time on Thursday — any later and I would have missed Jonah Barrows," my mother burbled. "My gosh, even the airport in Key West is adorable."

Olivia nodded without enthusiasm. "I flew into Marathon this time."

"Have you eaten here before?" Mom asked. "We just loved the trio of hummus. Though actually the croquettes were my favorites — these light little patties of crusty mashed potatoes with a tiny bite of hot pepper. They quenched the fire with a dollop of sour cream and chopped green

110

onions in exactly the right way. Hayley's boyfriend ordered those — such a guy thing — but we were all crazy about them. He's a detective with the local police department and just adorable."

I gritted my teeth to keep from correcting the boyfriend comment. Olivia Nethercut would not care about the status of my relationship, which after tonight hovered near ground zero. Better to jump on the food bandwagon and then steer Mom away as quickly as possible.

"The pita bread with the trio of dips was the best we've had outside of Athens," I said. Mom flashed me a grateful smile. "They put tons of lemon in the plain hummus, while the red pepper version was just the right spicy."

"Hayley's the food critic for *Key Zest* magazine," my mother announced to Olivia and her dinner partner.

"I'm sorry to say I haven't heard of that one," said Olivia.

Although she had heard of it — when I'd introduced myself the night before. But who could blame her for losing that fact in the discovery of the murder that followed?

"Local rag," I said before my mother could inform her it rivaled the *New York Times.*

Across the room, I noticed the waiter delivering the dessert we'd ordered to our table. "I would love to talk to you at some point over the weekend if you're available," I said to Olivia. "I'm doing stories on some of the folks here at the conference. What would be the best way to get in touch with you?"

She took an elegant ivory card from a small black satin bag and handed it over. "Text or e-mail — I'll get either."

"Wonderful!" I said, running a finger over the raised printing. "I'll be calling. We hope you enjoy your dinner." I gripped Mom's elbow and steered her back across the room.

"You see?" Mom said as she slid into her seat and unfolded her napkin. "You just need to put yourself forward a little more. Now you've got an interview with a hot-shot."

"She didn't really agree to anything," I said, though I did feel a hopeful glimmer of possibility as I tucked Olivia's card into my worn leather wallet.

My mother divided the desserts between our plates and spooned in a bite of the bread pudding, studded with enormous, fresh blueberries and garnished with vanilla ice cream.

"This is outstanding," she said. "And I

don't even care for bread pudding. Would you say that a critic should always order the restaurant's specials?"

I sighed. "I suppose. If that's what they're steering people toward, you ought to taste it, right?" But I had little appetite for either the bread pudding or the chocolate crepes, too wound up about both the conversation with one of my foodie idols and the evening with Bransford. Beginnings were hard — whether it was a relationship or the dream job you were desperate to succeed at. Endings were worse.

As we started our walk back to Bill and Eric's house, I deflected Mom's suggestion about a second go-around of dessert at the Better Than Sex Restaurant by pointing out that both of us had been forced to unhook the top buttons of our pants during dinner. After the detective left, of course.

We walked the length of Duval Street instead, Mom marveling at the young black boys playing a keyboard and singing at the top of their lungs who reminded her of the Jackson Five in their heyday. We cut away from the crowded bustle of Duval and headed into the residential neighborhood where my friends lived. It was after ten by the time we arrived at Eric and Bill's small cottage. We let ourselves in, surprised that all the lights were blazing. Toby the wonder dog threw all his fifteen pounds of wiry dog flesh at our knees, yapping with outrage.

"I'm home," Mom warbled cheerfully. "Is everybody decent? Hayley's here too. Dinner was amazing. Killer croquettes and the most stunning hummus. And oh, we actually talked with Olivia Nethercut. And Hayley's Nate is just adorable."

"He's not 'my Nate,' " I grumbled.

No one answered.

We walked through the kitchen to the open-air seating that overlooked the garden. Bill was pacing by the fan palms in the backyard, yelling into his cell phone.

"I don't need a lawyer tomorrow. I need one now!"

7

That's something I've noticed about food: whenever there's a crisis if you can get people to eating normally things get better.

— Madeleine L'Engle

Bill slammed the phone back into its receiver and sank onto the couch, burying his face in his hands. Toby leaped up onto the cushion beside him and tried to lick between his fingers.

"What's happened?" I asked. "Why do you need a lawyer?"

He explained in a hoarse whisper that three cops had arrived at the house earlier.

"For what?" Mom and I asked in unison.

"They wanted Eric to come to the station." He glanced up at us, struggling to hold back the tremor in his voice. "To be questioned about the murder of Jonah Barrows."

Mom and I exchanged horrified glances.

"Your boyfriend was one of them," he added, and I winced. Bransford had left dinner with us to pick up Eric and hadn't mentioned it? Not that I'd expect to get the update on every detail of his police business, but good gravy, he knew Eric was one of my best pals. Surely he could have given me a heads-up. It was hard to see how dating a cop in a tight-knit community was going to work out, no matter how cute he was.

"They dropped him off five minutes ago," Bill said, his voice so tight it almost broke. "He went directly to our bedroom and closed himself in."

"So, what were they questioning him about?" I asked.

"He wouldn't tell me *anything,*" Bill said. "But I've never seen him look so bad."

"He withdrew like that when his dad died," Mom said. "That was such a shock. They all took it hard. Because of the unfinished business about the divorce, I suppose. If you don't get these things sorted out at the time they happen, they fester. Eric barely spoke to his mom when he came home for the funeral."

"But he's a grown man now," I said, feeling a little impatient with Mom's amateur analysis. "This behavior makes no sense."

116

Mom nodded and planted herself on the couch next to Bill, circled one arm around him, and reached for his hand, ignoring Toby's warning growl. "He probably needs a little time alone to digest what happened. That's all."

Bill straightened his slumped shoulders. "But doesn't he understand that I'm worried sick too? It's not just him anymore."

"What can we do?" Mom asked, patting his knee. "How can we help?"

"I can call Detective Hotshot and find out what the hell's going on. That's what I can do." I pulled my phone out of my purse and punched in Bransford's number, which shunted me right to voice mail. "He is so not my boyfriend," I muttered while his "away from my desk" message played.

"It's Hayley Snow," I said after the beep. "I'm concerned about my friend Eric Altman. I'm at his house now. Could you kindly call me when you get a chance?"

"Say something nice about the date," Mom fussed from across the room. "She didn't even let him pay," she told Bill.

"Dinner was lovely," I choked out, rolling my eyes and deciding not to explain to my mother *again* that professional ethics demanded that I expense the meal. I slid the phone into my purse and went over to take a seat across from Bill and Mom. "Did Eric even know Jonah?"

Bill shrugged and wiped his face on his sleeve, looking as forlorn as I'd ever seen him. I hoped he was overreacting. After all, the cops had let Eric go after a short conversation, right? Maybe this mess involved one of his therapy patients, in which case he wouldn't be allowed because of professional ethics to divulge anything. Even to Bill.

"Okay if I try to talk to him?"

Bill shrugged again. "You can try."

I popped up, crossed the porch, and went through the kitchen, Toby bouncing behind me, his toenails clacking on the Dade County Pine floor. Remnants of dinner had been abandoned on the speckled gray granite counter — a nice piece of grilled salmon, barely eaten, potato salad, and *haricots verts*. I continued down the hall to the guys' room and tapped on the closed door.

"Eric? It's Hayley. We're all worried. Is there any way I can help?"

I paused to listen but heard nothing. Possible he was snoozing already, but not likely. He was a night owl and a restless sleeper, even in the best of conditions. Besides, Bill said he'd just arrived home. No one drops off to sleep that fast. Except for my ex-boyfriend, Chad, after you-know-what. Which had always been a point of contention and not worth one nanosecond more of my brain time. I shook my head to clear those unwelcome thoughts and tapped again, with a little more force. "Eric? We're here to support you, whatever you're going through."

"Thanks for that. I appreciate you guys coming over. I'll be fine."

He didn't open the door or offer to talk things over. What was the right thing to do? Would it help to remind him I'd been through something similar? Maybe he needed one more little nudge.

"We could brainstorm —"

"Right now what I need is space." His voice sounded flat and hopeless and utterly definite.

"You got it," I answered, and retreated down the hall to the others, stopping first to put the potato salad into the fridge. It looked too good to abandon to the ravages of botulism. Then I dipped a finger into a small bowl of mustard sauce — light and spicy with a touch of honey — considering what to say to Bill. Just the facts, I supposed.

"Like you said, he needs space." I wrinkled my nose and sat back down. Toby jumped up beside me and pawed at my hand until I scratched behind his ears. "This isn't like him. Isn't he the guy who always, always wants to talk things over?"

"Always," said Bill. He closed his eyes and rested his head against the cushion behind him.

Mom started to straighten the magazines on the coffee table, looking as helpless as I felt. There wasn't enough of a mess to clean up to contain her anxiety.

"Do you have butter and chocolate in the house?" she asked. "If anything will bring him out —"

"Fudge pie will," I said, moving Toby off my lap and getting up to help. If Mom and I had one thing in common, it was the urge to cook and eat during a crisis. Even the whiff of crisis brought a surge of recipes to our minds. I wasn't the least bit hungry after our enormous dinner, but just making the pie would feel therapeutic. And it would be something tangible we could leave behind as a token of our love and support.

I cleaned up the remnants of their dinner, tucking the plates and silverware into the dishwasher and scraping a few leftovers into the dog's bowl. Toby rooted through the food, pushed the green beans to the side, and snapped up the fish. Meanwhile, Mom

melted three squares of unsweetened chocolate and a bar of butter in the microwave
and began to beat some eggs. Bill paced a
few laps around the living room and collapsed back onto the couch.

"I can't understand how the Jonah Barrows business would have anything to do
with Eric," I said as I greased a glass pie
pan with butter and turned on the oven.
"What could possibly lead them to even
consider the possibility that he knew something about Jonah's death?"

"Or killed him," Bill called from the
couch, his face darkening like a summer
afternoon thundercloud.

He sprang up and strode off the porch
into their small garden. We watched him
lope down the path past the potted basil
and purple impatiens, then past the three-
tiered fountain and the ceramic-tiled concrete bench, over to the towering traveler
palm and an even taller stand of black
bamboo. A gust of wind blew, rustling the
stiff stalks of bamboo and causing them to
rattle like old skeletons. Bill bolted back up
the stairs, Toby circling through his feet,
yapping with excitement.

"Maybe he did know him. Why else would
he be acting so weird? If the police call you
in for questioning about a murder, why

wouldn't you tell them everything you know and be done with it?"

I could answer that question from personal experience. I'd had nothing to do with the murder of Kristen Faulkner, but under the pressure of the police investigation, I'd felt guilty as hell. If they'd had time to press me a little bit longer before I hired my buffoon of a lawyer, I probably would have confessed. My skeevy lawyer told me there have been hundreds of lawsuits filed — and won — against police departments for the kind of psychological pressure that caused innocent people to buckle.

"You think it would be easy — you didn't do it, so just say so. But you panic. And you start feeling and acting guilty even if you aren't."

"But why wouldn't he simply say he didn't know the man? Why lock himself away like this? It makes him look bad." Bill leaned on one of the barstools facing the kitchen counter, looking pale and shaky. "Remember how he came down with that terrible headache at the party last night and had to rush home? Since when does he get migraines? What if it wasn't a headache at all? What if he fought with Jonah Barrows and something terrible happened between them?"

Mom dropped the whisk and clapped her hand to her mouth, her eyes shining with sudden tears. "Oh my gosh, this is my fault. I'm the one who told the detective that Eric went to the grapefruit bitters table right around the time that man died."

I shook my head. "If he didn't know Jonah, he certainly wouldn't have killed him."

I stirred the beaten eggs into the cooled chocolate and added vanilla and flour, feeling sick to my stomach and, for once, speechless. Maybe he *was* involved somehow.

"Surely it was an accident, then," said Mom. She poured the batter into the pan and slid the pie into the oven. "Our Eric would never hurt someone on purpose. And he's not the kind of man who would run away from trouble."

"In seven years together, he's never shut me out," said Bill. "No matter how bad things got. I'm beginning to wonder if I know him after all." Bill got up, snapped a leash on his dog's collar, and stormed from the house.

Mom and I waited the twenty-five minutes it took the pie to bake, hoping Bill would return and Eric would get lured out of his room by the incredible scent of warm chocolate. But neither happened. We pulled the pie from the oven and hunkered on the back porch, listening to the night rustling, waiting for the dessert to cool. Finally we served ourselves small triangles and loaded dollops of French vanilla ice cream on top. Not that we needed rich pie on top of what we'd already consumed at Santiago's. But it was hard to know what else to do. We both picked at our third dessert of the night.

Mom dropped her fork on her plate and pushed it away. "It feels like rain," she said. "I hope he didn't take the dog too far." She sighed. "Should I pack up and come home with you?"

As cramped as Miss Gloria's houseboat would feel with three of us shoehorned in, I had to agree it was time for Mom to clear out. Whatever was going on with Eric, entertaining a houseguest would not be an asset in hashing things through. Even well-meaning and good-hearted company like my mother. She would straighten the kitchen and cook little treats and natter cheerfully about the weather and the interesting people she'd seen on the streets of Key West, but right now the guys needed privacy.

"I think that's a good idea," I said. She

124

went into the spare bedroom to pack while I called a cab and alerted Miss Gloria and left a note for my friends.

B and E: Mom came home with me for tonight at least. Let us know what we can do. The pie tastes amazing with vanilla ice cream. And maybe a shot of whiskey on the side. I drew a little smiley face and a row of *x*'s and *o*'s and stuck the paper to the refrigerator, where it would be hard to miss.

At the sound of the taxi's horn, I carved off a piece of the pie for Miss Gloria, wrapped it in foil, and helped my mother carry her stuff out to the front stoop. Ten minutes later, the taxi driver dropped her at Tarpon Pier and I pulled in behind on my scooter. As we walked up the finger, the moon glided out from its cover of clouds, causing sparkles of light to dance on the water like a thousand pearls of tapioca. We could hear the deep cowbell clank of the wind chimes on the Renharts' boat, and the answering silvery notes from Connie's front porch. Miss Gloria bounced out on the deck to meet us and I hoisted the suitcase from the dock to her porch.

"What fun having your mom visit — it's a hen party!" Miss Gloria said, clapping her hands. Ninety-seven pounds of exuberant welcome. She reached for the foil packet

Mom was carrying and peeked inside. "And good heavens, you brought chocolate too!"

Hard to imagine all was not right with the world.

8

Unlike cooking, where largely edible, if raw ingredients are assembled, cut, heated, and otherwise manipulated into something both digestible and palatable, writing is closer to having to reverse-engineer a meal out of rotten food.

— David Rakoff

Just after six the next morning, I dressed quickly and scribbled a note for Mom, telling her to hire a cab and meet me at the conference at nine. Then I grabbed my backpack and headed out on my scooter in search of Cuban coffee. It felt strange to be riding in the morning darkness, a little lonely, a little spooky — and chilly. It had rained half the night, and then the front cleared out, leaving colder air and wind. I wished I'd worn an extra layer.

I was feeling bone-dog tired too. Miss Gloria's couch was as lumpy as I'd expected and my housemates had snored through the night in stereo. And I was edgy — Bill had texted me around midnight, thanking me for being understanding and respecting their privacy. And for the chocolate pie, which he rated five out of five stars. But he didn't mention Eric, nor had there been any word from him.

On top of that, I had gotten a worrisome text message from Bransford: *Thx for dinner. Sorry can't say more about your friend. Encourage him to hire a lawyer.*

The idea that Eric could really have been involved with Jonah's death was eating me alive. Why else would Bransford think Eric needed legal representation? Only slightly less worrisome was the probability that my mother had tipped the police off to Eric's possible association with Jonah. I hadn't wanted to make her feel worse than she already did by jumping on that bandwagon, but she *had* fed that information directly to the detective.

I sputtered across White Street and down Southard to Five Brothers and parked my scooter on the sidewalk. The small, idiosyncratically stocked grocery and sandwich shop was already busy with early risers: construction workers, retirees, cops, and the homeless. The smell of powerful coffee and grilling bacon and egg sandwiches on Cuban bread lured me to the back corner, where I ordered one of each, thinking I could save half of the sandwich for Danielle. I moved aside to wait for my order and nearly tripped over Officer Torrence.

"Good morning," I said. "You've got the early shift."

"Crime never sleeps," Torrence said, baring his teeth and straightening the badge clipped to his shirt.

We'd spent so much time together the night Jonah Barrows died. Had he warmed up to me the slightest bit by the end? Would he tell me anything more than Bransford could about the case? Probably better to ask in general terms.

"Any progress on solving Jonah Barrows's murder?"

"We're following leads," he said. "I suspect there will be an arrest soon."

"That's it?"

He laughed, wiping a skim of steamed milk off his mustache. "You don't quit, do you?" He bit into his sandwich and chewed, and then tucked the remainder into its foil wrapping. "You should try one of these — delicious."

I just stared.

"I'm sure you want to know about your

friend. Mr. Altman is a 'person of interest,' as they say on TV. I believe that's as much as I'm authorized to divulge. But it's hard to dispute physical evidence." He shrugged, gathered up the remains of his coffee and sandwich, and started out of the shop. "Have a nice day!"

My food and coffee arrived shortly after he left. I packed it into the crate on the back of my scooter, determined not to ruin the morning by fuming over the Key West Police Department. If they were about to arrest someone, and Eric was a person of interest, was he about to get arrested? And what physical evidence could he possibly be talking about?

If I could keep my focus, I'd have a couple of hours at the office before the conference started to rough out a tribute to Jonah, begin the piece about the conference luminaries, and think about my review of Santiago's Bodega. Then I could concentrate on asking questions about who — besides Eric — might have had it in for Jonah. I hiked up to the second floor and retreated to my office, really a cubbyhole the size of a small walk-in closet, and booted up my computer. I unwrapped the sandwich and began to eat, the melted cheese oozing over the crispy bacon and egg, the fresh roll toasted a nice light brown. After wolfing down half the sandwich and licking the bacon grease off my fingers, I started to work. But the thoughts I was grasping for were floating just out of reach. I had words and sentences and even a couple of paragraphs. But nothing anyone would consider insightful. Or even publishable. Nothing that would snatch my precarious job from the slavering jaws of Ava Faulkner. So I ate the second half of the Cuban sandwich, the part I'd planned to save for Danielle, and buried the wrappings in my trash can.

Around seven thirty I heard her whistling in the reception area, then the whoosh of water as she filled Mr. Coffee, followed by his answering burble.

"Do I smell bacon?" she called.

"Must be from downstairs," I answered, feeling guilty and piggish.

Wally came into the office minutes later and stuck his head into my cubby.

"You're up and at 'em early. Love to see that in my new hires." He grinned.

I got up and stretched and followed him into the reception area, where Danielle passed us mugs of coffee. "You look like you've hardly slept." She batted her eyelashes suggestively. "How was your date?"

I blew on my coffee and shook my head.

"I've had better. He's a bit of a bully."

"He is a cop," said Danielle. "Occupational hazard."

"And having my mother along didn't help," I said, pleating my lower lip between my thumb and forefinger and wondering how much to say about Eric. I liked my coworkers a lot, but did I know them well enough to share everything? I spilled part of it, rat-a-tat-tat, leaving out the disturbing story about Eric getting ferried down to the KWPD and how he'd retreated to his bedroom and refused to come out. I skipped right over to how I'd run into Officer Torrence this morning and how he said an arrest was imminent, based on some sort of physical evidence. Again, I didn't mention Eric.

"I need to find out more about Dustin Fredericks. Yoshe King said that he'd had a short romance with Jonah. Everyone I took to lunch seemed to have the idea that it had ended badly, at least from Dustin's perspective. After lunch, he got called out of the conference so the cops could ask him about the missing bird statue."

"How did you hear about that?" Danielle asked.

"Back up just a minute," Wally sputtered. "How many people did you take to lunch?"

"Only two," I said. "Plus my mother. And of course I'll pay for her meal."

Wally glowered. "I need the receipts for anything you've spent this week."

Danielle ignored him. "Definitely talk with Cory Held. She's a Realtor right downstairs," she said. "She was on the advisory board for the Key West Loves Literature Seminar, but she quit last year." She lowered her voice as if she might be heard through the floorboards. "I think Dustin finally drove her batty."

Wally cleared his throat and pushed his glasses up the bridge of his nose. "Hayley. I have two words for you. Ava. Faulkner."

I blanched, feeling the breakfast sandwich churn in my stomach.

"Your beat is food, not murder," he continued. "If you could keep that in mind, I'd appreciate it. I need a draft of your article about the legacy of Jonah Barrows by tomorrow morning. And make it a clean copy — you're not leaving me much time to edit. I'm sure the cops can get along without your assistance. And those receipts — pronto."

"Righto," I said as Wally retreated to his office. But I was too worried to concentrate and the bacon, egg, and cheese continued to somersault in my gut. I grabbed my purse and a notebook and trotted downstairs to the Preferred Properties Real Estate office. The receptionist directed me down the hall to Cory Held, a small, pleasant-looking woman with dark auburn hair, a sprinkling of freckles across her nose and cheeks, and vibrant red lipstick. She was eating fruit salad and studying the latest listing updates on her computer.

I introduced myself, explaining that I was a new addition to the *Key Zest* staff and that I'd been assigned to write articles about the food writing conference this weekend. "Danielle from upstairs said you might be willing to give me some background information on the seminar and Dustin Fredericks." I watched her face carefully as I said his name, looking for any telltale signs of her previous connection — any twitches, any winks, any snorts of derisive laughter.

She just nodded and snapped the lid shut on her Tupperware container. "I'm sure Danielle told you I resigned from the board this year. Are we talking unofficially?" she asked.

"Absolutely off the record," I said, and perched on the comfortable chair in front of her desk.

"I'm sure you've deduced that Key West

Loves Literature likes to consider itself literary."

I nodded. It was pretty much there in the name — they hadn't called it Key West Loves Hack Writing. And if that wasn't clear enough, the choice of panelists made it even clearer.

"In the past, Dustin took that too far. He insisted on inviting authors who might have had the highest literary standing, but honestly, their books were so dense, they were practically unreadable. What followed from those decisions is that the program sailed over the heads of many of our prospective attendees. It boiled down to this — Dustin has been trying to hawk hypermodernist fiction to a crowd that loves Oprah's book club picks. Attendance started to fall off over the last few years, and the conference has had trouble breaking even. But he didn't want to hear about that. Not from me anyway."

I wrote down "hypermodernist" and "trouble breaking even." "But this year's topic seems a lot more accessible. And at least for opening night, the crowd was standing room only."

She nodded vigorously. "He simply couldn't afford a misstep this year. That's why he agreed to focus on food writing. But trust me, we've been to dinner many times to discuss business and he's no foodie. He orders only what's safe — steak, chicken, chocolate. Never touches a piece of fish or a chef's special."

"And who's in charge of his hiring and firing?"

"The board," said Cory. "I'm certain they're watching the bottom line very carefully this season."

"And the bottom line means?"

"Filling the seats and keeping the sponsors happy."

"And his contract —"

"Is up for negotiation in February. Whether he is invited to continue will depend very heavily on how the next two days go."

She handed me a business card and stood up. "I have to get to a showing. But feel free to contact me if you have any other questions. Or if you're in the market for a house or condo." The skin around her eyes crinkled pleasantly as she smiled.

"Don't I wish?" I said. I considered myself vastly lucky to have a rent-free room on Miss Gloria's boat, as long as I kept an eye on her and helped her with errands. I couldn't afford the down payment on a parking space in Old Town Key West.

As I left the real estate office, my phone

rang. Wally. "I didn't want to say this in front of Danielle, but you need to know that Ava Faulkner has insisted on a meeting first thing Monday morning. She intends to go over everything — receipts, articles, reviews, anything to do with your position. She wants us both there. I can't defend you if you give me nothing to go on. I can't defend any frivolous expenses."

"Understood," I said, working to keep the shakes from showing in my voice. "I appreciate your confidence."

"Huh," he answered, and hung up. Which left me wondering how much confidence he actually had. Was he getting tired of backing me up?

I had forty-five minutes to kill before the conference. I could march back up to my office and try to fit the same five hundred words I'd been struggling with all morning into some reasonable facsimile of a hard-hitting food editorial. On the other hand, my brain felt like overcooked oatmeal. And scribbling more random words would only ratchet up the spiral of my anxiety. And thinking of anxiety made me think of Eric.

It occurred to me that he usually met with two therapy patients on Saturday mornings. If I surprised him at his office, might he tell me what had driven him into seclusion the night before? Worth a try.

I drove back up Truman Avenue, which was already alive with blasts of noise and diesel from the weekend traffic. I parked in the lot behind Eric's office building, wondering whether to ring his doorbell. For reasons of both privacy and safety, he monitored carefully who entered, admitting only folks he expected or grilling them over the intercom first.

As I deliberated over whether surprise or a direct attack would produce better results, a UPS man rang the bell for the upstairs law firm. I drafted in after him and settled into Eric's outer waiting area, listening to soft classical flute music and leafing through *Modern Yachting* magazine, the latest issue. Eric developed seasickness just looking at a boat, but maybe his customers needed the sense of possible escape while waiting to spill their darkest secrets. His office door swung open and he appeared with a welcoming smile. The smile fell off when he saw me.

"Hayley. What are you doing here? I'm expecting a patient any minute." He looked at his watch. "In fact, he's late. If he gets here and finds you in the waiting room, we'll have to spend the next six months talking about how I double-booked him."

"Can I come in for a second? I swear I'll be in and out. I just want to be sure you're all right."

His gaze swept the room and he looked again at his watch. "Two minutes," he said as he whisked me into his inner sanctum. A jungle of orchids bloomed on the shelves around the window, and in the corner, a soothing babble of water washed over beach stones in his Zen fountain. I reacted the same way I had the few other times I visited — my stress dropped instantly. No wonder his patients loved him.

"I'm sorry to bust in on you like this, but we're all worried," I said after he'd closed the double doors behind us. "Mom, Bill, Toby, me, even Miss Gloria."

"Please don't worry about me. I'm fine," he said with a tight smile.

But he didn't look fine. His skin had a grayish pallor, his tailored white shirt was wrinkled, and his hair stuck up in little tufts along the part line, as if he'd forgotten to comb it once he'd stepped out of the shower. Not fine. No way.

"Okay, so, what happened with the cops last night? Obviously you didn't kill Jonah Barrows. So, what's all the drama?" I tried to keep my voice light, thinking he'd be more likely to respond to that than to direct pressure. This wasn't the way things usually went in our relationship — usually I was in some kind of trouble and he was talking me through it.

His eyes closed, he rubbed the back of his hand over his chin so I noticed the patches of whiskers he'd missed when shaving this morning. Then he blinked them open and focused on me.

"Hayley. The police don't have a leg to stand on. They're doing the usual, casting about for suspects when they don't have a clue whodunit." His laugh sounded thin and a little bitter. "You know what that feels like."

"Of course I do. That's why I'm worried. When I was a murder suspect, I had a darn good motive for the crime and no alibi. They weren't targeting me randomly."

He squeezed his hands together and looked away, his lips pinched into one straight line.

"Okay, what about this? Mom's scared to death that she sicced the police on you by telling them you were getting a drink near the dipping pool right around the time of the murder. But how does that make any difference if you never met the guy? So, did you know him?"

His eyes got wide, but at that moment the

buzzer rang with the arrival of his first morning patient. "Gotta go, Hayley," he said. I stood up and he strode across the room to open the parking-lot-side door for me. He gave me a little push. "I'll talk to you later."

9

Each time I see a Michelin star in a small town, I say, well, that's a boring place, and it always is.

— François Simon

I left Eric's office and hustled over to the San Carlos Institute, heartsick at the thought that Eric had really been involved in this murder. Gentle, thoughtful, and above all, self-contained Eric: From everything I knew about him, it was impossible to imagine.

But why wouldn't he defend himself?

And who else might have done it? Had Jonah threatened to expose something about the conference infrastructure? And did Dustin love his job enough to consider killing a man over it — a man he'd been involved with, by some reports? Soured love was famous for inciting rage. He had certainly sounded angry the first night when

I'd gone looking for him at the opening reception. On the other hand, if he'd been entertaining a cluster of sponsors, he couldn't very well have killed Jonah. How could he have managed to get to the other side of the Audubon House grounds, swing that statue, and mow Jonah down? It would require not only ice in his veins but lightning speed. Another puzzling question: Why would Jonah have wanted to ruin the very conference for which he was the featured speaker by disclosing its financial woes?

While I waited for my mother to show up for the first panel, I rustled through my backpack, looking for a piece of gum. I caught sight of my brand-new, unsigned copy of *You Must Try the Skate,* which I'd been carrying around for three days without a chance to read it. Most likely Jonah Barrows wouldn't have mentioned Eric or Dustin in his memoir, but maybe I'd recognize some kind of connection in their history. Skimming through it, I was reminded that Jonah's honesty kick was really nothing new — more of a loud revival of sorts. Like accidentally hitting the volume on the TV clicker and blasting yourself out of the den.

The first three chapters were devoted to his family and their complete lack of interest in food. His mother produced a weekly rotation of meals that began with a well-done roast accompanied by mashed potatoes on Sunday, moved on to hamburgers fried to hockey-puck consistency, and ended with "Oriental Night": slimy chop suey glopped out from a large can to the pan on the stove top and heated to lukewarm. The only saving grace was the crunchy noodle topping. Vegetables also came limp from a can, and the family's weekly salad consisted of a wedge of pallid iceberg lettuce doused in bottled Wishbone Russian dressing. There was no talk about food over the dinner table — there was no talk, period. Jonah's father had been a bricklayer who preferred to eat in silence. Cooking was one of his mother's chores; food was fuel for the family, nothing more. There was no room at the table for a sensitive son's passionate interest in all things culinary.

His upbringing could not have been more different than mine. Every meal that came out of my mother's kitchen had been fresh, local, and made from scratch, except for the very occasional box of macaroni and cheese. And even that had been Annie's certified-organic, rather than the bright orange mixture I craved because it was served at my friends' homes. Over dinner, my parents discussed flavors and recipes and brain-

144

stormed about variations that might turn out even better. After we recovered from the tectonic shock of Dad moving out, I took over his role as appreciative food critic.

An entire new world had opened up for Jonah during his first job as a dishwasher in New York City. As he scraped the remnants of patrons' plates into the trash, he took the opportunity to taste their upscale meals. That led him to choose a program in hospitality at New York University and then to a gig as a sous-chef in a French restaurant in the city. And then followed his famous application for a job as a *Guide Bouchée* restaurant critic. During his interviews, he so wowed them with the accuracy of his taste buds and the novelty of his descriptions that they hired him with practically no experience whatsoever.

In the next chapter, Jonah went on to discuss his training in France and England and the apprenticeship that followed back home in New York. "At first, I savored my work with the *Guide Bouchée*. They helped me understand the importance of what I chose from a menu — the dish should represent a challenge to the chef without being too fussy or peculiar. I learned to spot critic traps on a menu — dishes that no ordinary diner would select. I had some

145

astonishingly good meals and others that were marginally edible. And some memorable bouts of food poisoning. I was taught to notice the restaurant's ambience, the service, the presentation of the meal, the freshness of the ingredients, and finally, their preparation.

"But the life-and-death matter of awarding the stars — this began to weigh heavily on me. Many people will have read about the two well-known cases of chefs driven to suicide after their slide in ratings. One was demoted from three to two stars; the other had his star stripped altogether. Which is not to say there may not have been other personal issues contributing to depression or despair — a perfectly balanced person would not choose this profession to begin with."

I could imagine Jonah cackling with laughter as he wrote this.

"But to contribute to the possibility of a man's despondency and ultimate suicide . . . that was no longer acceptable. And of course, lying or even stretching the truth about food was never an option.

"And finally, the secrecy demanded by the Guides began to press upon me like a lead apron. Because how can prospective diners judge the criticism rendered upon a restaurant if they have no idea who's provided it? Would you choose your spouse or your hometown or even a movie based on anonymous recommendations?"

I skimmed over the next chapter, in which Jonah had quit his job as restaurant critic, moved to the West Coast, and founded a restaurant in L.A. He described the same grinding schedule that I'd heard other chefs talk about, but he did not mention using alcohol or other drugs to keep up the pace. And I doubted he would have held that information back. The chapter after that was devoted to his life through the distorted lens of love.

"Like Keith Richards of the Rolling Stones — if you can believe the words of a heroin addict — I never put the moves on someone else. I preferred to stand back and let things develop. Let the tension mount until it felt almost unbearable, and then watch the other party's reaction.

"Take Z," he said, "a brilliant chef who lurched toward me and ravaged me like a starving grizzly. Or A, ebullient on the page but more like a trembling schoolboy approaching his principal when I met him in person. When I noticed myself rating these last two men as though I would be responsible for writing up their performance (no stars at all in these cases), I knew it was time to take a break from 'love.' "

Feeling a little sickened by that much personal disclosure, I marked my place in the book and leafed through the program, checking to see which writers he had been scheduled to appear with today. I imagined that all of them had secrets they would be loath to expose, but which ones were worth killing over? What about zero stars in the romance department? I would definitely feel murderous if I were Z or A, who'd had their amorous advances described and rated in a best-selling memoir. I really, really hoped that one of those letters didn't stand for Eric.

Mom slid into her seat as I reached the page in the program detailing this morning's session: "Food as Metaphor: The Resurgence of Food Writing as an Expression of Culture."

"Sorry I'm late," Mom whispered. "I took Miss Gloria to breakfast. Wow, can that lady eat! Have you had any news about Eric?"

"Nothing really," I whispered back. "I did see him for a few minutes at his office, but he wouldn't say much. I'll tell you more at the break."

Dustin burst onto the stage from the wings and strode to the podium, a wide, forced smile on his lips. "How's everyone doing this morning in beautiful Key West?" he inquired. "We've planned a glorious day to go along with this glorious January weather!"

But the energy in the audience had wilted — only a few audience members called out in response. He went on to make some general announcements about the day's events, while the panelists mounted the side stairs. Sigrid Gustafson came first, barging across the stage as though she couldn't wait to sit down. Two other women we didn't recognize took their places on either side of Sigrid.

"Isn't Yoshe supposed to be on this panel?" my mother asked, tapping my open program.

I shrugged. "I guess they're switching everything around with Jonah out of the picture."

Dustin assured us we were in for an amazing day, a day that would leave us wrung out and famished. "Those students who have signed up for a special restaurant meal tonight should remember to appear at their chosen venue at seven o'clock sharp. Unfortunately all seats have been sold out, but of course you are all warmly invited to our closing luncheon tomorrow. And breakfast

149

as usual before our final panels. How about our catering company? Aren't they doing an amazing job?"

Tepid applause rippled through the crowd, surely more of an indication of low energy than unhappiness with the food because everything I'd sampled had been delicious.

"Should you need a restaurant recommendation for this evening, please don't hesitate to flag one of us down," Dustin continued. "And don't forget that we are taking deposits for next year's seminar, 'The Art of the Mystery.' "

Apparently he had taken to heart the advice of his board and chosen another topic that would appeal to a mass of common readers. Though I had to wonder if this was the right topic, following on the heels of a suspicious death right here at the conference.

"Now on to our first stellar panel." Dustin looked at his notes, frowned, and then introduced the three women on the stage.

For forty-five minutes we listened to the three writers bat around the topic of food as a metaphor for changes in culture — many of Sigrid's comments we'd heard already at lunch yesterday. A second woman hailed from Colorado and had a lot to say about cowboys and beans. The third woman, a writer from Thailand, broke into tears several times as she described the process of cooking her grandmother's food and how it brought childhood memories to life.

I got up to stretch and run to the ladies' room during the break. As I came out of the bathroom, Dustin waved his arms furiously from across the room. I wove between the clusters of attendees until I reached him, surprised that he would single me out to chat when we barely knew each other. When in fact our only interactions this weekend had been unpleasant conversations around Jonah's death.

"Have you seen Yoshe King?" he demanded in a low voice. His skin was a deep color of violet and the veins on his neck throbbed ominously. "Sigrid Gustafson said you appeared to be friendly with her. She missed her morning panel altogether and now she's scheduled for a reading from her memoir." He looked at his watch, a cheap plastic item whose hands were shaped like a knife and fork. "She's supposed to be on that stage alone in fifteen minutes and I haven't heard a word. We could cover for her in the panel — God knows all of those women abhor a vacuum. But when she's supposed to be performing solo . . ." He rubbed a chubby hand across his face.

"We're very, very clear that every panelist is supposed to be in the greenroom at least fifteen minutes before they go onstage. I've called and texted her — nothing!"

"I haven't seen her today," I said. He seemed like he was about to bust a gut with worry — I should do what I could to calm him down. And maybe a small kindness now would pay off later in a private interview? "Would you like me to look around the auditorium? There have been so many adjustments to the program. Probably she just got mixed up."

"I've looked everywhere," he said. "She isn't on the premises."

Mom appeared at my side. "I know exactly where she's staying. I took her home yesterday after lunch and she showed me her room. They upgraded her to the most magnificent view. Not that you could do any better than your houseboat," she said to me. She reached over and tucked my bra strap under the neckline of my shirt. "My daughter lives right on the water — it's so soothing," she explained to Dustin. "I slept like a baby. Never even heard the squall that blew through."

"Mom," I said, gripping her elbow. "He's not in the mood to hear about my living arrangements or your sleeping experience.

He's worried about Yoshe missing her solo reading and ruining the day."

"You're right," she said, and smiled at Dustin. "I was just trying to say that I know where she's staying. If you'd like, I can run down the street and tap on her door. She probably overslept."

I whooshed out a breath. In case anyone wondered where I got my nosy streak, they could see it in its full genetic expression right here. "You can hardly run down the street and get back in ten minutes," I said.

"Go!" said Dustin, ignoring me and giving her a little shove. "Call on my cell if there are any issues at all. If she's not coming, I'll have to do some damn fancy dancing." He recited his phone number and then Yoshe's too. I punched them both into my contacts directory as Mom bustled off through the crowd.

I followed her outside, not sure who I was more annoyed with, Mom for butting in where she didn't belong, or Dustin for taking advantage of her.

"Come on," I told her. "My scooter's right around the corner. I'll run you over."

She hesitated for a minute — she had never approved of the idea of me riding a motorcycle, even though a scooter was about as far from a motorcycle as Jonah's childhood chop suey would have been from one of Yoshe's Asian noodle recipes. But curiosity and her Good Samaritan streak overrode her nervousness. We walked quickly to the side street where I'd left the bike, and I fastened the helmet on Mom. "Just keep your feet up on these little footrests and hold on tight."

She slung her leg over the body of the bike and clamped me around the waist.

I twisted around to look at her and grinned. "I gotta be able to breathe, Mom."

We sailed the length of Whitehead Street past Hemingway's house to the Southern-most Point on the island and in the continental U.S., marked by an enormous black-, yellow-, and red-striped buoy. At almost any hour of any day, you could find tourists lined up to get their photos taken at the closest point from the U.S. to Cuba. Ninety miles, the sign said. Even today, with the wind whipping the waves so they crashed against the break wall and sprayed the buoy and the people, a queue of visitors in vacation clothes too cool for the weather jostled for position.

"We'll make sure to get this shot before you leave on Tuesday," I hollered over my shoulder to Mom.

We stopped in front of Yoshe's bed-and-

154

breakfast, two blocks past the Southernmost Point on South Street, exactly overlooking the private South Beach and not so private Atlantic Ocean. I parked the scooter on the sidewalk outside the three-story yellow Victorian home with white gingerbread trim and a green-and-white-striped awning. Mom staggered off the back of the bike, removed the helmet, and shook out her curls. She had to shout to be heard over the sound of the waves crashing on the rocks next to the beach.

"That was kind of fun."

I smiled and followed her into the building, decorated with white wicker furniture and miniature palm trees. A wall of wooden cubbies holding mail and metal keys hung behind the reception desk. And an old-fashioned copper bell and a collection of tourist destination pamphlets sat on the polished pine counter.

"Hello!" Mom called, but no one appeared. She rang the bell: still no answer. I peered over the counter into the office behind the cubbies. A computer screen flashed on a cluttered desk, but there was no one working.

We looked at each other. Mom shrugged and darted up the sweeping staircase, me trotting behind. We were both panting a little by the time we got to the third floor.

"Down here." Mom took a right-hand turn and walked briskly to the room at the far south end of the hallway.

"This is it," said Mom, tapping on the whitewashed wood. We listened. Dead quiet inside. She pressed her ear against the door and then tapped again. Nothing.

I took a turn, rapping loudly. "Miss King? Yoshe?" I pulled the phone out of my pocket. "Let's try calling." I dialed the number that Dustin had given us. Through the wooden door, we could hear the answering echo of her phone.

"That's just odd," Mom said. "If we walk around the side of the building, we may be able to see up to her balcony and then try to wave her down. Her porch overlooks the rocks right in front of the water. She could be out there having coffee or doing yoga and not be able to hear a thing. She doesn't strike me as the kind of woman who has to be in reach of her phone every instant."

"Like me, you mean," I said, feeling a prickle of irritation.

"Your generation is different from ours," Mom said over her shoulder. "We like to focus on the people we're spending time with, not the ones we might imagine are having more fun. Wherever else they might be."

I ground my teeth and tried to breathe evenly — one long, slow breath in, one seething whistle out. Sometimes Mom had a way of couching her criticisms and suggestions so gently you could hardly notice them. Other times, especially when she was stressed or a little bit anxious (like now), subtle as a meat mallet.

I followed her back down the stairs and along the red brick path that led around the side of the building. Mom pointed to Yoshe's third-floor, far-corner room. I climbed onto the low cement wall surrounding the grounds to get a better sight line. A heart-wrenching shriek nearly made me fall; I turned quickly to see my mother stagger back off the wall and crumple to a heap on the sidewalk.

"What's wrong? Mom, are you okay?"

"That's her," she wailed, pointing to a messy pink-and-white pile on the rocks below Yoshe's balcony. A big wave sloshed against the boulders, drenching the colorful rags with salt water.

"Don't panic. That can't be Yoshe," I said, crouching down next to her and gripping her hands, and then helping her to her feet. I brushed off the sand sticking to her black trousers. "We probably crossed paths on the way over here. I'm sure she's up onstage at the conference talking about her childhood in China and how she carries those memories into every recipe. Competing like mad with the Thai lady we just heard and furious to get upstaged." I smiled, aware I was babbling but hoping it was in the most soothing way. I smoothed her hair. "There's no reason for her to be on those rocks."

"That's the exact outfit she showed me yesterday," said my mother, wrapping her arms around her torso. Her teeth began to chatter. "Pink and white. She said she was so tired of everyone wearing black — she wanted to stand out for this reading, look young and fresh. I swear it's her, Hayley." She burst into more weeping and sank back to the pavement. I looked around for someone to flag down — in this town you were rarely alone. But now, when I needed help most, there was no one.

"I'll go take a look. If I signal to you, call 911. In fact, call them right now anyway and tell them what's going on. Or Bransford. He's in my contacts list." I pressed my phone into her palm. Detective Bransford was going to love being called out because my mom saw a pile of pastel rags on the beach, but better safe than sorry.

"Oh, please be careful," my mother croaked. "I'd feel so awful if she was in trouble and we did nothing. But it's not worth you getting hurt too."

I hopped over the retaining wall and began to crawl hand over hand across the rocks, which were more damp and slippery than they had looked from a safe distance. I crept a little closer, just near enough for the pale face and dark hair to materialize against the pink clothing. Yes, Yoshe. And her neck was crooked at an unnatural angle. An enormous gray gull glided in and settled on the rock next to her head.

"Get away, you stupid bird!" I hollered, imagining him pecking at her. Not wanting to imagine where he'd start. I waved my hands until he flew off. "Call the cops!" I screeched back at Mom, gripping the slick coral beneath me. "Better let Dustin know too."

10

It's so beautifully arranged on the plate —
you know someone's fingers have been
all over it.

— Julia Child

Within half an hour, the block was thick
with police cars, emergency vehicles and
personnel, and a fire engine. My mother
and I had been stashed in the backseat of
one of the patrol cars, with its engine running and the heater blasting. We'd been
asked to stick around until they secured the
area and had time to question us about our
gruesome discovery. My hands and pants
were stained green by the crawl across the
rocks, and Mom was doing her best to clean
my palms with a spit-dampened tissue. It
gave her something to do other than stare
at the scene outside the cruiser, so I didn't
object.

A rap on the window caused us both to

startle. A tall woman carrying a bamboo tray of steaming mugs and a plate of cookies motioned for us to open the door. Gripping her collar closed and breathing hard, Mom tapped on the window until the officer standing guard nearby unlocked our door.

"I'm Reba Reston, the manager here," the woman said, pointing to the bed-and-breakfast. "I thought you might be able to use these. This is such terrible news about Ms. King." Then she handed us each a cup of peppermint tea and slid the cookies onto the seat beside me.

Chocolate chip. Homemade or from a package? Without thinking, I picked one up to nibble. Homemade. The tiniest bit dry, though just about anything would taste like sawdust right at this moment.

"We appreciate your concern," I said automatically.

"I'm so sorry I wasn't there to help," said Reba, wringing her hands. "I was in the back office answering phone calls and confirming bookings, and before that was breakfast, so I never heard anything out of order. And then I had just gone to the restroom when you ladies arrived. Such a terrible thing to happen. Do you suppose she was a drinker?"

161

Mom sputtered, nearly choking on her first sip of tea. She swallowed hard and straightened her shoulders. "We have no idea what happened. Whatever gave you the idea that Miss King was a drinker?"

"Just that it wouldn't be easy to topple off that balcony. They designed it chest-high on purpose even though some of our guests complained that it ruined their sight line when they were seated in the deck chairs. But of course, it was most important to avoid exactly this kind of thing." She wrung her hands again. "Maybe if you were really, really drunk you could do it," she mused. "Or intent on doing yourself in."

The thought came to mind that she was positioning herself to defend her establishment against possible lawsuits.

"I wouldn't have pegged her for either," Mom said. "A drinker or a suicide. And besides, if you truly wanted to do yourself in, there must be better ways. You could count on breaking some bones — that's about it. Unless she dove headfirst. . . ." My mother shuddered.

A cop approached, talking into his phone. He motioned Reba away from the cruiser and slammed our door shut. She melted back into a small crowd that had gathered like vultures circling roadkill. We both sniffled a little, watching through the cruiser's windows as the paramedics reached Yoshe's body. After the police photographer finished taking pictures, they loaded the body onto a stretcher, silent like an old movie. Behind them, the sun slid out from its cover of wispy clouds, and the water slapped happily against the breakwater. Two policemen stayed behind, searching the area around the rocks, where the body had been. One pointed up at her balcony, where a third man was studying the railing. I put my arm around my mother, who couldn't seem to stop shivering.

"I'm betting that woman was just trying to cover her behind," I said.

"This makes no sense," she said. "Yoshe was so excited about reading from her memoir. And there's no way she'd get drunk in the morning anyway. I'm not a dietician or a psychologist, but she was a health nut. She told me all about it when I walked her home yesterday. Why bother to eat right if you're thinking about killing yourself anyway? And she prided herself on taking the stairs. That's why she specifically asked for a room on the third floor. Though the view wasn't bad either."

"She looked like she was in good shape," I said.

"You have to take care of yourself as you sled through middle age — that's what she told me," said Mom. "She said Sigrid thinks those extra pounds will never catch up with her."

I pictured her lumbering across the stage without much grace. "They already are."

Mom sighed. "I got the idea that she'd been nagging Sigrid about her weight. Which I don't think you'd do with someone you barely knew. Would you? Did you notice at *La Crêperie* she tried to steer her toward a salad?"

"I noticed. It didn't work. In fact, it back-fired."

Mom snuffled and blew her nose into a clean tissue. "Yoshe was most of the way through another cookbook. Asian-style flavors like her others, but this was going to be home cooking. She traveled around China, collecting ideas from local chefs and grandmothers and the remnants of her own family. It sounded so good. And now I'll never have access to those recipes."

"Mom, the publisher will make certain it gets finished. She's a big moneymaker for them. People are crazy about authentic family connections — especially these days when the world is in such turmoil. The publisher would no more let her recipes languish than if they found a long-buried manuscript of Julia Child's."

But I knew the tears were about something else altogether — the shock of losing someone she so admired and had begun to know personally. The absolute horror of finding someone dead. Two people in the span of three days in my case.

I was distracted from those morbid thoughts by the arrival of Detective Bransford. He appeared rumpled and tired, as though he'd been shorted in the sleep department the night before. But not unattractive. In fact, his unfinished appearance made him seem a little more vulnerable. Almost human. Like he could use a hug. Which made me realize that as bad as finding a body was for us, maybe it was worse for him. Because he was ultimately responsible for protecting his island and the people on it. And things were going horribly in that department.

The cop who'd been talking on his phone gestured at us. "They're in the back of my cruiser," he told Bransford, loud enough for us to hear through the window.

The detective came over, opened the door, and peered in, frowning. "Hayley, Mrs. Snow." He shook his head. "I can't believe you're here. I hardly know where to start."

"Isn't it just awful?" Mom asked. "She was such a talented cook and writer. It's a terrible loss to the food community. Even ordinary cooks who wouldn't otherwise have had the nerve to try an Asian recipe adored her. She helped make foreign food accessible."

"I don't think that's what he means," I said, taking Mom's hand, my kind feelings toward Bransford ebbing away. "I think he's finding it hard to believe that we've discovered a second dead person within the span of three days."

"It does pique my curiosity," the detective said. "Suppose we begin with why you happened to end up here."

"We were doing Dustin Fredericks a favor," Mom said. "Yoshe didn't show up for her panel and I knew where she was staying, so I volunteered to pop over and knock on her door. Only she wasn't in her room. And then we thought maybe she was snoozing out on her deck or running through a few rounds of the sun salutation and didn't hear us. And so we came out here. And that's when I spotted her." Mom's composure cracked and she began to cry. I scowled at the detective, who ignored me.

"And how did you happen to know where

her room was?"

My mother explained that she'd walked her home the day before after having a lovely lunch on Petronia Street. She started to describe the dishes we'd sampled, but he cut her off.

"Would you say you were the last one to see her alive?"

"I couldn't say that and be sure it was true," Mom said, pressing both hands to her chest. "Though no one at the conference remembered seeing her this morning. I imagine your pathology experts would be able to pinpoint when she died. Don't you think?" Before he could answer she continued. "We certainly don't think she threw herself over the railing. The manager wonders if she was drinking, but again, your people could be the judge of that should you decide an autopsy is in order. Which in this case, I imagine, would be a slam dunk."

"Was the door open when you arrived? Unlocked?" asked the detective, who seemed a little flustered by losing control of his interview to my mother.

"We didn't try the door," I said. "We were not interested in breaking in. We only wanted to remind her she was due at the conference."

"Something different for you," said Brans-ford.

"No need to be snippy," said Mom. "We're all a little tense. It's been a terrible morning."

At that moment, Dustin Fredericks roared up on his scooter, no helmet, thin hair wispy in the wind. He weaved through the crowd around our cruiser and wobbled to a stop, looking distraught. Like a man who saw his livelihood ebbing away, I thought suddenly. His face paled as he saw the stretcher bobbing over the rocks, Yoshe's body draped in a silver blanket.

"What the devil?"

"It's definitely Yoshe King," Mom said sadly. "We found her on the rocks below her balcony." She turned back to the detective. "It occurs to me that if I were wondering whether someone pushed her over that railing, the question that naturally comes before that is whom she would have let in the door."

The faces of both Dustin and the detective tightened to alert.

"Pushed over?" Dustin asked. "You mean she was murdered too?"

11

A weariness has settled in and taken root, helped along by the gray and frigid weather and the aftermath of a headache, a blousy, bilious feeling, dense as pound cake.

— Meredith Mileti

Once the police had finished interviewing all of us, and Yoshe's body had been loaded into the ambulance and driven away, Dustin got back on his bike and roared over to the conference. To Mom and me, it didn't seem right to return to listening to panelists talk about food, no matter how much we'd paid to attend. And no matter how much we'd looked forward to the weekend. The air had leaked right out of our enthusiasm. Most of the day was shot anyway. And for some reason I couldn't quite pinpoint, Mom felt responsible for Yoshe's death. If only she'd thought to look for her earlier, or

169

had called to check on her the night before, or half a dozen other equally unreasonable possibilities. So sightseeing was also out of the question. Even a tour of Hemingway's place, former home to the most tragic and morose figure on the island, didn't tempt her.

I could think of two things that might both calm Mom down and cheer her up. One was cooking. And eating what we'd made. After all, other than a couple of slightly dry cookies and the too-sweet tea, we hadn't had a thing since breakfast — and for me that egg sandwich had come very, very early.

The second was a tarot card reading by Lorenzo. I offered Mom the two options. She was in favor of both.

"Lorenzo sets up at the sunset celebration on Mallory Square almost every day, and we're a little early for that," I said. "But he's usually there ahead of time."

"Let's try," Mom said. "I've been dying to meet him."

Mom was a tarot fortune-telling addict — she rarely made a move without consulting her Rider-Waite tarot pack. Her entire divorce agreement with my dad had been negotiated by tarot. And the decision to sell her own mother's house — same thing. Since moving away from home, I'd found myself sliding in the same direction. Only my results hadn't been consistently friendly — the cards I'd been dealt recently scared me half to death.

"You could read for us just as well," I said, feeling a sudden flush of trepidation. Mom wouldn't tell me really bad news, even if she saw it in the cards. "He's not always on target."

"No one's always right," she said. "Sometimes it's nice to get someone else's energy involved in a reading. Especially in times like these." She perched on the rear seat of my scooter, one hand on my waist, much more relaxed about the ride than she had been on the way over.

When we reached Whitehead Street right near the Courthouse Deli and the Green Parrot Bar, she tugged on my shirt and pointed for me to pull over. Surely we weren't going to start drinking this early in the afternoon?

"Hayley, I think it's time I rent my own wheels. That way I won't be relying on your generosity to get around. And I can have a little independence."

"But you hate motorcycles," I said after a stunned pause.

"It's hardly a motorcycle." She laughed. "More like a bike with a toy engine. I can

171

handle it, dear." She rubbed my back, hopped off the scooter, and handed me the helmet I'd loaned her. Then she marched over to the nearby rental hut and accosted a tanned man wearing a faded Hawaiian shirt, his blond hair pulled into a ponytail that hung almost to his waist. His head was bobbing to music we couldn't hear. She motioned to him to remove his earbuds.

"I'd like to rent a scooter. And a helmet. Both of them pink if possible."

"Hmmm. Pink is popular," he said, studying my mother with a bemused smile. "I think I rented the last one." Mom's face fell. "But I did take delivery on a new machine yesterday."

They combed through the rows of motorbikes until he found a Euro-style moped with a locking trunk — cotton candy pink — and a pink paisley helmet to match. Not a scratch on either one. I didn't have the heart to mention to the attendant that my mother had never driven — or even ridden on — a scooter before today. From the wacky driving I saw here on the streets every day, this did not seem to be a prerequisite anyway. After taking her license and credit card information, the man pushed the scooter into the middle of the parking lot.

Now Mom looked nervous and flustered:

I suspected a case of cold feet. "My daughter thinks this might be over my head."

"Pffft," he said with a flick of his fingers, "you just get on it and ride. It's not like operating the space shuttle." He explained how to start the bike, accelerate, and most important of all, how to brake. "You should use both front and back brakes, but in an emergency, rely on the front. You'll stop quicker. But don't brake too suddenly — I've seen the mechanisms lock and dump the rider right over the handlebars. Usually after a few beers." He squinted at her, looking a little more worried.

"I don't even like beer," Mom assured him. She putt-putted around the parking lot for twenty minutes until she pronounced herself ready and then rolled the pink bike out onto the street behind mine.

"Thelma and Louise, meet Hayley and Janet," she called out as she fastened the helmet's strap under her chin. Not an image I found comforting.

"Scan the road and the sidewalks all the time," I warned her. "Look for bicyclists, cars, pedestrians, chickens . . ."

"Thanks, dear," she said, smiling as she gunned the engine and swerved past me into the flow of traffic.

Ten minutes later we reached the Customs

House Museum, where I showed her how to park the bike and pull it up onto its stand, a detail that the hippie rental agent had failed to cover.

"Always, always remember to take the key," I added.

She linked arms with me. "I know I said this before, but it's still true. I'm having so much fun with you." Her eyes filled suddenly. "Even with all that's going on."

"I know. Weird how you can feel two such different things at once," I said.

We followed the brick path between the Westin Hotel and the water, admiring the yachts tied to the closest moorings. On the largest boat, three stories high with a deck the size of Miss Gloria's entire home, workers dressed in white shorts and shirts polished chrome and swabbed mahogany while the owners sipped wine and looked out at the world.

"Don't you think it would feel like being in a zoo?" Mom whispered. "Speaking of zoo animals, where did you live with Chad?"

"Nice transition, Mom." I snickered — I knew she'd been dying to ask about my ex but trying to hold back — and pointed to his whitewashed building a block to the left. But then I flashed on the possible horror and humiliation of running into my old

174

boyfriend while showing his gorgeous place to my mom. "I can't take you any closer because of the restraining order."

She pulled away, her hazel eyes widening to the size of quarters.

"Just kidding. Let's go find Lorenzo." I gripped her arm and guided her in the opposite direction. It took us almost fifteen minutes to get to the main square because Mom wanted pictures of everything: the bar that looked like a trolley car, the Cat Man of Key West setting up for his feline acrobatics show, the slightly sad aquarium. She walked over to take yet more photos of the cruise ship getting ready to cast off from the dock.

"Howdy, Hayley," called a man from his perch on a cement wall bordering the square. I waved back at Tony, a homeless guy I'd met before Thanksgiving. We'd bonded when he helped me find the real killer of my ex's girlfriend. He'd been keeping a loose eye on me ever since. In exchange, I gave him leftovers and spare change whenever I had them.

"Who the heck is that?" my mother asked.

Grubby and marginally groomed, he didn't look like the kind of friend a mother would want her daughter to cultivate. And the two men lounging on either side of him looked worse.

"He's homeless," I explained, trying not to sound defensive. "He helped me out with that business about Kristen Faulkner. He's a nice enough guy but rough around the edges. And to be fair, he's lived through some hard life experiences. He isn't about to follow some random authority's rules."

Tony sauntered over and I introduced them, cringing a little inside.

"Wouldn't your mother like a photo of us?" Tony asked. "We're pretty good local color." He broke into a big smile that showcased his missing incisor.

"Yes, of course I would," said Mom. "Thank you for suggesting that." After she had arranged the three bemused bums into a photogenic pose, she gave them each five dollars and we moved on to find Lorenzo.

"This is such an interesting place to live," my mother said. "I love all the different kinds of people you've gotten friendly with. Makes me feel like I did something right as a mother."

Lorenzo was setting up shop in the large open area between the Waterfront Theater and the harbor. He straightened a deep blue cloth edged in gold fringe over his card table and pulled on a vest decorated with the stars and the moon. His tie was pinned to his shirt with a large silver question mark. And a rhinestone the size of a golf ball dangled from his black turban almost to his heavily made-up eyes.

"Hayley!" he called out, then placed his fingers to his forehead, as if concentrating deeply. "This must be your mother." He hurried over to hug her. "I didn't read that in the cards," he whispered to Mom. "She told me you were coming. Welcome to sunset in Key West. Your daughter is one of my favorite customers."

"That means I've paid him a small fortune," I said with a laugh. "Can you give us each three cards?" A three-card reading would offer us a quick glimpse into our past, present, and future. I laid a twenty-dollar bill on his table and rustled in my backpack for another.

"This one's on me," he said, waving the money away and escorting my mother to the chair across from him. He waited for her to sanitize her hands, then placed his deck in her open palms. She shuffled the cards and handed them back, a look of hopeful anticipation on her face. He dealt out the ten of pentacles, the nine of cups, and the two of cups.

"So interesting," Lorenzo said, leaning over the table to get closer to the cards and visibly slowing his breathing. "As you probably know, the ten of pentacles, the card in your past position, represents a good home life, security, prosperity, and happiness . . . on the surface. But look a little closer" — his finger grazed the card's border — "the family crosses paths, but they are not together. They don't appear to appreciate the richness and blessings around them, which are symbolized by the stars or pentacles."

Mom looked down at her hands, brushing the empty place on her left ring finger where her wedding band had been. "That's so true," she said sadly. "I took too much for granted."

"Dad had a role in that too," I told her. "It takes two people to ruin a marriage."

Lorenzo raised his thick eyebrows, causing the rhinestone to sway, and tapped on the second card, a seated man with nine chalices arranged on a ledge behind him. "But here in the present you are happy and comfortable. Life is your banquet right now!"

He smiled broadly, as though delighted to shift gears to some cheerful news. What a burden to have to constantly tell people the bare truths about their lives. Like working as a shrink, only worse, because folks probably put more stock in Lorenzo.

"And here." He pointed to the third card. "Ooh-la-la! I see love and friendship — a new relationship based on passion and understanding. You will feel a connection experienced by few others. And could you possibly be discussing marriage?" His eyebrows arced almost to the line of his turban; his black eyes twinkled.

Mom giggled, flustered, and covered her eyes with one hand. "You must have given me Hayley's card — she's the one with the boyfriend. I'm all washed up in the romance department."

Lorenzo just grinned and passed me his bottle of witch hazel hand sanitizer. I spritzed my hands and shuffled the cards, the feeling of dread in the pit of my stomach mushrooming.

Lorenzo turned over my three cards: the devil, the tower, reversed, and the emperor.

I groaned. "I knew I should have skipped this today."

Mom patted my leg, a worried frown playing on her lips. "It's only cards."

But I'd seen how happy she looked when Lorenzo turned over the two of cups and explained that true love lay in her future. She believed completely in this stuff. Two new customers, middle-aged women wearing tropical sundresses and heavy tans, approached Lorenzo's table and peered over my shoulder.

"Oh my gosh, she's got the tower," said one to the other, and then they backed away.

"The devil in us keeps us chained to other people's expectations," Lorenzo explained, speaking quickly as if he was suddenly pressed for time. "In the past, you may have been bound by your fears or by a situation that was unhealthy for you. Even an addiction of some kind."

I grimaced and nodded like a good sport. He probably hated giving me a lousy reading almost as much as I hated receiving it. And hadn't everyone been bound by fear at one time or another? For me lately, it had been the fear of relying on myself, rather than a man.

"Now, the tower in the present position" — he shifted in his seat and tried to smile with reassurance — "represents the structure of defenses you've built around yourself. A shocking truth can shatter your perceptions. While it may seem that there is chaos all around you, you should consider welcoming the challenge, the change from the restrictions of your previous card. Some people say that moving on and rebuilding can only happen after such destruction has occurred," he said hopefully.

"The restrictions of the freaking devil." I sighed, barely able to listen to him yammer about my third card — the emperor. Something about a paternal figure and a quest for mastery that might not be progressing.

It made no sense to let myself react so strongly to a couple of colored cardboard cards, but the last time Lorenzo had turned up the tower, I'd nearly been killed by a crazy woman.

12

The best moment of the day, he says, is when your knees are under the table.
— Colman Andrews

We were both exhausted after our readings, though I tried not to show just how shaken I felt. "I'll stop by Fausto's Market on the way back. You go on home and have a glass of wine with Miss Gloria. What do you want to make for supper?"

After some discussion of possibilities that left me salivating even though I wouldn't be eating with them, we settled on Screw the Roux Stew, an old faithful recipe Mom had coaxed out of her cousin MK in Texas. She started back toward Tarpon Pier on her pink scooter, promising to chop the onions, celery, garlic, and peppers and start them sautéing before she and Gloria broke open the wine. I drove to Fausto's, the tiny grocery store halfway up Fleming Street, and hurried inside. I selected a roasted chicken, a length of smoked sausage, a half pound of Key West pinks — our local shrimp — and some frozen okra. Impossible to find decent fresh okra in January, even on a tropical island.

By the time I reached the dock and parked my scooter, I could smell the vegetables cooking from seventy-five yards up the finger. Mom and Miss Gloria were sitting on the deck of the houseboat, sipping white wine out of tiny cut-glass snifters, our two cats lounging beside them. When I got to the boat, Evinrude meowed and then sprang up and wound between my legs, half greeting, half complaint. Sparky leaped onto Miss Gloria's lap, splashing wine on the blue Conch Republic flag emblazoned across her white sweatshirt. She dropped him back on the deck and shuffled inside in her green rubber Crocs to help me unload the groceries.

"Are you sure you won't trip in those things?" I pointed to her clogs, and then instantly felt bad about saying anything. We were still working out the boundaries of our domestic partnership. I hated to insinuate that she was decrepit or frail, but on the other hand, her son was counting on me to keep her safe. And his confidence in me was all that stood between her and an old age home in Detroit.

"You want her to wear old-lady lace-ups?" Mom asked as she followed us inside. "Give her the sausage, Hayley. I'll take the chicken."

"I made up my layered lime-carrot-pineapple Jell-O mold this afternoon," Miss Gloria announced proudly. "I haven't really cooked in years, but you ladies inspire me. We can have it for dessert since I finished eating your chocolate pie this afternoon."

Jell-O mold? Mom and I exchanged rueful grins behind her back and I suspected she was hoping, as I was, that one of the layers didn't turn out to be a jar of mayonnaise.

"Shall we invite Connie too?" Gloria asked.

"The more the merrier," said Mom. She began to shred the roasted chicken while Miss Gloria chopped the sausage and I shelled the shrimp.

Connie arrived as the rice was almost done and the stew bubbled on the stove, filling the houseboat with luscious, spicy smells. I dumped in the frozen okra, turned down the heat, and we settled on the deck with freshened drinks. Every evening spent on Miss Gloria's porch, tiny lights winking, water gently sloshing, made me feel as though I couldn't get any luckier.

"How's your business going?" Mom asked Connie.

"Not bad," said Connie. "Hayley helped me land some weekly cleaning contracts at the Truman Annex, and those are starting to kick in now with the snowbirds arriving in town. Before Christmas, it's more maintenance and getting places ready." She glanced down at her clasped hands and then up at us, grinning. "But I have some news. Ray and I are engaged!"

Mom shrieked and leaped up to hug her. "Hot dog! I'm so thrilled for you! Hayley's told me all about what a sweet man Ray is. Let's see the ring."

Connie held out her hand, where a slim gold band studded with a small ruby circled the ring finger. "We were out fishing this morning early. He'd hidden it in the tackle box and it got caught on the hook of one of his skitter pop lures. Almost a goner."

I laughed and came over to hug her once Mom let her go. "That's so Ray. I'm happy for you — you landed a keeper."

She hugged me back. "Thanks. He says I'm worth a big whopping diamond, and if his paintings ever catch on, that's what I'll get." I felt the tiniest twinge of envy, wondering if I'd ever find a guy who loved me the way Ray adored Connie.

"If there's any way I can help at all," my mother said. "With the wedding or anything. This is such a happy time, but it must be hard without your mother."

Connie nodded, her eyes bright with tears. Her mom had died of breast cancer when we were college roommates. We didn't talk much about the empty space her mother's death had left in her life, but I could imagine how lonely it would feel not to be able to share a moment like this. Which made me appreciate Mom even more. In spite of my intermittent urges to wring her neck.

"You haven't told us anything about your date last night," Connie said to me.

"He's pretty much impossible," I said.

"You haven't given him much of a chance," Mom protested. "He's a traditional kind of guy — like your father was. For heaven's sake, let him pay the check once in a while. Or maybe if you feed him dinner instead of going out all the time — that's how I won your dad over."

I choked back my first response, which was that Mom wasn't perhaps the very *best* person to give advice on this topic. Dad's parting words when I was ten were burned into my brain like a chop steak seared in a hot cast-iron pan. I had crouched on the landing above the living room, listening to them argue.

"Life isn't all about dinner parties and recipes, Janet," he'd said. "I always thought you'd find a career, develop your intellect and your interests. Not stay home permanently as a housewife." His lips had curled in mild disgust. "We have nothing in common anymore."

"We have Hayley," Mom answered, and then begged him to give her another chance. But ten years of an unfulfilling marriage were enough for my father. He hadn't wanted a stay-at-home wife. He'd expected my mom to challenge him — and herself — and contribute to the household. Once it became clear that his picture of marriage would not materialize, he wanted to move on while they were still young and had prospects of meeting someone more compatible. Soon after they split, he had met someone.

My mother spent the first few weeks without him in the local hospital's psychiatry unit. No wonder I'd always felt like he could manage life without me in its center, but her? Unlikely. The highlight of Mom's life seemed to be talking to me on Sunday evenings. We chatted a lot more often than that, but on Sundays Mom settled in her living room with a cup of tea and the phone to catch up on everything. Everything.

"Men are different animals," said Miss Gloria, interrupting my thoughts. "They need a lot more support than we do. And compliments too. And the funny thing is, they don't even realize it." She clucked her tongue and set her empty glass on the table. "My Harry always thought he was looking after me, but in truth, it's a good thing he went first." She told a story about a time she'd been laid up after her son's birth. Harry had flooded the laundry room and then started a fire in the oven when he'd tried to bake a casserole in a plastic container. "Three trucks responded and all those big fire department lugs came tromping through my kitchen. I knew I had to get up and take over or the house would be destroyed."

I was embarrassed to realize I hadn't imagined Miss Gloria as anything other than a senior citizen. Spunky, yes, but elderly all the same. I'd filed her away in the old lady slot in my mind, not thinking she'd been my age once, with big hopes and dreams for her life and her family.

"You should start dating someone, Janet,"

Connie said.

"Whoa!" I said. "Ding, ding, ding. Major off-limits conversation alert!"

"Hayley's father was one in a lifetime," Mom said, sipping her wine and smiling at me. Then a funny expression crossed her face, which I took to mean subject closed.

"Awww," said Miss Gloria. "That's so romantic."

And slightly pathetic, I thought, realizing yet one more time why establishing my career felt so important. A girl shouldn't rely on a man to give her life meaning. "Soup's on," I said.

We moved to the card table we'd set up in Miss Gloria's tiny galley. She'd covered the table with an old lace tablecloth, faded blue linen napkins, and the remnants of her good china. Mom ladled the stew over bowls of rice while I retrieved the cornmeal-cheddar scones I'd taken from the freezer and warmed in the oven. I took just a small taste of everything. At this point, I would have preferred to stay home, but I'd paid dearly for the special seven-course dinner offering at Louie's Backyard. If I didn't write it up, there would be no turning in the receipt to *Key Zest* and no restaurant review. And no insider buzz about the conference — or the murders — from the other diners.

Connie and Miss Gloria proclaimed the stew and the biscuits delicious.

"Better with fresh okra, if you can get it," Mom said. "If you make this for your new husband, take care the sausage isn't so strong it overwhelms the rest of the ingredients." She waggled a finger at Connie and grinned. "I'll write out some of my recipes for your trousseau. Never mind the fancy underwear."

"How was the conference today?" Connie asked.

Mom and I exchanged glances. "Not great," we said at the same time. The sickening vision of Yoshe King's body splayed out on the boulders, drenched in seawater, rushed to mind. I sighed, and described our discovery.

"That's horrible!" said Miss Gloria, then added, "Why didn't you tell us right away?"

"There's nothing to be done about it now," said my mother. "I suppose we were resting from the day." Connie leaned over and gave her a quick hug.

"Who's killing the food critics of Key West? Wasn't that a movie?" By now Miss Gloria sounded a little tipsy — I was sure her son would not approve.

"We shouldn't assume the two deaths are related," I said, standing up to clear the

190

table and make room for Miss Gloria's wiggly mold and a plate of cookies. "Or even that she was murdered."

"If someone didn't kill her, what happened?" asked Connie when I returned with bowls and spoons. I took a tiny taste of the mold to be polite.

"Delicious," I told Miss Gloria with a smile. "The lady at her bed-and-breakfast wondered if she was a big drinker," I said. "It's possible that she got up on the railing for some reason and then slipped and fell. Or it could have been a suicide."

"Is there any evidence for those possibilities?" Connie asked. "Sounds unlikely that she'd climb up on the railing, doesn't it?"

"And she didn't seem sad to me," Mom said. "She was a marvelous chef and writer — at the height of her career."

"So different on the outside from Jonah Barrows." I described the highlights of what I'd read in his memoir earlier today — the rough upbringing, the lovers, the rivals, his sharp opinions about everything.

"They both had difficult upbringings, but for different reasons. Yoshe's parents emigrated from China," Mom said. "She took the legacy of that hard life, the heart of her Chinese family, and parlayed it into something truly memorable and universal."

I got up to clear the table, stacking the bowls and carrying them to the sink.

"Don't you have a dinner to get to?" Connie asked. "I'll help with the dishes."

"Never you mind. You'll have enough of that as a married lady." Mom stood up and squeezed her shoulders. "What are you wearing?" she asked me, her eyes lighting up like this might finally be the moment I'd emerge from my unfashionable cave and snag a husband myself.

"Basic black," I said.

"At least borrow my chunky turquoise necklace," she called after me as I disappeared into my — our — bedroom. "It will give your outfit a focal point." As though she were an interior designer and I were the empty room.

My phone rang as I was getting ready. Bill. "Have you talked any more to Eric?" he asked after a halfhearted stab at pleasantries.

"I tried," I said, pulling a black T-shirt over my head and shaking out my hair. "Did he tell you I dropped by his office this morning?"

"He's saying nothing," Bill said.

I put my cell on speakerphone so I could fasten my earrings and apply a little mascara.

"He came home and took the dog out. I'd

192

made a special dinner, but he hardly ate a thing. Said he had another, quote, *migraine* and went to bed in the guest room. But when I was at the dog park earlier today, one of the other small dog owners told me there's a rumor circulating that Eric may have been the last person to see Jonah alive."

"Who would even know enough to say that?"

"You don't really need facts to make wild guesses on the Coconut Telegraph," Bill said. "But why won't he talk to me about any of this?"

It was hard to know how to reassure him because Eric's behavior was so far out of character. "Call me the minute you hear anything," I told him. "We're here for you." I made a smooching noise and signed off.

I kissed Mom and Connie and Miss Gloria and gathered my helmet, purse, and a little notebook. I needed to keep my eye on my career ball and not get entirely distracted by the world going to pieces around me. Connie followed me out to the dock.

"I hope you're okay with me and Ray," she said shyly. Since Chad dumped me last fall, she'd heard me moan about my single state as a slew of our college friends announced sequential engagements over the holidays.

"Of course I am!" I flung my arms around her. "I couldn't be happier."

She grinned, looking mischievous. " 'Cause I want you to be my maid of honor. It'll be a small wedding and very casual," she added quickly. "Flip-flops on the beach at Fort Zachary Taylor Park."

"Phew," I said. "No pouffy pink bridesmaid gown that makes my butt look like an anvil? It would be an honor."

She started up the finger toward her houseboat and then came a few steps back. "I heard something from Ray about Bransford. He heard it from one of the other artists at the Studios of Key West. It might explain why you're finding him a little prickly. I wasn't sure whether you'd want to know."

I nodded, my heart sinking. He had another girlfriend? A wife? A man friend? "Definitely. Secrets are toxic." Per Eric, who was now apparently keeping a whopper.

"Bransford was married when he started out as a rookie cop in Miami. They had a particularly ugly divorce — they had to go to court to get it resolved."

"That's brutal. Who was the unreasonable party?"

Connie shrugged. "Unclear. After that, he moved down here to the island. Ray suspects he's never really gotten close to a woman since. So be forewarned."

Another mantra from Eric: All of us are wounded somehow in the course of our lives. But some of us are better than others at licking those wounds and rebounding.

13

Who goes after her lover with a paring knife? She was completely unbalanced. She did teach me how to cook.
— Allegra Goodman

Connie's news about Detective Bransford's disastrous romantic past swirled through my brain as I raced across the island, late for the fancy foodie dinner. How did a person establish a normal relationship after a lousy divorce? My own father had managed it, my mother not so much. Where did you find the optimism to start over? Was I the first woman Bransford considered dating since he split from his ex?

More likely, seeing as how he was handsome, accomplished, and single, he'd made other forays. And maybe gotten derailed by his memories and the knowledge of what could be lost, and how much he had paid emotionally by getting close. Maybe like my father, he was resigned to paying alimony for life. Which I had to admit had always bothered me a little about my mother.

Or maybe I was overreading everything. Maybe the whole theory was bull-hooey.

As I approached the ocean side of the island, I could hear the waves rolling in, and the grace notes above that — tinkling glasses and laughing guests. Louie's Backyard appeared down the block, a pink-sided building with white trim and white lights wound around the small property's palm trees. I parked, removed my helmet, finger-combed my hair, and then went inside, feeling flutters of anxiety about the night ahead.

A slender hostess with almond-shaped eyes and a deep tan directed me up the stairs to the outside deck. The second floor opened over the restaurant below, which was dotted with green umbrellas, its weathered wooden furniture packed with diners. To the right of the bottom floor, a woman with three black dogs threw tennis balls into the dark sea off a tiny beach. I could hear the splash as the dogs burst through the surface of the water and then barely make out the black dots of their heads as they swam. I'd seen this view before, but still it was glorious — one hundred eighty degrees of Atlantic Ocean. The lights of the White

Street Pier sparkled off in the distance, marking the sad terrain of the AIDS memorial. Key West had been hit hard by that pandemic.

Five tables seating eight had been laid out perpendicular to the water. As the wind died down to a whisper, the voices eddied louder. I picked out the deep bass of Dustin Fredericks, Olivia Nethercut's husky alto, and Sigrid's piercing soprano. There was no way to judge how much these folks tended to drink at a social gathering, but most of the dinner party appeared to be on their way to sloshed. And maybe to be fair, the drinking was a by-product of two deaths in one weekend. Certainly my head was throbbing with all I'd seen and heard.

A black-haired waiter offered me a flute of champagne and I floated to the nearest group of guests, none of whom I knew. It didn't take long to realize that two writers were dominating the conversation, still playing to their conference audience, telling funny stories about food in their lives. But the anecdotes felt brittle and flat and the attention of the listeners was drifting.

I moved on to another cluster of guests, including Olivia and Sigrid, where the talk was all about Yoshe's death. It sounded like many of them had squirmed under Bransford's crime-fighting microscope today. His questions seemed to have centered on whether her friends and associates would have described her as depressed or morose. Did she have any personal problems they were aware of? In other words, did she take her own life?

A tall blond woman clinked a fork against her water glass and asked us to take our seats. I found my place in the middle of the second table, identified by a name tag written in fancy calligraphy. Olivia Nethercut took the seat beside me, offering a quick smile that gave the impression she still had no idea who I was. Dustin remained standing as the blonde clanged her glass again.

"I'm pleased to introduce Christine Russell, who will be your hostess this evening," he explained. "We are delighted that you chose to partake in one of our special dinners. I wish I could stay because the menu looks incredible." He sighed. "Unfortunately, duty calls and I must make appearances at the other dinners taking place around the town tonight. *Bon appétit!*"

"Thank you," Christine said as he left the room. "We'll be enjoying a pairing of wine with each course of dinner. These wines hail from the Dennis Jensen Vineyard, down the road from Solvang, California, a town most famous for the movie *Sideways*. After tonight, I trust you'll remember our wines rather than the movie." She waited for the polite laughter from the guests to die down. "I'll describe each of them as the night progresses, leaving time to answer any of the questions I've neglected to cover."

I groaned inside. I could listen to descriptions of food forever, but someone droning on about how long a wine sat in a cherry-flavored oak barrel shaped like a mushroom bored me to weeping.

"Bor-ing," said Olivia, snorting softly. She unfolded a white napkin edged in white crochet and spread it across her purple pants.

"I'm Hayley Snow. We met in Santiago's Bodega?" I said, not wanting to go through the embarrassment of having her fail to recognize me. Again.

"Of course," she said, vague recognition finally crossing her face. "I'm so upset about the news of poor Yoshe — my synapses just aren't firing clearly. One day we're having a lovely time visiting a tropical island and the next — two of my colleagues are dead." She chopped a finger across her neck, shiny pink nails flashing, nearly knocking over my wineglass at the finish. "I can hardly think or talk about anything else."

"Horrible," I agreed, noticing her struggle to keep her lips from quivering. "Did you know her well?"

"All of us food writers are on the speaking engagement circuit together," she said.

"There's a food writers' circuit?" I asked.

Olivia nodded. "A group of us were at the Greenbrier last fall — not Jonah, of course — he would have been too big for something like that." She made air quotes with her fingers around "too big." "I had the most heavenly spa treatment involving a salt rub and a big hose. But anyway, don't let me drone on about that silliness. The point is, we know one another. As much as you can know someone from watching them yakking onstage or drinking coffee in the greenroom before an event or wine in the bar after."

She paused. Maybe realizing her description was on the harsh side?

"Yoshe was an exceptionally talented cook and writer. Not in the realm of Julia Child or Jonah Barrows, but definitely top tier. It would seem she had a lot to live for, but one never really knows. . . ." She cocked her head. "I haven't seen you around much."

"I'm very new to this business," I admitted. "I was hired as *Key Zest*'s food critic right before the holidays, so I'm still getting up to speed. It's been amazing to spend the weekend with all of you guys." I swallowed my last half inch of champagne, hoping I wasn't chattering stupidly with anxiety and especially wishing I'd quit mentioning my neophyte status.

"So you didn't know Miss King?"

"Barely — my mom and I did have lunch with her yesterday. Mom was a big, big fan. Sigrid Gustafson joined us too." I tipped my head to the end of our table where Sigrid was slathering butter on a piece of bread and loudly describing her recipe for kick-butt goulash. Her tips included browning the cubes of meat in a full stick of butter — never olive oil — adding extra onions and garlic, and simmering for hours.

"That must have been telling," said Olivia. "Get those two women together, and the competitive juices fly."

"Thinking back, there was some talk about the fat content of each dish Sigrid considered ordering," I said. "Yoshe tried pretty hard to steer her toward a salad."

"And that would make Sigrid certifiably loony," said Olivia, sotto voce. "She's been on every diet known to mankind and some you've never heard of. And still she's big as a house. And trust me, those caftans don't disguise anything. She couldn't stand the fact that Yoshe seemed to eat so much and stay so slender." She patted her own plywood-flat belly. "And Yoshe's books sold much better than hers too. Have you read her novels?"

I shook my head. "I read the first one, but I haven't gotten to *Dark Sweden.*"

"Two words," Olivia said. "Deadly. Tedium."

A trio of waiters circled around us to fill our second set of wineglasses with a white wine and deliver the first course. "Stone crab with Ibérico ham and calamondin," the second waiter muttered as he set the plate in front of me. I had no idea what the last item was, but I certainly wasn't going to inquire within earshot of Olivia Nethercut. I already felt like a food nincompoop in her company.

"We are pouring you our signature sauvignon blanc," said Christine the wine maven. "See if you notice the penetrating aroma of melon, and lemon verbena, which is grown in the field next to our vineyard."

I kept my gaze pinned on my plate to reduce the chance I'd roll my eyes and embarrass myself by snorting with laughter in front of the other diners, who seemed to be taking the wine talk more seriously than me.

"This particular sauvignon blanc is aged for seven months in French barrels, which adds a gentle oak integration to the wine. We chose it to complement the stone crab, of course."

The room fell mostly silent except for the scrape of forks on heavy-duty china. I gobbled the crab and the Spanish ham, determining that calamondin must be a kind of citrus with a fancy name. The combination was delicious and the wine wasn't bad either.

Olivia laid her fork on her plate and patted her lips with her napkin. "Did the chiseled detective call to inform you about Yoshe's death as well?"

I startled, then smiled at her description of Bransford. " 'Chiseled' is a good word," I said, thinking it applied to both his chin and his body. "But it was much worse than that. My mother and I discovered her body."

"No way," said Olivia. She touched slender white fingers to her throat, which pulsed like a captured bird.

I nodded, taking a gulp of wine and feeling again the horror of that moment, as that colorful pile of rags had come into focus. "It's true. And the police were pressuring my mother pretty hard, poor thing. She was absolutely devastated when we spotted

Yoshe on those rocks." I shivered and nodded to the waiter who'd circled around the table with another bottle of wine. "Mom came down for a vacation and instead she stumbled into the middle of a murder investigation."

"Murder? I heard it was suicide," Olivia said, her eyes widening.

"What do I know, really?" I said. "But it wouldn't have been easy to throw yourself over that railing. Though I suppose she could have stood on a chair. In that case, the cops would have found the chair positioned on her balcony." I shuddered. "If that's true, imagine how desperate she would have been feeling."

Olivia turned a little more pale — it must have felt dreadful to have a colleague in that much distress and have noticed nothing.

I added quickly, "But I can't say what avenue the cops are pursuing."

We worked our way through hogfish and shrimp steamed in lettuce, duck breast with capers and marrow, plus a chardonnay and a pinot noir. Our plates were cleared yet again and a fourth course delivered, along with glasses of red wine. "Braised oxtail with potato gnocchi," the waiter whispered.

"Our Insignia wine combines cabernet sauvignon, petit verdot, and merlot wines," said Christine. "The grapes are harvested early in the morning and soaked for five days. After that comes forty days of maceration and twenty-four months of aging. See if you recognize the hints of dark-roasted coffee and graphite."

Feeling slightly hysterical after a little too much wine and way too much ornate description, I choked back a rush of giggles. Who wanted to taste graphite in expensive wine? This dinner was, if nothing else, a good reminder to keep food jargon to a minimum in my reviews. I took a sip of the excellent wine and started in on the braised oxtail. Better than any beef stew I'd had in years. Even rivaled Mom's.

The woman across the table from me addressed Olivia. "Tell us more about your Bread for Kids Foundation. It sounds like such a marvelous idea."

Olivia laid her fork down and smiled. "Over the past few years I realized how much money gets poured into the high end of our food industry. For example, there are people who will pay forty dollars a pound for ham, or a hundred fifty bucks a head to eat out at a restaurant without blinking an eye." She said that with a straight face — we'd all paid close to that for tonight's dinner. "Shouldn't we make sure that some of this money trickles down to the kids who don't have enough to eat on a daily basis? It's that simple. A hundred percent of our income goes to feed children — and best of all, no politicians are involved." Laughter rippled around the table and she resumed eating.

"Sounds wonderful," said the woman who'd asked the question, and then excused herself to visit the restroom.

Olivia swirled one last fat lump of pasta through the deep brown gravy on her plate. "If they think it was really a murder, do they have any leads?" she asked me, the pale white skin of her forehead gathering into lines. "That detective wouldn't tell me much."

"Their technique is a little heavy-handed," I said. "Just because you were the last person to see the dead person alive doesn't mean you did her in."

She looked horrified.

"That sounded bad. What I mean is, they seem to be pressuring people who have nothing to do with the crime. First my friend Eric. And then today my mother. Actually I don't think they have a clue. But two deaths in one weekend — they must be related, don't you think?" Now I was really blathering — this was exactly what I warned my mother not to say. Even if I did think it was true.

"I can't imagine what those two would have had in common, other than food, of course," Olivia said. "Yoshe was controlling and particular and meticulous about how she dressed and spoke. You could tell she cooked exactly by the book. Jonah, on the other hand, threw in a dash of this and a pinch of that. And I doubt he ever spent a minute thinking before he spoke." Then an odd expression flitted across her face, but before I could ask anything else, Christine broke into our conversations again.

"For dessert and our final wine, we are asking some of you to switch places so you'll have a chance to experience the company of others at your table." She came around and tapped some of us on the shoulders and had us trade places.

After a few minutes of chaos, we were re-seated with new napkins, plates, and cutlery. This time I found myself at the table next to Sigrid, who was holding forth on her own theories about the deaths of Yoshe and Jonah.

"I suspect both of them could have been killed by rabid fans," she said. "No offense to anyone here, of course."

She cackled with laughter and I fidgeted

with my fork and shifted uncomfortably, thinking of the e-mails Jonah had rebuffed.

"I don't suppose the franchise he was talking about will get off the ground now," she said.

"The franchise?" I asked.

"Oh," she said, "it was an utterly plebeian idea. He wanted to take what's best about Key West cuisine and bring it down to the lowest common denominator."

"I didn't know him personally," said a woman across the table, "but that doesn't sound like a project Mr. Barrows would endorse."

Sigrid rubbed the tips of three plump fingers together. "Anything for the right price. Besides, Jonah was always trying to stir something up," she continued. "No wonder at all that someone had it in for him. He looked for whatever mattered most to somebody else and then stabbed holes in it. You should have seen the review he wrote on my first novel. My agent had to talk me off the ledge on that one — she's the one who helped me realize that a scathing review reflects a whole lot more on the person writing than the author of the book. And it turned out to be excellent publicity."

"Sure, Jonah loved controversy," said the man on the other side of Sigrid, a twig in comparison to Sigrid's spreading live oak. "But I wouldn't say the same about Yoshe. She was a lady."

Sigrid twisted the white napkin, her pink cheeks flushing darker. "She was no lady. She was simply more subtle than Jonah. Unless you were the target of her commentary, you might hardly notice how vicious she was." She put the napkin down, picked up her dessert fork, and plunged it into the apple praline tart that had just been delivered. "Nothing subtle about that."

After a small silence, talk turned to where the party would move next. Once I'd demolished my tart and taken a few tiny sips of the dessert wine to satisfy the wine lecturer, I said good-bye to my tablemates and slipped out. Not that anyone begged me to join them. Besides, I had more work to do than I could fathom, and a late-night hangover would not help. Olivia Nethercut followed right behind me, stumbling slightly on the last step.

She grabbed the railing and caught her balance and we made our way out into the crisp night. "Do you think that detective is single?" Olivia asked.

"The detective? Oh, Bransford." I nodded. "I believe so. Probably divorced."

"Maybe I'll give him a call. He was definitely hitting on me," she said. "You know that feeling you get when someone is doing their job but at the same time sending the signal that if it was after hours, they'd jump your bones?" She smiled and tripped down the street toward Duval.

Mom was still awake when I got home at eleven, standing by the deck rails and looking out at the harbor. The water had picked up to a good chop, but she was handling the rocking like an old salt. It felt like high school days, when Mom waited up most nights when I was out. I never quite figured out if she was checking on my state of mind. Or just lonely. Tonight with almost three glasses of Dennis Jensen Vineyard wine down the hatch, I might not have passed her high school sniff test. Luckily, I'd eaten enough to sop up some of that alcohol before driving home.

"How was your night?" she called when she spotted me coming up the finger.

I hopped from the dock to the boat. "Food was amazing. And the company most entertaining." I described my chat with Olivia, and then Sigrid's mention of Jonah's attack on her novel and his new franchise. "But the tension we noticed between Yoshe and Sigrid while we were at lunch? We definitely didn't make that up. Though Sigrid's conclusion was that rabid fans killed them both."

"Convenient," Mom said with a laugh. "She only wishes she had a few fans like Yoshe did. I'm glad you had fun. What was the best thing you ate?"

I told her about the braised oxtail stew with its partner gnocchi swimming in gravy.

"Sounds delicious," she said. Her eyes narrowed as she looked me over from top to bottom. "But you seem a little down."

She patted the seat beside her. Might as well tell all — she'd sit here grilling me until I spilled out the truth. I sat.

"On the way out of the dinner, Olivia mentioned that she thought the detective hit on her today. She's planning to call him."

"Your detective? That would surprise me," Mom said. "Sounds more like a figment of her imagination than anything else." She squinted and brushed a strand of hair off my forehead. "I never would have said that she was his type. Besides, he's sweet on you. I'm sure of it. And she must be closing in on forty, don't you think? Even though she's very glamorous, she's getting long in the tooth. Like me."

"Forty's not old," I said, grinning. "You're older than that and you're in the prime of your life. Miss Gloria and Lorenzo are right, you know. You should consider dating."

She started to say something but stopped, her face frozen. Then she bobbed her head and clucked her throat clear. "Well, I might as well tell you." She took my hand and squeezed the fingers. "I am dating. I mean, I've gone out a couple of times with a very nice fellow. The other ones hardly count. . . ."

"The other ones?" I stuttered, my mouth feeling too dry to form the words cleanly.

Mom laughed. "It's a jungle once you get started on Match-dot-com. All these fellows winking at my profile. It took me a couple of weeks to realize I could pick and choose. I wasn't obligated to chat with someone or even have coffee, if their profile wasn't appealing."

"M-M-Match-dot-com?" More stuttering.

"I started with eHarmony," she explained. "It seemed more civilized. I thought those nice people would screen the men for me and tell me exactly which ones I was compatible with. But I couldn't make it through the questionnaires." She giggled. "They wanted so many details. I figured any man who was willing to fill out this much information on a form couldn't possibly be my type. Sam seems like a dear man, but I'll keep you posted. If it really turns into something, I'll introduce you next time you're home. Or bring him down here." Her expression brightened. "Now, that would be fun! Don't worry. We'd get our own place."

I watched in horror as her face blushed a fierce pink.

14

I wonder if a certain sort of chromosomal stodginess can ever really be completely leached out of the Michelin guide and the system.

— Frank Bruni

I woke up before anyone else to the sounds of the Renharts fighting about the size of their electricity bill. Last night on the way home from dinner, I'd seen them sitting by the open window of the Bull and Whistle Bar on Duval Street. He'd had his arm slung around her shoulders and they were singing along with the featured Elvis impersonator, who undulated onstage in a blue-sequined jumpsuit. But this morning, without beer and music and the congeniality of a Duval Street bar, their marriage had lost some luster.

I twisted restlessly on the sofa bed, hovering on the edge of a headache myself from too much wine. And too much information from my mother. This was the kind of day I could have happily spent in bed with the Sunday papers or a good novel or best of all, a couple of new cookbooks. But my bed was occupied by a snoring parent. Instead I dressed in jeans and a long-sleeved T-shirt and zipped down the island to *Key Zest.*

After making a pot of coffee, I rummaged through the minirefrigerator and came up with half a blueberry muffin, probably Danielle's. She had a terrible time resisting the baked goods at the Old Town Bakery on her walks to work, but she was almost always hit with buyer's remorse part of the way through eating them.

Then I started to rough out the review of Santiago's Bodega. I'd been studying reviews from well-known restaurant critics, searching for how they described the nuts and bolts of the food while adding the stamp of their personalities. I wanted to write the truth. I wanted to use zingers that would capture readers' attention. But without hurting anyone's feelings. Maybe the combination was impossible. For the next forty-five minutes, I struggled to hammer out the first paragraph, despairing of ever getting it right. My cell phone rang — Mom.

"Good morning, darling!" she chirped,

probably relieved to have dumped the details of her secret life on me. While I was, to be honest, still reeling.

"You've been scooped," she said. "Do they still call it that? Go online to the Metro section of the *New York Times,* page one."

I saved the file I'd been working on and clicked over. "Tropical Tapas Make Key West Top Ten: Santiago's Bodega by Olivia Nethercut," the headline blared. She'd reviewed the same restaurant where we'd seen her two nights ago, including a few of the dishes we'd suggested, even using some of our words. My spirits sank to a new low as I read her piece.

"The best chickpea dip outside of Athens . . . pita bread as a litmus test of the meal to come . . . Maybe not a standout in New York City, but a fin's distance above the competitors swimming in this small fishbowl."

I couldn't really blame Olivia for writing the review — she had chosen to eat there, not gone on our recommendation. And she hadn't asked for our help or our opinions — probably hadn't even realized she was including them. All that said, I was going to have to learn to be more ruthless and guard my words in front of the competition.

"Don't feel too bad about it," Mom said.

"It's a tough business and chances are your audience is entirely different from the *Times.* But anyway, that's not why I called. Did you check your e-mail? Did you hear that the panels this morning have been canceled? The only thing left standing is lunch at one p.m. And then the tribute to Jonah and Yoshe afterward. Can you imagine how mad all the attendees are going to be at Dustin? Well, I suppose he made the best decision he could. Shall I meet you there?"

"Fine," I said. "I'm going to turn off my ringer until lunch, okay?"

Half an hour later, the *Key Zest* landline rang, and my mother's cell phone came up on the caller ID. What now? She knew I was working — but what if it was something important? So I picked up, feeling hassled and annoyed. And underneath that, worried.

"Have you checked your messages?" Mom asked.

I tried not to snap churlishly. "I'm working, Mom. I turned the ringer off so I wouldn't get distracted. Some of us don't have alimony for life to fall back on." I was sorry I said those words the moment they tumbled out. Mom was silent for a moment.

"And I didn't want to bother you, but I thought you'd want to know: The police arrested Eric for Jonah's murder. Bill hired a lawyer who's headed to the jail at the sheriff's department. He told Bill to stay home and wait for him to call with news."

"I'll meet you at their house," I said, and she hung up. I saved the file I was working on and ran down the stairs and out to my scooter. Business was starting to pick up a little on Southard Street, mostly people having breakfast, or mainlining coffee, or in line at the ATM. It's easy to run through your cash on a Saturday night in paradise.

Mom arrived at Bill and Eric's place at the same time as me, looking utterly confident on her pink scooter. We knocked on the door and barged right down the main hall despite Toby's yapping protests. Bill was sitting on the couch on the back porch, the newspaper spread across his lap, his face devoid of expression, eerily calm.

"Oh, poor Bill," Mom said, plopping down beside him, grabbing his hand, and pressing it to her lips. "You've had a horrible week! What in the world happened?"

Bill sighed, folded the paper, and shifted a couple of inches away from Mom. "As I said in my message, two police officers picked Eric up this morning. Our lawyer thinks it's likely that he will have to spend the night in the clinker, this being Sunday. Hard day to get the cogs of justice rolling. I hope he doesn't have to share a cell with one of his patients." He barked out a strangled laugh and brushed away the Yorkie, who was leaping at his knees.

"So you've already got a lawyer," Mom said, throwing a worried-sick glance my way. "What else can we do for you?"

"Nothing really."

The dog raced to the door, yapping, and then careened back to Bill.

"We could take Toby out for a spin," I suggested. This worried me most of all — usually Bill channeled their dog's needs like an experienced psychic.

Bill shrugged. "Fine."

I snapped the leash onto his harness and he trotted out ahead of Mom and me, lifting his leg on a bougainvillea just off the front porch. We followed him around the block, stopping to let him sniff and relieve himself, and bark at the neighbor's tortoiseshell cat and a squashed Cuban tree frog he found in the gutter.

"I think Bill's in shock," I said. "I hope his lawyer is competent. The one I had last fall was a real loser."

"How in the world could Eric be mixed up in this murder?" Mom wondered. "And why isn't he speaking up for himself? This

220

isn't how he'd tell one of his own clients to handle a crisis."

When we returned to the house, Bill was on the phone, pacing back and forth across the porch as he talked. "I have no idea, Edna," he said squeezing his face into a horrible grimace. "He won't tell me anything. Yes, I'll call you the minute I hear something." He dropped the phone into the receiver and collapsed onto the couch with a heavy sigh.

"Eric's mother. I don't know what to say to her," he said. "Your son may be a murderer? But I'll keep you posted?"

"It's so upsetting to be completely in the dark," I said. "He still wouldn't say why the cops would think he's involved?"

"Nothing. Not one word," said Bill with a deep frown.

"What if I call Edna back and ask her if she remembers anything about this Jonah?" Mom asked. "You know she lives in the same neighborhood as me at home. I wouldn't say we were ever close-close because Eric's mom worked and I didn't have to." Her gaze flicked over to me, then back to Bill, unleashing in me another surge of guilt over the ill-considered alimony comment. "But I always liked her — we were friendly."

"I don't want you two to get more involved than you already are," Bill said. "I'm sure with our lawyer's pressure, the police will find out what really happened and clear Eric. If Mrs. Altman knows something about Jonah Barrows, she'll tell the detective."

"Nonsense," said Mom. "Citizens have to fight for themselves. Eric isn't helping his case by keeping secrets. I'll express my condolences and explain that we're looking for leads to the real killer."

I didn't really like the idea of my mother meddling, but what were the chances that Mrs. Altman would spill her guts to a random cop calling from Key West? Not good. I plucked the phone from its cradle and brought it to her. She carried it out to one of the wicker chairs facing the garden and dialed.

"Edna, how are you? It's Janet Snow. I'm in Key West, visiting Hayley. Can you imagine? What's the weather like up there?"

"Mom," I warned. "Just get to the point."

But she put a finger to her lips, listening intently to the high-pitched rant on the other end of the line.

Back in our neighborhood of immaculate split-level homes with neat lawns and elaborate swing sets, the Altmans' weedy yard and peeling tan paint had plain stuck out. Mr. Altman had bolted for a new life in California when Eric was five. But unlike my father, once he started his second family, he quit paying regular child support and rarely contacted his son. Mrs. Altman took a job in the local hardware store and covered her despair with a hearty cheerfulness when she was out in public. Obviously Eric couldn't confide in her about his problems — she had all she could manage just to keep their family fed and housed. And he knew it. But every once in a while both of them talked to Mom when their emotional dams were ready to burst.

My mother explained to Mrs. Altman our thoughts about Jonah's murder and how, of course, Eric couldn't have killed him — he didn't even know him. Then she listened for a few more minutes.

"Is that right?" my mother was saying, a shocked note in her voice. "When he lived in New York? And you're certain his name was Jonah?"

She murmured into the phone for several more minutes. "No, no, I can't think that it would help for you to run down here." Bill made a wild slashing motion across his neck and my mother smiled and nodded. "I swear, Edna, we will get to the bottom of all this. We will make sure Eric doesn't go to jail." She finally hung up and let out a big whoosh of air. "That was something," she said. "More than I expected, really."

"Tell us," I said.

"Well. Edna says that Eric had a connection with a man named Jonah that went way back. She isn't sure what exactly their relationship was — Eric was in graduate school in New York and he didn't tell her much about his life. He was coming out back then and it was hard on everyone, especially him. And her." She smoothed the fabric on Bill's shoulder and looked at me. "You probably don't remember, but he was on an honesty binge for a couple of years. He began to needle his mom about family secrets and the way she and his father never talked about things that were important and difficult. He told her that keeping quiet because it was easier was just wrong."

"He's mellowed since then," I said, thinking this sounded an awful lot like what Jonah had preached to the opening-night crowd.

15

It's a cabbage rather than a rose, a tangy ring of bologna rather than a sirloin. Side effects may include heartburn.
— Dwight Garner

Within a few minutes, we'd hammered out a plan with a new urgency. None of us could believe that Eric was involved with Yoshe's death. He had little interest in Asian cooking. He was not a celebrity stalker. Their lives would not reasonably have intersected prior to this weekend. But if we could find out what had happened to Yoshe, we might find out what really happened to Jonah, and thus clear Eric.

Bill would stay home to field phone calls with potential news. Someone needed to stay put, and frankly, he seemed flattened by Eric's arrest, drained of vitality like a root vegetable that had spent too many months in the crisper. Mom would ride over to the Key West library and do some research on Yoshe's background, looking for a possible connection between the deaths, including the franchise that Sigrid had mentioned. Before this, Mom had felt awful about Yoshe's death. But now she was on a personal mission: No neighbor of hers was going to suffer with her son in prison if there was anything she could do about it. For my part, I would return to *Key Zest,* finish my review, and surf the Web for information about Jonah's activities in the late 1990s, back when Mrs. Altman thought Eric might have met him.

After half an hour glued to my keyboard, I finished the review draft for Santiago's Bodega. I e-mailed it directly to Wally so I couldn't obsess any further or make grim comparisons between my own work and that of Olivia Nethercut. When I'd been in the business as long as she had, I could beat myself up about the speed and brilliance of my writing. Now it felt like a victory just to get a story finished.

I typed "Jonah Barrows" into the Google search bar and came up with the usual potpourri of intriguing but useless links — a kid with a similar name had won a chocolate-pudding-eating contest. Samantha Barrows had appeared as a character on *Days of our Lives.* And Jonah Barrows himself had ten thousand something fans on his Facebook fan page, and twice that number of Twitter followers. Sidestepping the temptation to get sucked into reading all the posts and tweets these fans must have generated, I skimmed over news headlines from the 1990s about the crack epidemic in New York City, various murders, and the death of a New York University undergraduate. How could any of this be related to Eric? Waste of precious time. I set up a Google alert so I would be informed of any new developments that came along about Jonah.

Then, wishing I wasn't so curious but unable to stop myself, I typed "Detective Nathan Bransford" into the search bar. I scrolled through several pages of news about crimes and public relations in Key West before coming across this headline: "Miami Rookie Police Officer's Wife Held by Hostage."

The article explained that a Miami drug dealer out on bail had gone to the home of the arresting officer and taken his wife hostage. After twelve hours of failed negotiations, a SWAT team entered the home through a basement window and shot the alleged dealer to death after a barrage of gunfire was exchanged. Officer Nathan Bransford's wife, Trudy Bransford, was not injured in the incident.

Whoa. I couldn't imagine the guilt and rage that he must have experienced, realizing that his wife's trauma and then her decision to leave him were directly connected to his work. This was much worse than a garden-variety nasty divorce.

Stomach gurgling a hungry lament, I rummaged through the office refrigerator, looking for something else to tide me over to lunch. Wally had tucked a tin of mixed nuts into the far reaches of the bottom shelf with his name printed on the label in neat block letters. Clearly off-limits. I scooped out a small handful and smoothed over the top to disguise my looting. With my brain feeling slightly fortified and a little less sluggish, I returned to the computer and brought up the Match.com Web site. Spying, yes — and I would have melted from embarrassment if anyone caught me. But I couldn't help myself — I'd been dying to look ever since Mom had mentioned this last night.

A small colored box popped up on the screen, asking for my age range and zip code. I typed in forty to fifty, and 07922, my mother's information. Another box materialized, asking me to register with the site to begin trolling for prospects. But a page was shadowed behind the registration form, including photos, screen names, ages, and cities of local prospects. My mother was one of the prospects: LetItSnow, 46 — Berkeley Heights. I groaned and closed the window on the computer.

Pacing around the small office, I tried to force my focus back to helping Eric. Obsessing about Bransford and my mother's dating life was not helpful. Then I thought of calling Stan Grambor, the psychologist who shared Eric's office space. We'd met at Eric and Bill's open house after their recent home renovation. I remembered finding him low-key and approachable — the kind of shrink I'd consider hiring if I ever considered hiring a shrink to replace Lorenzo. Not likely.

He answered the phone on the first ring. "Stan, it's Hayley Snow. I'm a friend of Eric Altman's." I explained how we'd met and then plunged right in to describe Eric's arrest and what had happened to Jonah Barrows. If anyone could keep a confidence, it ought to be Eric's suitemate.

"That's dreadful! I'm stunned. How can I help?"

I explained that my team and I were collecting information that might help the cops find the real killer. No need to tell a psychologist that my team consisted of me and my mother. And Bill, who was essentially deadwood at the moment. And that the cops couldn't be less interested in my theories.

"The problem is, he refuses to exonerate himself. So I'm wondering how he seemed to you over the past few days."

"He was quiet this week," Stan said. "And busy. He didn't have time to schedule lunch as we often do. Houseguests, he said. You know how that goes!" He brayed with laughter.

I sure did — Mom. "Can you think of any reason why he wouldn't try to defend himself?"

Stan cleared his throat a few times. "Let me puzzle over that a minute. Hmmm."

In my limited experience, shrinks don't jump to conclusions quickly. They like to sift through all the data and then generate a tentative hypothesis and then —

"The best question might be, whom is he protecting with his silence?" Stan said. "It could be himself. But more likely, someone close to him?"

I thought of Bill, who was acting almost as oddly as Eric himself. Eric would do anything for Bill. But since Bill had never entered the Audubon House grounds, I didn't see how he could have killed Jonah. Nor did he know him. "Maybe Eric was quiet this week for some other reason. Was he especially worried about any cases? I know you can't tell me specifics."

Stan hummed tunelessly to himself, like the hideous canned music you're subjected to when you're put on hold trying to straighten out a bill. He stopped humming and said, "He asked me in passing if I'd ever lost a client."

"And then?"

"I haven't, but I told him what a supervisor once told me — if you stay in this business long enough, it's bound to happen. Some folks you just can't save. They are too far down the tunnel and simply can't see the smallest flicker of light." He clicked his tongue and sighed. "Then my ten o'clock came in and I never did get to ask Eric why he'd inquired. I'm sorry. It sounds like I should have been paying better attention. I hope I didn't miss anything — I haven't seen news about a suicide in the *Citizen*."

"Speaking of that," I said, "there was a second death related to the food writers' conference — a woman found on the rocks below her third-floor balcony." I felt my throat close up with the memory of finding the body. "We've been trying to imagine what frame of mind she'd have had to be in to throw herself off."

This was the kind of question I'd have asked Eric, had he been available. Only I wouldn't have been reluctant to let him see and hear how sick I felt about finding Yoshe. How the horror of crawling across the rocks to confirm her identity seemed to mushroom as the hours ticked by. And he would have known the things to say to ease me forward. But Dr. Stan didn't know me and I couldn't expect that from him.

"Terrible — I'm so sorry to hear that!" A bit of silence on the phone again. "If this was a suicide attempt, she didn't think it through," Stan said. "Not like hoarding pills for weeks or months, for example, and then swallowing them with a fifth of whiskey for good measure. Nor would it be a certain death — she could have escaped with broken bones, no? Or even snapped her back and ended up a paraplegic. If it was a cry for help, without true intent to die, it reeks of desperation and a histrionic personality. Are you certain it was a suicide?"

"Not really," I said. "We're not certain about anything."

"Any problems in her life that might have looked insurmountable?"

"I don't know enough to answer that," I said. In the background, I heard the dull buzz announcing the arrival of one of Stan's patients.

"My patient's here. Please do call if you have any other questions. And I'll keep an eye on Eric when I see him next," he promised. "I'm certain this will all turn out to be a terrible misunderstanding."

I hung up, wishing I could borrow his optimism, and tried to imagine whom Eric might be protecting. Had he actually been arrested for the death of one of his own clients rather than Jonah? I felt certain that wasn't what Bransford had told me. Was Bill so distressed that he'd completely butchered the story?

I twirled in my desk chair until I felt dizzy. And feeling dizzy made me think of Sigrid. There had been no love lost between her and Yoshe — that much was clear from the lunch we'd all shared. Or Sigrid and Jonah, for that matter. If I ever had a book published, I didn't think I'd be quite so willing to talk to strangers about getting lousy reviews. Even the ones I thought were agenda-driven garbage. I pulled Amazon .com up on my computer screen and typed "Sigrid Gustafson" into the search bar. One of the featured reviews for her new novel had been written by Jonah and was titled "Fictional Culinary Buffoonery."

"The concept is intriguing, a novel set in Sweden depicting a dysfunctional family whose problems are reflected through their dinner preparations over a long holiday weekend, and then a murder mystery. But Gustafson loses her way and her readers by stooping to a combination of cliché and melodrama. Her attempts at humor fail to enliven the plot, just as lingonberry jam fails to lighten a heavy stew. The characters exist merely as a vehicle for the author's ramblings about Nordic food archetypes. The execution is dry and the recipes, drier still. The plot is thin in a way that the author herself can never aspire to."

Whew. I would have felt the stirrings of a murderous rage after reading this excoriation of my novel — I was willing to bet Sigrid had too. And it wasn't one of her older books, as she'd told me at the dinner party last night. It was *Dark Sweden,* the newest — the one her career trajectory now rested on. What might have happened the first night of the conference between her and Jonah? The review was dated earlier this week, so likely this would have been the first time she'd seen him since its publication. With a flash of insight, I remembered her being in the bathroom as I attempted to chat with Olivia. Had she looked flushed or sweaty or otherwise guilty? I couldn't recall the details. But I could honestly picture her losing her temper, grabbing the metal bird, and swinging it at Jonah. Maybe surprising herself when she connected. But why not report the incident as a terrible accident?

If she'd been terrified to confess, she must be terrified about being exposed. Did Jonah hold a secret of hers worse than the lousy review? Suppose she feared that Yoshe had learned some ruinous truth about her. Suppose she marched to her room a day later and pushed her off the balcony. I ran my fingers through my hair and sighed. I knew a little about everyone and not enough about anyone. If Sigrid had killed Jonah, what could be her motive for killing Yoshe? Rude comments made at lunch? Ridiculous. Why even assume both writers were killed by the same person?

I glanced at my watch — eleven thirty. I still had an hour before I was due to meet my mother. Where would the underemployed food panelists be hanging out? Most likely at the scene of the conference, hoping to sell a few last books to the foodie enthusiasts who might stop by. Maybe Sigrid would be among them.

I walked from my office to the San Carlos Institute on Duval, figuring the exercise would balance out consumption of an extra cookie or two at lunch. Wally's mixed nuts and Danielle's half a muffin were not holding me over very well — I was starving. And feeling terrible that I'd thrown a dart at my mother about lifetime alimony. The financial dealings between my parents were none of my business. Though, on the other hand, I couldn't picture how a person would justify dating one man while living on the largesse of another.

As I'd wagered, the doors to the building were open and the bookstore inside was buzzing with panelists and customers. Sigrid sailed by like a steamship on a billowing wave of flowered cotton and positioned herself near the stacks of her last two books, which seemed almost as tall as they had the day before. Her eyes were rimmed in red and she'd bitten most of her orange lipstick off except for a flaky patch on the top lip. I followed her over to the books, plucked a copy of *Dark Sweden* off the pile, and handed it to her.

"Could you sign this for my stepmother?" I asked. "Her name is Allison and her birthday is coming up. She's not much of a cook — don't say I said that — but she loves to eat. And I think her father's side of the family hails from Sweden, so this will be perfect."

Sigrid scrawled *Happy birthday, Allison* on the title page along with her name and handed the book back to me.

"What a disappointing weekend," I said.

"Dreadful, discouraging, disastrous, dispiriting," she said, although she sounded more furious than discouraged or any of those other *D* words.

"I hope the book sales are going well anyway," I said, touching my palm to the teetering pile.

Sigrid's plump cheeks flushed a terrible red. "A mere trickle. You can't expect to sell merchandise if the customers are prevented from attending the panels and getting to know the authors. If only Dustin could be privy to the things I'm hearing this morning. If only he was interested! People are incensed about the cancellation of the morning sessions. Do you know how much they paid to come to this conference? Do you know how much time and energy it took each of us to get to this godforsaken island? I could have been home writing. My agent has been badgering me for weeks to finish up the proposal for a new novel." She stopped to take a breath and pat her face with a tissue. "Did you say you were a writer?"

"Journalist," I said. "Food writing and restaurant criticism. I imagine fiction must be so much harder."

"It's getting worse and worse," she said. "The publishers are in sheer, babbling panic about how to maintain their grip on the industry while every talentless wannabe scrambles to publish their so-called literature directly to the Web. Agents are foaming about their financial interests too. Mine informed me on Friday that unless the numbers pick up soon on *Dark Sweden,* she will find it 'challenging' to sell any others, at least for a decent and livable advance."

A tiny white-haired woman approached us timidly from the side. "Miss Gustafson, may I get you to sign this book for my sister?"

Sigrid grabbed the book from the woman's hands, radiating an enormous, phony grin. "Absolutely delighted. What is your mother's name?"

"Sister," the woman peeped.

Best wishes, Sister — hope you enjoy the read! Sigrid wrote.

I muttered, "Good luck" and backed away to give her space with her fan. I felt no closer to knowing her secrets — if she had any. She seemed to wear her feelings on her sleeve and have no problem expressing them, even to total strangers. Once the other woman left, I moved in closer again.

"You may not remember," I started, "but we were both in the ladies' room around the time that Jonah Barrows was killed. Do you remember seeing anyone else leaving the area when you did?" Watching her eyes narrow, I added, "I'm sure the police have asked you already, but one of my friends has been implicated in the murder. . . ."

"I don't know anything about that," she said in a low voice that invited no further questions. "Many of us were not particularly fond of Jonah, but that doesn't mean we'd kill him. I'm trying to make the best of a grim situation here. We all are. If you don't mind, I have work to do." She whirled around, nearly taking out two women nearby who were perusing cookbooks. "I'm Sigrid Gustafson," she told them as they regained their balance. "I write Nordic culinary novels. May I show you my latest?" She pressed the copy she was holding into the hands of the closest woman.

As I left the makeshift bookstore, I spotted Dustin on his cell phone near the entrance to the auditorium. He too must be feeling fragile because of the terrible turns his conference had taken this weekend. If I pushed him a little, might he spew more about Jonah's murder than he'd been willing to share previously? I ticked off a list of questions in my mind and hurried across the room.

"No, it would not be convenient," he was saying to the person on the other end of the line as I approached. "We have a closing luncheon to endure and then the tribute to our fallen warriors. And the bookstore is open the rest of the afternoon. You can call tomorrow and we'll make an appointment like normal people do."

"Excuse me," I said as he ended the call. "Hayley Snow. With *Key Zest*?" I added in case he was too scattered and frazzled to remember me. "I'm finishing up my profile on Jonah Barrows and had a few last-minute questions. I realize that you must have a personal connection to all these folks, but it seems like you might have been particularly close to Jonah?"

"Jonah is killing me," he said grimly. "Stone-cold dead and he's still managing to ruin my life."

"I heard from one source that there is some question about whether your contract will be renewed for next year."

"What source?" he demanded, his face

closed and wary.

I squirmed, wondering what I could say. The investigative reporter identity did not suit me very well. "The Realtor Cory Held mentioned —"

"That woman is a liar!"

His eyes narrowed to slits. "Now I recognize your name. You're not a real writer — you were the one who was stalking Jonah. And now you're starting with me. Are you intent on executing a Key West version of *Fatal Attraction*?"

I backed away from him, speechless, and retreated to the bathroom to wash my face and do some emergency deep breathing. In Dustin's anger and panic, he'd hit my neurotic sweet spot: a pervasive sense of insecurity about my competence as a food writer. The sense that I'd never belong in this company. I blotted my face dry, trying to convince myself that his comments said a lot more about his state of mind than about me.

I hurried down Duval Street toward the Oldest House Museum. The closing lunch was taking place in the backyard of this cozy 1829 home, a white clapboard eyebrow house with black shutters and a lovely front porch, only missing the rocking chairs. Most people walked right by this little patch of history without noticing it — it didn't call attention to itself amid the sidewalk salespeople hawking two-for-one drinks, or T-shirts, or rides on a Jet Ski or a sunset cruise. But the garden behind the house was a true gem — another secluded oasis of tropical plantings and brick walkways.

I'd agreed to meet Mom there by twelve thirty so we wouldn't fall too far back in the line of ravenous diners. Our experience the first night had taught us that those late to the party had better be prepared to eat lightly. I trotted along the queue that already stretched two blocks, embarrassed about my altercation with Dustin and bursting to describe my conversation with Sigrid to my mother. And to apologize about the alimony comment. But she was neither in the line nor waiting at either entrance.

I talked my way past the volunteer guarding the gate by explaining that my mom sometimes got a little flustered and misplaced herself. In the backyard, food workers in white aprons tweaked the buffet — a gorgeous display of salad, soup, bread, and an entire double table groaning with cookies, heavy on the chocolate. But no sign of my mother. I slunk by the dessert table and palmed one macaroon. I nibbled the cookie on the way out — strands of toasted coconut drenched in dark chocolate. Definitely swoon-worthy. Half a block down the line, I spotted Olivia Nethercut, bright with animation as she chatted with several carefully coiffed women in pastel suits.

"Hi-ho, Hayley," she said with a friendly wave.

Which seemed to offer an opportunity to get a little information. I ratcheted up my energy to mirror hers. "Good morning. It was fantastic to visit with you last night. I learn so much chatting with more experienced writers. And the idea of your foundation is brilliant."

We talked a little about the food at Louie's Backyard — she had been mad for the duck, done rare, exactly to her preference, while I most enjoyed the gnocchi. Which could start to explain why she was so slender and I was trending toward pleasantly plump. When the timing seemed right, I added, "After we changed seats last night, I heard something Sigrid said about a franchise that Jonah Barrows was trying to get started."

"Oh, the pseudo Margaritaville," she said. "I suspect with Yoshe and Jonah gone and Dustin's future in jeopardy, it won't get off the ground. It was a ludicrous idea anyway. Didn't they realize that Jimmy Buffett's

243

people had already done that?" She touched her fingers to my wrist. "Don't tell me you were interested in investing?"

"Not investing per se," I said, thinking my savings wouldn't be worth one share of one dinner at this point. And wondering how I could get her to say more about Dustin. "More looking for foodie news. For my beat." I grinned. "What did they have in mind for the restaurants?"

"An imitation of Margaritaville, modeled on the restaurant up on Duval. Their plan called for serving cheeseburgers, shrimp, key lime pie, conch fritters, margaritas, of course — and playing Jimmy Buffett tunes round the clock. Dustin thought the tropical island thing might take off. They have Hard Rock Café in Key West. Why not paradise in Peoria?"

"Sounds like a good concept," I said. "One that would be popular with the general public." I wouldn't be caught dead eating at a place like that, but I was definitely a food snob when it came to chain restaurants.

"The majority of Americans don't care whether their food is better. They care whether it's familiar. So in that sense, the concept was a winner. But when you get artsy types involved in business endeavors, you can be sure the financial statements are not their strong suits. And in the end I believe the biggest concern was the possibility of a lawsuit. The Margaritaville name is very closely protected. Jonah couldn't get past that."

"Jonah was worried?"

She gave a dismissive flick of one wrist. "He was utterly conservative. He didn't seem to realize that some members of his foodie tribe don't have the kind of income stream he did. They aren't all in demand as keynote speakers and authors."

The lunch line began to inch forward.

"Oh, by the way, I did manage to reach the sculpted detective and persuade him that dinner with me this evening should be on his docket," Olivia added. She grinned and plumped her bangs. "Not that it took too much persuasion. He suggested Michael's. Is that a place you'd recommend for a date with a macho guy?"

I opened my mouth to say something pleasant, but nothing came out. Michael's was one of the more expensive restaurants on the island. No water view, but a sweet outside dining courtyard and amazing steaks, flown in daily from Chicago. Traditional and romantic — perfect for a date. I didn't have any claim on Bransford — he could see whomever he wanted. But that fact didn't shield me from feeling swamped by a wash of disappointment and envy. I licked my lips and tried again. "I bet you'll have a lovely time. He'll be happy there — no surprises on the menu, so he'll be able to concentrate on the conversation. Not always his strong point."

I backed away, mustering a weak smile, and continued down the block looking for my mother. With still no sign of her, I tried her cell again, which rolled right over to her voice mail. I left a brief message, circled around the grounds again, and then called home to Miss Gloria.

"Have you seen Mom? We said we'd meet for lunch at twelve thirty, but she isn't here. I wonder if she got mixed up on the time."

"No," Miss Gloria said. "When she got home from the library, she showered and dressed. She was very excited about the lunch and looking forward to copping a few more autographs and photos. She made some phone calls, including to that Sam, her boyfriend back in New Jersey. He sounds like a winner, doesn't he? Did you know that he's a venture capitalist? He must be loaded because he invited her to go on a Mediterranean cruise this summer. Separate cabins, of course." Miss Gloria giggled.

"That sounds nice, even if a little early for their relationship," I said, hoping I didn't sound like a killjoy old fart. "But where is she now? What time did she leave the houseboat?"

"Around eleven, I'd say. Yes, eleven. Because I'd gone down to put some clothes in the washing machine and I had to look at the clock to remind myself to move things over to the dryer. You know how people blow a gasket if you don't take your stuff out the minute the machine stops spinning. She'd gone to the library to do her research, but of course this being Sunday morning, it was closed. Let's see now . . . She told me she was going to have tea with a lady at the bed-and-breakfast where the dead writer stayed."

"Tea? You're sure about that?"

"I'm sure," Miss Gloria said. "As sure as I can be about anything these days. I'm going to miss her so much. Do you think there's a chance she'd stay on? We could set up bunk beds in your room."

I swallowed, reaching for words that would sound polite but firm. "Bunk beds?"

Miss Gloria snickered. "Joke. I got you on that one. But I will miss her."

"Me too," I said.

"You two are a lot alike," said Miss Gloria.

"I never had a daughter. Only sons. But if I had, I'd want her to be like you. I'd want a relationship like the one you two have."

"Thank you," I said, feeling a little teary. Our relationship had certainly hit its bumpy patches over the years, but I wouldn't trade my mother for anyone. "Did it seem like she was mad at me?"

"I wouldn't have guessed that. And she didn't say so."

I hung up, considering the possibilities. Mom had had a wreck on her scooter on the way back across the island. She'd taken a tour of Hemingway's house and lost track of time. Or she was still visiting over a cup of Earl Grey with the manager of the B & B. That last seemed the most likely and the least histrionic. So with a sigh of regret over missing out on the steaming bowls of chowder, I left the grounds, trotted back to the office to fetch my scooter, and drove across town.

16

But the bitter truth we critics must face, is that in the grand scheme of things, the average piece of junk is probably more meaningful than our criticism designating it so.

— Anton Ego

Reba Reston, the manager, was working on the computer in the back office behind the reception area when I came in. She looked up, peering over a pair of sparkly silver reading glasses.

"I'm Hayley Snow. My mother and I were here yesterday? With Yoshe."

"I remember," she said, pushing the chair away from the desk and getting to her feet. "Absolutely devastating. In every way." She twisted her hands together, looking as though she might cry.

I nodded sympathetically — she must certainly be spooked about the death. And worried about the possibility that it would smear her business's reputation. Particularly if Yoshe had been murdered. Though a suicidal plunge from one of her best suites would be no public relations picnic either. "I'm looking for my mother. A friend said she was headed this way around eleven?"

She swept off her glasses and came out to the counter. "She did stop in. Such a lovely lady. We had a cup of tea and talked all about your career — she's so proud of you! Then she told me about her home in New Jersey and her new boyfriend."

I suppressed a groan. Would I be forced to endure hearing about my mother's love life all over town? "Was there something in particular she seemed to be looking for? I know she was upset about Yoshe's death."

Reba nodded slowly. "She was certain that I knew more about Miss King than what I told the police. She wanted to review everything that I'd noticed about her yesterday. She said she'd read a hundred times over how this works in mysteries. The smart police ask you to go over your day from stem to stern because you just don't know what's going to turn out to be important." She tapped her glasses on her front teeth. "And you know what? She was absolutely right."

"About what?" I asked, ready to shake her until her fillings rattled. Two people were dead and my mother was missing, and she was yammering like a cheap music box. I smiled with encouragement.

"She asked me if Miss King seemed anxious or afraid about anything."

"And you said . . ."

"Not at first. She came down for breakfast yesterday just like normal." She pointed across the room to the table where Yoshe must have been sitting on the day she died. "And she had a cup of tea while she worked. She travels with her own tea and a strainer. Even though I have a very good selection. But this is something special — from her childhood in China. Lapsang souchong. She said it has a strong, smoky flavor and most people don't care for it." She pressed her hands against her cheeks. "Listen to me, talking about her as if she's still here."

I bobbed my head with encouragement, trying to be sympathetic, but wondering if she'd ever get to the point.

"So, as I told your mother, she nibbled on one of our croissants from the bakery down on Eaton Street. We've switched over to them lately and I've gotten a ton of compliments."

"So she seemed normal at breakfast. Tea

and pastry. But then . . .”

"But then she got a phone call on the house phone. One of the girls who helps me with breakfast and cleaning the rooms answered it and called her over. I did quiz my girl about this, but all she remembers is that the voice was female." She paused and slid her glasses back on. "Do you think it's okay for me to be telling this to anyone who asks?"

"Not just anyone. Naturally you should tell the cops if you remember any details you didn't tell them yesterday. But you see, my mother is missing." I tapped two fingers on the counter. "And I'm wondering if she might be following up on something that the two of you discussed."

The manager squirmed, suddenly making herself very busy with straightening the sightseeing literature on the rack.

"There's something else?" I asked, holding the fear out of my voice, trying to keep my tone pleasant and nonchalant so I didn't spook her into silence.

"I did let her look through Miss King's belongings." She pointed to an upholstered suitcase and a brown snakeskin briefcase stashed under a table in the back office. "It's the high season," she explained. "Miss King was scheduled to check out this afternoon anyway, and I really couldn't afford to leave her belongings all over the bedroom. We have another guest coming in today. So once the police were finished and gave me the go-ahead, I packed everything up. Her niece is arriving midafternoon to retrieve her bags. I wished I could have offered her a free room, but we have a full house. And she said she didn't want to stay in the establishment where her aunt died, so not to worry."

I steered her back to my initial question. "Mom looked at this stuff and then took off? Did she find something in particular?"

The manager shrugged. "I wasn't watching very carefully. Maybe she said she was looking for her passport? But that doesn't seem right. Miss King may have looked Oriental, but she's as American as you or me. So maybe it was a diary or a date-minder." She nibbled on her thumbnail. "I did mention to your mother about the tea and how Miss King said her grandfather used to smoke this kind of tea on his farm in the Hunan Province of China. And your mother said that was odd, as she recalled the tea originating in the Wuyi Mountains."

"That's my mother," I said. "She knows a lot about food. Do you mind if I take a quick look at Yoshe's belongings?"

"I'm not really authorized —"

"The horse is already out of the barn door. Don't you think?" I asked her. "Look, Mom's disappeared and I'm worried. I'm sure you don't want another death associated with your bed-and-breakfast."

The woman paled and stepped aside so I could go into the office. I quickly shuffled through the clothing in the suitcase, feeling a little ill as the citrusy scent I'd noticed Yoshe wearing on Friday wafted from the fabrics. At the bottom, I found a copy of Jonah's memoir, *You Must Try the Skate*. I riffled through it, taking note of the pages that Yoshe — or someone — had dog-eared. Underneath Jonah's book there was a manuscript labeled with dozens of small yellow sticky notes and marked up with a red pen.

"Your mother was very interested in that, now that I think of it," said Reba, hovering close behind me as I picked the papers up. "I think it was a version of Ms. King's new cookbook."

Of course my mother was interested in this — she'd lamented several times the possibility that it wouldn't be published posthumously. I skimmed a sample of the comments from the copy editor — *recipe needs to be double-checked, tastes different than your description* — *is this person related to your ancestors? Cannot find* — I couldn't make out the rest of the words, but in general, it looked like a load of revisions would have been required to meet the publisher's standards. The last page in the stack was an editorial letter.

Not up to your usual standards . . . question the authenticity of a number of the recipes . . . four weeks to make substantial revisions or contract will be canceled.

Serious, horrifying notes for an author. Maybe even enough to have made her feel suicidal. "You said Ms. King took a phone call. Could it have been from someone at her publisher?"

"I simply don't know. But your mother asked the same question," said Reba. The phone rang at the front desk and she hurried off to answer it.

Without thinking too much about the ethical dilemma, I folded the editorial letter in quarters and slid it into my pocket.

17

I left the bed-and-breakfast, tapping down little niggles of worry that sprouted up faster than I could squash them down. I sat on my scooter for a few minutes, my face lifted to the midday sun, trying to decide what should come next. What was my mother's theory about Yoshe? And how was she pursuing it? And most disturbing of all, why hadn't she called me? What I really wanted to do was go to the police station, burst into the detective's office, and beg him to put his best men out looking for my mother. Of all people, wouldn't he know what it felt like to almost lose someone you should be taking care of?

On the other hand, it was really too early to worry. I'd feel totally ridiculous when Mom turned up, having spent the afternoon admiring and photographing the descendents of Hemingway's cats. Or lowering her blood pressure with a spin through the

Butterfly Conservatory. Which would explain why her cell phone was silent. Though a dead battery would explain that as well.

And besides, Bransford had made a dinner date with Olivia Nethercut. Which made the possibility of blathering in front of him very unappealing.

I zoomed back to the oldest house in Key West and combed through the tables of conference folks who were now chowing down on conch chowder and salad. No sign of Mom anywhere. Though the soup looked incredible, a briny, milky broth studded with potatoes, celery, onions, and bits of orange conch. At the table farthest from the buffet line, Fritz Ewing, the culinary poet, recited doggerel in between bites to a group of star-starved women.

"This is a pseudohaiku called 'Conch Chowder,' " he said to the ladies. "Golden conch," — slurp — "shoe leather texture" — slurp — "trophy wife after humble clam."

His tablemates snorted with laughter; the blonde next to him patted his shoulder with congratulations. I recognized two of them as the women Mom had befriended the first night at the opening reception. Crouching down between them, feeling like a children's cartoon character, I asked, "Have you seen my mother?" Neither had. I asked them to have her call me in case she made a late appearance.

I left the grounds, walked west on Duval, and turned up the block to Whitehead toward the Audubon House, thinking I could distract myself by reviewing the facts of the first murder. Surely the cops would have thought of this, but might someone from one of the neighboring properties have witnessed an altercation involving Jonah and the killer? Considering the noise level of the party that night, it was unlikely that any nearby residents could have retired early. And it had been a lovely evening with a spectacular full moon — a perfect evening for sitting out on the porch, any porch, and thanking the universe for winter in Key West.

I hadn't noticed before that a tiny clapboard house with a full porch and a miniature front yard outlined with conch shells was tucked in between the Audubon House and the much larger time-share condominium on the other side. Two dirty white cats slept on faded striped cushions on the porch swing in the shade of an enormous banyan tree. I hesitated for a minute, wondering if the weathered "Private Property" sign stabbed into the lawn really meant no visitors ever. The larger of the cats lifted his head, blinked green eyes, and mouthed a silent *meow.* Taking that as a sign of welcome, I unlatched the gate and approached the front porch. "Hello!" I called from the bottom of the stairs. "Anybody home?"

After several minutes, a man creaked down the center hallway to the door, leaning on an aluminum walker with tennis balls on its legs. He peered through the screen, white-tufted eyebrows lifted, a wary look on his craggy face.

"So sorry to bother you," I said, one foot on the bottom stair, smiling like a stewardess delivering peanuts to coach passengers. Which is to say, I gave him the best I had under the circumstances. But he looked like the kind of guy who would doubt that a food writer had any business nosing around in the aftermath of a murder. A reasonable conclusion.

"I'm attending the writing conference," I told him, and rattled off my name and credentials. "You've probably read the news that we had a death this weekend. And I'm sure the police have already asked, but I wondered if you might have heard anything unusual Thursday night? Say around nine o'clock or a little later?" I pointed to the tangle of overgrown shrubbery that separated his lawn from the far end of the manicured Audubon House grounds. "There's a tiny pool right over there behind your bushes. And that's where the dead man ended up."

The man lifted one shaky hand to rub his chin and then pinch together his cracked lips. At least he wasn't chasing me out. Yet. He pushed open the door and struggled onto the porch with his walker. "I did hear the sirens," he said. "Right close yonder." He pointed to the roof of the Audubon House, barely visible through the greenery.

"Anyone arguing?" I asked. "Maybe just before the sirens?"

He leaned into his walker and took another step. "Sometimes with the TV running, I don't hear so good. My daughter's always telling me I'd do better with hearing aids, but I heard too many horror stories about the damn things. Those companies are just out to cheat the old folks. So I turn up the volume and put on the TV captions and I get along just fine."

I kept the encouraging smile plastered on my face, but my heart was sinking. An elderly, hard-of-hearing man with a hearing-aid conspiracy theory and his TV cranked to max wouldn't make much of a witness, no matter how sweet he turned out to be.

"Maybe you were watching TV between nine and ten — maybe *America Has Talent*?" I suggested, trying to get him thinking about Thursday night. "Or *Dancing with the Stars*?" I had no idea — the few programs I watched were cooking shows, showcasing the only talent I really cared about.

"I think I saw a crime show this week," he said. "There was a murder and some cops on the take." He snickered. "Not too original, hey?"

"They do all start to run together," I agreed. "Did you go outside at all that night? Maybe during commercials? The evening I'm talking about, the moon was full. The paper made a big fuss about how high the tides would be and all."

He lifted his walker an inch off the wooden floor and banged it down. The fat white cat thumped to the floor and sauntered over to wind between his legs. "That's right! I came out to look because that columnist I like in the *Citizen* said you wouldn't see anything like it but once in a lifetime." He looked wistful. "I don't have all that much time left."

I nodded sympathetically. "So you had a good view."

"Good enough. Those branches" — he pointed to the big tree in front of his house

— "keep things private so I can look out without everyone in the world peeping in."

Nodding again, I said, "I'm sure it gets crazy here most evenings, lots of people trooping by. Did you notice anyone who seemed out of place?" Leading the witness, but so far, he wasn't following.

His eyes lit up and he swiveled his wobbly head and pointed a trembling finger at the sidewalk behind me. "Right here a young man came barreling down that sidewalk so fast he would have run me down if I'd been out there."

"Are you sure it was a man? Would you be able to describe him?"

He scratched the back of his neck and scowled. "More tall than short." He touched the rim of his heavy tortoiseshell frames, so old-fashioned they were coming back in style. "With glasses."

Which really didn't narrow things down in the way I had hoped. If he'd said a heavy-set woman, I'd have thought of Sigrid. Or a tiny Asian woman — Yoshe. Or a stocky, lumbering, round-faced man, Dustin. Unfortunately, tall with glasses fit Eric's description. But then I remembered Fritz, the meat poet. He wore glasses too, like a lot of men. This old man's recollection didn't have to mean anything about Eric. I tore a deposit slip from my checkbook, blacked out the account numbers, and jotted my name and cell phone number on the back of it, reminding myself to remind Danielle that I needed more *Key Zest* business cards. Assuming I still had a job at the magazine come Monday.

"In case you think of anything else." I handed over the paper, leaned down to stroke the dusty tomcat, and then wished the man good night. If he'd seen one person running down the street in the space of forty-five minutes, chances were there'd been a dozen more. And that man could have been anyone. Going anywhere. And coming from any place, not necessarily the Key West Loves Literature opening night party.

On the way back to the office to collect my bike, I passed a raucous crowd spilling out onto the sidewalk from Sloppy Joe's Bar. A woman in shorts too small for her ample behind was waving at the webcam and shouting into her cell.

"Can you see me now?" she shrieked. "I'm wearing jean shorts and a white top. You should have come. We're having the best time!" A florid-faced man stumbled out from the bar to join her, thrusting a bottle of beer at the camera and handing a second bottle to his lady friend.

"I don't ever want to come home!" the woman yelled at the camera. The couple clinked their drinks and toasted their missing friend.

I skirted around her, thinking of how many thousands of people in the cold North had been subjected to the braggadocio of sunburned tourists over the years. I'd done the same thing when I first moved here — called up everyone I knew to insist they look at the Duval Street webcam so they could see me in summer clothes while they suffered in their winter parkas. I walked back to the office to get my bike, and then decided I would stop in to regroup. I vaulted up the stairs. Danielle's reception area was dark and quiet, but Wally's form was silhouetted through the blinds that shielded his glass-enclosed office.

"Your restaurant piece is terrific," he called out to the reception area.

Feeling a momentary rush of euphoria, I paused in his office doorway on the way to my cubicle to bask in his praise. A pool of light spilled from the lamp on his desk, illuminating neat stacks of articles, a steaming mug of coffee, and several newspapers. Should I mention Olivia's *New York Times* review of Santiago's Bodega? I was terribly afraid mine would look tired and amateurish in comparison. On the other hand, what if I said nothing and he discovered it later? Or even worse, what if Ava Faulkner found it and used it against me? I couldn't stand feeling like a fraud. Best to spill it right out.

"Thanks," I said. "I was worried you might not want to use the review because Olivia Nethercut beat me to it."

He waved a couple of dismissive fingers over his head. "I'm going to make a few little edits and we're good to go. What's really strong about the writing is the way your status as an outsider who now lives here allows you to see the food and the setting in a way an insider might miss. Someone who grew up here might not feel the same excitement about the flavors of Key West worked into the tapas. But you've been here just long enough to understand our culture without taking it for granted. Olivia Nethercut missed the importance of the local angle altogether. For her, everything is compared to New York. She seems to think she never left."

He grinned and then glanced up. "What's wrong? You look like you've seen Hemingway's ghost."

I heaved a great sigh and slumped in the wicker chair beside his desk. According to

Danielle, he'd refused a tropical upholstered chair like the ones in the reception area because he didn't want visitors lingering. But I needed to talk to someone. And he'd asked. . . .

"I'm worried about everything," I said.

"Such as . . . ?" he said.

So I filled him in about the latest on the two deaths and what I'd learned about the folks at the conference and why they might have wished either Jonah or Yoshe dead. I skipped lightly over Eric's arrest, assuring Wally the police were way off the mark on that one. I only left out the part about the detective making a dinner date with Olivia — way too humiliating to discuss with my boss. And also Dustin's stinging remarks about me stalking Jonah. Ditto on the humiliation factor. I wrapped up with the troubling fact that my mother was not answering my calls and had not appeared at lunch as planned.

"My mom's like me: she doesn't miss meals," I added with a shaky smile.

"You need to get organized," Wally said.

He pulled a new yellow legal pad from his drawer and began to sketch out a chart, with the names of the two dead writers across the top of the page and the people with connections to them down the left margin:

Yoshe, Sigrid, Dustin, Fritz, Olivia, and finally Eric. "The two deaths may be related or may not, correct? For example, it could have been Yoshe who killed Jonah and someone else who did her in."

"Possible," I said. "But hard to imagine. She was so tiny. Hard to picture her swinging that bird statue with enough oomph to knock him out."

He jotted *physically small* in the box where Jonah's name intersected with hers.

"And Yoshe's death could have been a suicide or an accident, but not Jonah's. On the other hand, if they were both murders, neither seems meticulously planned," Wally said. "Especially the first one. You couldn't assume you wouldn't be seen whacking Jonah — there were hundreds of people at the party, no?"

"Yes. But if it was an accident, or the person didn't mean to hit him — or at least not that hard — why not let someone know? Get help and limit the damage? Maybe even save the man's life." I flashed back to my feeble attempts at CPR and how dreadful it felt to have failed.

"People do this all the time — act in some utterly stupid way and then panic and try to hide it." Wally lined the pad up with the edge of his desk and tapped his pen on

Jonah's name. "On television, it's all about love, money, or revenge. With politicians, it's power."

I nodded, trying to massage away the headache that had begun to brood behind my forehead. "So if I could figure out what each of them came to the weekend hoping would happen," I said, "maybe I'd have an answer." I closed my eyes and ran my mind over what I thought I knew. "To begin with, every one of them appeared to need a career boost." I described Yoshe's troubles with her new manuscript: the deep shame she would feel if it failed — or if the editor refused to publish it at all. And Sigrid's tanking book sales and bad reviews — she'd flat-out told me her career rested on this new novel. And Dustin's waning performance as the director of the seminar. Where would he find refuge on this little island if his dream crashed? And Fritz's dreadful meat-themed poetry: In spite of his audience at lunch, it had to be going nowhere fast. No one had specifically pointed to him as a suspect, but good Lord, poetry about protein? Deadly.

Wally wrote summarizing notes in each square on his grid.

And Eric? His practice seemed to be in fine shape, and his relationship with Bill humming along . . . but who knew? He simply wasn't talking. "I can't think of anything for Eric," I said. "I thought his life was going just fine."

"How about Olivia?" he asked.

"The only thing Olivia needs is a man," I answered grimly. "And it looks like she's on the way to snagging one." I drummed my fingers on the notepad. "Though why she'd be interested in a small-town Key West cop is beyond me." Wally scribbled *single and desperate* in her section, which made me smile until I realized the same words could be applied to me.

"A couple of folks mentioned a Key West restaurant franchise that several of these writers hoped to invest in." I explained about the proposed fast food restaurant that the founders had hoped would spread paradise from Pasadena to Providence.

"I hate that idea," said Wally. "Either you're in Key West eating something wonderful or you're not. It's like eating Italian or Chinese in the airport. No one believes that's real ethnic food — just something you have to tolerate if you forgot to bring your own sandwich. Why would a perfectly wonderful chef or writer want to tag onto a project like that?"

"You sound like Jonah," I said. "Only less

crazy." I grinned. "I think the only plausible answer is money."

Wally added dollar signs to the notes he'd made in Yoshe's, Jonah's, and Dustin's columns. "So, why do you think Jonah was killed?" Wally asked. "Some vague threat about honesty doesn't seem like enough of a reason."

I thought back to the first night, the food writers arranged onstage behind him like a Greek chorus. And the palpable discomfort that radiated from the writers when he turned to them with his warning: *"Caveat emptor — my policy of utter transparency will be in full effect."*

"I got the feeling he planned to be quite specific. He hated the path today's food writers are taking and he believed he could change it by exposing their truths this weekend. He was going to go even further than he had in the memoir. He told us that on opening night."

"Someone felt so threatened by what he *might* say that they killed him?"

"Something like that." I squirmed, thinking about the editorial letter I'd stolen from Yoshe's briefcase. I wanted to show him, but it felt wrong. It *was* wrong — he might very well fire me for lousy ethics.

Instead, I described my conversation with

the elderly man next door to the Audubon House — how he thought he might have seen a man with glasses running from the direction of the party, past his little house and on toward Duval. And then another idea clicked in. "What if the killer was captured on the Duval Street webcam?" I sighed, my enthusiasm ebbing away as quickly as it had rushed in. "We'll never know. The police could access the archives, but they certainly aren't going to show them to me."

"You don't need the cops for that," he said. "You need access to the right Web site. Or a friend with that access." He raised his eyebrows and grinned, then typed in a Web address on his computer. A photo of the sidewalk outside Sloppy Joe's came up on the screen, along with a bar for choosing the time interval you wished to view. "When would this person have been running?"

"Say it was nineish when I found Jonah? Maybe as late as quarter to ten. Let's start fifteen minutes before that."

For the next ten minutes, we squinted at the antics of tourists and street performers passing down Duval Street, but recognized no one. In the background, the noise from the bar roared in a fuzzy way, with oc- casional blasts from car horns and mufflerless motorcycles passing by. Then came a familiar figure. More tall than short. With glasses. Walking quickly, almost at a trot, looking horribly worried.

I felt sick to my stomach, really sick. Like the night I ate an entire order of bad oysters and spent the next eight hours hugging the toilet. And the twenty-four hours after that lying in bed like a wet rag.

Eric. I shrugged carelessly, hoping that nothing showed on my face.

"Oh well, I can look at this later, make sure none of our suspects passed by. But even if they had, it doesn't mean anything, really." I sprang up from Wally's folding wicker chair. "Right now I better get back to work. My boss is a bear and I owe him a big article," I said.

18

Usually the food that meets your hunger sends you into a calmed and expansive state of deep satisfaction, but I instead sat in that café and became quite heavy and defeated.

— Gabrielle Hamilton

I closed my office door, even though doing so shut out the only natural light and usually left me quivering with claustrophobia. I woke my computer and typed in the Duval Street webcam address again. I watched Eric trot down the street several more times, reentering the time and date stamp, trying to decipher the look of panic on his face. And the way he kept looking over his shoulder. He did not look like a man who'd come down with a sudden migraine. Had he seen something he shouldn't have that scared him badly? Or had he done something awful? But if that was the case what possible reason could my friend have had for killing Jonah?

My iPhone buzzed. *Private caller* came up on the screen — usually the sign of a badgering telemarketer, or worse. But I couldn't take the chance of missing news about my mother. "Hello?"

"Hayley Snow?" The words quaked and shimmered. "You told me to call you if I thought of something else."

"Who is this?" I barked. Then I recognized the raspy voice of the old man who lived next door to the Audubon House. "Yes, thanks so much for calling."

"I did think of something I forgot to mention. The cats and I had breakfast early the other morning, just like always. I shouldn't give them milk — my daughter says it's bad for their digestion, but they look forward to it."

"A tiny splash won't hurt them," I said, trying to be patient while his story unfolded. "My Evinrude loves milk almost more than he loves me."

The old man laughed. "Evinrude, that's a name you don't hear often."

"He purrs like a well-oiled engine," I said. "Always has, since he was a kitten. But anyway, you were saying you forgot to tell me . . ."

"After breakfast, Boris and I were walking the perimeter of the property and I saw him stop to rub his jowls on something in the bushes. You know how they like the way that feels, the way we like our neck and shoulders rubbed?"

I could picture the big white cat stalking around the yard behind the old man with his walker, stopping to scratch his cheeks on a tree limb or an old paint can or . . . I hoped it didn't turn out to be something gross. "Uh-huh. So, what did Boris find?"

"It was a big metal statue of a bird. Only the legs were broken off. Couldn't figure out how in the heck it got on my property, half-buried in the weeds. But I guess people throw all kinds of trash around in this town. So I picked it up and dragged it back to my porch. And that's where the police officer found it."

My heart started to pound. This had to be the egret that had disappeared from the scene of the crime on Thursday night. The bird that went missing and made me look like a fool. "Which police officer was that?"

"The detective with the horse face. Some name like Bran Flakes."

I burst out laughing. In less than twenty-four hours, Bransford had been demoted from "chiseled" to "horse-faced." And his name had morphed from some distinguished European heritage to breakfast cereal.

The old man chortled along with me. "He came back around again yesterday to ask what else I might have seen or heard. I guess they figure one old man can't remember much, but if you go back a second time he might dredge something up. Or make it up, even." He chuckled again. "Lucky thing Boris found that bird. And like I said, the detective saw it on my porch and his eyes got so big, I thought they might pop right out of his head and roll off into the dirt. So then he asked me if he could take it and I said, why not? It don't belong to me. And he wrapped it up in his jacket and carried it off. I should have thought of this when you were here, but sometimes my brain just don't go where it should."

"Not to worry. Thank you so much for calling," I told him. "You and those cats enjoy the sunshine today."

I hung up and sank back into my chair. Somehow the bird had to be connected to Eric's arrest. Was this the physical evidence Officer Torrence had mentioned? But what were the chances Bransford would tell me anything about it? Slender. Still, I packed up my belongings and headed out — the chances of my getting any more writing done here were even more slim than that.

I drove superslowly on my way to the police station, looking down all the alleyways off Eaton Street and in the parking lots too, hoping I'd spot Mom or her bike. Of course, she could have gone anywhere — into New Town for grocery shopping at Publix or a quick sandwich — or even buzzed right off the island. But why, when we'd had lunch plans as clear as plastic wrap? And why not call me? None of it made sense. Unless she was in trouble. Or angry. I drove with a piercing sense of dread — and I wasn't going to feel better until I spotted my mother puttering up on her bright pink scooter and knew Eric was safely back home, the arrest a nightmarish mistake in the past.

I parked in front of the peach-colored police department and picked up the intercom phone that hung outside the front door. A gruff male voice answered, "KWPD."

"I'm hoping to catch a word with Detective Bransford?" I said, wishing my voice didn't sound like a lost little girl's.

"He's not in."

"Are you expecting him later? It's about a missing person." And clearing my friend of

277

murder, I thought but didn't say.

"Doubt it," said the gruff man. "Torrence is covering the desk. I'll put you through to him."

I groaned aloud and considered slamming the phone down and running. But before I could make that move, Officer Torrence appeared at the double glass doors, pushed them open, and poked his head out. "Can I help you, Miss Snow?"

Too late to bolt. "My mother's missing," I said, and horrified myself — and probably him — as a trickle of tears started down my cheeks. The opening salvo for what felt like many more.

"Come in," he said, swinging one of the heavy doors open wide and waving me through. "Coffee? It's been sitting on that burner a couple hours, so I don't recommend you say yes." He smiled and I followed behind him down the greenish blue cement-walled hallway to his office. When we were settled, me on a folding chair, him behind his desk, I scanned the framed citations for bravery and excellence in community relations and marksmanship on the wall above his head.

After a minute, he asked, "So, about your mother?"

Now, in spite of my efforts to keep them

inside, the trickle of tears turned into a torrent as the stress of the weekend gained purchase. Two deaths too close to me. And two of the people I was closest to in the world, one in jail, and the other maybe in danger. I put my face in my hands and leaned onto his pristine desk blotter and cried. Finally I gathered myself and peeked through my fingers. Torrence, looking thoroughly alarmed, had nearly overturned his chair while flapping his hand behind him for a box of tissues.

"Let's start fresh," he said, grabbing the box and pushing it over to me.

I wiped my face and explained how Mom had failed to meet me as promised. And then, because why would he take me seriously otherwise, I told him that before she disappeared, she'd been asking questions about Yoshe King's unfortunate death at the bed-and-breakfast near the Southernmost Point.

"I assume you know that we found her body on the rocks," I said, parrying his disapproval before he could say anything. "I hope my mother didn't get in over her head with her inquiries. She's a little bit nosy, in a creative kind of way." He looked annoyed now, his face darkening and fingers gripping the arms of his chair. "It's not that we

279

don't trust you guys to do your job —"

"But?" he asked, leaning back in his chair until it squawked and the buttons on his shirt threatened to pop.

"But it's gotten personal," I said. "Our friend Eric Altman is in jail and we're positive he didn't kill anyone." I sniffled away some tears for the second time in ten minutes. "Can you tell me why he was arrested? Just a hint maybe? Does it have something to do with fingerprints on a bird statue?"

His dark eyebrows undulated and he licked his lips as his chair snapped upright. "That would be an excellent reason to arrest someone," he finally said. "As for your mother, it's too early to file an official report, but I can let our patrol officers know to keep an eye out for her."

He jotted some notes about her appearance (auburn curls and hazel eyes like me, only twenty-plus years older and without my father's widow's peak) and what she might be wearing. This I had to guess from what I'd seen in her suitcase, but I assumed she would have dressed up for the luncheon. When he'd gotten all the details along with my phone numbers, he promised he'd let the detective know I'd come by.

"Not necessary," I assured him. Bransford

wouldn't be calling me back tonight — he'd be drooling over a bloodred rare steak and garlic mashed potatoes in the cozy courtyard at Michael's. Washed down with a bottle of expensive wine and then Olivia Nethercut for dessert.

I left the PD and drove the short distance to houseboat row. Water glinted in the sunshine, wind chimes tinkled, and the steady hum of someone power-washing their home pulsed in the background. Odd how life could look and sound exactly normal, when the truth couldn't be more different. I felt acutely alone — meeting with Torrence had done little to dispel that — and eager to see the cheerful face of my elderly housemate.

I parked the scooter near the Laundromat and trotted up the finger to Miss Gloria's place. "Helloooo!" I called. No answer. I jumped onto the deck and hurried into the houseboat. The living area was pin neat, the pillow and bedclothes I'd left tangled on the couch folded away, the breakfast dishes upside down in the drainer, papers on the counter tidied into a neat stack.

I put the kettle on for tea and nibbled at the last remnants of strawberry-rhubarb cake, thinking sorrowfully of the lunch we were missing. Then I noticed a note

scribbled in Miss Gloria's old-fashioned
script lying on the counter near the fridge, a
copper-speckled rock on the corner for ballast.

Up the dock playing cards with Mrs. Dubis-
son, the note read. *Bill called. Eric's mom is*
coming into town this evening. Then in
parentheses: *Should we offer to put her up?*
She can share my double bed. I'll let you call
and suggest it.

Four women in this tiny space, all sharing
a bathroom no bigger than a closet? "Absolutely not!" I yelped aloud, and then jotted
on the paper: *I'm sure Bill will want her to*
stay with him or maybe get her a hotel room
up near their home. We'll have them over for
drinks or dinner, okay?

I poured hot water over the green tea bag
in my mug, and sorted through the stack of
yesterday's mail. Most of it was addressed
to Miss Gloria, including a few bills, cata-
logs, and a postcard from Cory Held at
Preferred Properties.

Who says real estate doesn't move over the
holidays? We sold four homes last month!
was splashed across the top of the card.
Underneath were snapshots of two condominiums and two wooden conch houses, all
staged to look adorable and tropical with
red SOLD banners slapped across the

photos. Someday. I restacked the mail, added honey to my tea, and dug the letter I'd lifted from Yoshe's belongings out of my backpack.

Settling into a wicker chair out on the deck, I sipped my tea and read the letter again, slowly. I'd never seen actual correspondence between a writer and her publisher, but this seemed unusually harsh. The editor had taken issue with Yoshe's food and her writing, but even more interesting (and probably devastating to Yoshe) were the questions about the authenticity of her recipes. I wondered if the call Yoshe had taken at breakfast had been from the publisher. But why call the bed-and-breakfast's house phone instead of her cell? How would they even have that number?

I wished I knew more. My gaze swept over the letter again, pausing on the letterhead. Certainly this person would not talk to me. Unless I called and impersonated Yoshe's next of kin? But I didn't even know her name.

Then I remembered that Yoshe's niece was expected at the bed-and-breakfast — maybe she had arrived. And maybe she'd have some insights about her aunt's state of mind before the tumble from her balcony. Should I phone ahead? I hated the idea that she'd refuse to speak to me or that the manager would think I meant to stir up more trouble about the death in her establishment and tell me not to come. Better to take my chances in person.

Back inside the boat, I smoothed out the editorial letter, tucked it into a clean envelope, and put it in my pack. Not that I intended to hand it over, because how in the world would I explain where it came from? As I searched through my room for an official business card to offer Yoshe's niece (because even I realized that a deposit slip with my name and cell number scratched on it looked sloppy and unofficial), my phone rang. My stepmother Allison's name came up.

"Hey, how are you?" I asked, ready to dance around why it had been too long since I called. Allison and my father have been married over ten years, but she and I had kept each other at arm's length until last fall when she used her chemistry expertise to help me solve Kristen Faulkner's murder. That definitely warmed things up between us.

We chatted about her job and mine, and the veterinarian's annual checkup report on her dog, a dachshund named Alphonse. Not that he and I were close — he bared his pointy white teeth and growled every time he saw me — which probably stemmed back to the time Evinrude had pinned him on his home turf. He'd never gotten over the humiliation of getting whipped by a cat, and in his linear dog thinking, he seemed to place the blame on me.

But despite our small talk, Allison sensed something was up with me. "You don't sound like your usual chipper self, Hayley," she said, sounding just like my mother. Which honestly, under the present circumstances, felt like a relief.

So I told her about Mom's visit, my impending job review, the two murders, Eric's arrest, and finally admitted that Mom was missing.

"What an awful weekend," she said. "I'm sure the police will find your mother. Or she'll show up with a dead cell phone."

"I know. I keep telling myself the same thing."

"How can I help? Do you want us to come down?"

"Not yet," I said, feeling a rush of gratitude, tinged with a little shiver of horror. Three parents on the scene would be two too many parents to manage. Even if one of them was MIA. "I'll let you know if I need you." But then it occurred to me that she might be able to help figure out what was going on with Eric.

"I do have a favor. Any chance you could run over to Eric Altman's house in Mom's neighborhood? Mrs. Altman is coming to Key West later on today and apparently she's quite hysterical. Maybe you could help her sort through Eric's boxes and see if she has any old yearbooks or letters or diaries from the years Eric spent at graduate school in New York? I'm looking for any clue about his relationship with a guy named Jonah Barrows."

It sounded stupid and hopeless even as I asked her — whoever heard of a graduate program with a yearbook? Did I think Jonah would have inscribed a secret message to Eric on his photo like we did back in high school? But I was feeling desperate.

"I'll call ahead and tell her you're coming."

19

Let things taste of what they are.
— Alice Waters

After ten minutes trying to calm the frantic Mrs. Altman, I ran out to my scooter and puttered back over to the bed-and-breakfast, keeping an eye out for my mother all along the way. Tourists were everywhere, enjoying the temperatures in the seventies and the blue, blue water and cups of Cuban coffee and relief from their frozen realities back home. I squeezed my hands into fists, pumping myself up to fib as needed, and marched into the lobby.

Reba, the manager, was tucked into the back room with a slender Asian woman wearing stylish New York clothes — a short, belted dress and black leggings, boots so tall they extended above her knees, a fluffy sheepskin vest that looked hot as Hades, the shiniest black hair I'd ever seen. And me in red high-tops and tight jeans — face it: everything was a little snug these days, considering the way I'd been eating. How could I make a connection so she'd answer my intrusive questions?

"There was no computer in the luggage," Reba was telling the Asian woman.

"Yoshe brought it here with her," the woman insisted. "That's why I flew down instead of having you ship the stuff. She told me she was planning to work in her downtime. It was a MacBook Air, practically brand-new. She kept it in a soft-sided Burberry case."

Reba shook her head. "I'm terribly sorry about the circumstances, but I don't remember seeing anything like that. You understand that we can't be responsible for missing items. As I explained, I locked her purse in our house safe. If the computer had been with her things, I would have put it there for safekeeping."

"Yoo-hoo," I called from behind the desk, thinking this conflict could work to my advantage.

Reba looked up but frowned when she recognized me. "Did your mother turn up?"

"Not yet," I said. "She didn't stop by here again, did she?"

Reba shook her head.

"Since I was in your neighborhood, I came to talk to Ms. King's niece. As we discussed." Which we hadn't, but what could she say with me right there?

"I'm so sorry for your loss," I added to the young woman, barging around the counter with my hand outstretched. "My mother is the biggest fan you can imagine. And I adored your aunt's recipes too — practically grew up on Yoshe King's vegetable lo mein and her crispy fried chicken. We spent some wonderful time with her this weekend. I'm Hayley Snow."

"Mary Chen," she said with a faint smile, placing a limp hand in mine.

Two women in flip-flops and bathing suit cover-ups rang the bell out in the lobby. Throwing a warning glare at me, Reba left the office to help them.

Up closer I could see that Yoshe's niece's eyes looked sunken and dull in spite of the thick band of eyeliner and multiple coats of mascara she'd applied. Food and caffeine, I thought, of course. I was desperate for both, but maybe she was too. And maybe while I plied her with calories and coffee, I could get her to talk about whether Yoshe was depressed. Or angry. Or frightened. Anything that might help explain her terrible death. And possibly my mother's disappearance.

"You must be drooping after that trip. There's nothing worth eating in the Miami Airport — that's for sure. Want to grab a bite to eat before you tackle this?" I waved at Yoshe's luggage. "The Banana Café is like two blocks from here and they make the best breakfasts and coffee."

She clicked her tongue against her teeth. "I'm catching the plane back to Miami at five."

I glanced at my watch — almost one. "We've got plenty of time for brunch. I don't know about you, but I can't think well if I'm hungry."

She stared at me for a few moments, finally heaving a grateful sigh and nodding. I grabbed her elbow and steered her past the desk. "Back in a jiffy," I said to Reba.

The hostess led us to a table on the rooftop — just high enough to feel removed from the noise and grit but still enjoy watching the buzz of activity on the sidewalk below. A large green umbrella shielded us from the midday sun. Shortly after being seated, we ordered — an omelet with fried potatoes and caramelized onions and cheddar cheese for me and La Formidable crepe for Mary:

sausage, tomatoes, peppers, onions, and cheese. A mimosa for her and a coffee for me.

"This beats January in the Northeast, right?" I said after the menus had been whisked away and Mary's drink delivered. "I moved down here from New Jersey early last fall. Never looked back."

"Fifteen degrees and incredibly windy when we took off," Mary said, sipping the mimosa. "Not that I'm planning to stay long enough to get used to it. There's no point. And now this place gives me the creeps."

"I really am so sorry about your aunt."

"And how did you know her?" Mary asked, her face tipped toward the sun like a delicate bird's.

"My mom and I took her to lunch on Friday with one of the other writers."

"So you don't really know her," she said, furrowing her forehead and clutching her purse as though she might walk out. "Why are you so interested in speaking with me?"

I suspected that only the awful truth would keep her talking. "We found her body," I said. "My mom and I. Honestly, we won't feel right until we know what really happened."

Mary grasped her stomach and winced, her face puckered in pain like she'd been socked in the gut. Then she straightened, pursing her lips and tapping a glossy finger-nail on the wooden table. A large tear rolled down her cheek, dropped off her chin, and sparkled on the hair of the faux-fur vest. "I can't believe she killed herself like that."

I leaned across the table to take her hand. "See, I'm not so sure she did." I explained that my mother and I had been making some inquiries about conflicts among the panelists, and were wondering if someone might have pushed her off that balcony to the rocks below, though of course I didn't put it that way.

"Was she worried about anything as far as you knew?"

Yoshe's niece shook her head mournfully as our meals were delivered. "Nothing out of the ordinary. Obviously, a food writer doesn't always generate what you'd call reli-able and lucrative income. Last year I would have said she was down — it had been several years since she had something new published. But then she had that fabulous idea about recipes from the ancestors and scored the contract for the new cookbook. I hadn't seen her this happy in a long, long time. Even though she had to work at warp speed to make the deadline. And she was so pleased to be invited to this conference."

She tucked a napkin into her black sweater and finally shrugged off the sheepskin.

Thank goodness, I was burning up just looking at her. She swallowed the rest of her mimosa and signaled for another.

"How did she seem to you? Emotionally, I mean," she asked, buttering a piece of whole wheat toast and then discarding it on the plate next to her crepe. Her eyes glimmered with unshed tears again and she fought to hold them back. Like she needed some good news.

"Spunky. Feisty. I would never have said she was depressed, though I know people can hide things. On Friday, she seemed upbeat, in spite of the dreadful start to the weekend with Jonah's murder." I told her about his opening lecture and described how the other panelists had been placed on the stage behind him like theater props. "I think all of the panelists were a little worried about his honesty manifesto. Maybe worried that they were in his bull's-eye. And I'm certain some of them were."

I took a small bite of my omelet, savoring the creamy browned onions in melted cheese and sighing with satisfaction. Food did amazing things for me even if the circumstances were completely dire. Mary had cut her crepe into tiny pieces, but so far I hadn't seen her eat a single bite. Nor was she telling me much. So I kept talking.

"Even I — and trust me, I must be the lowest writer on the totem pole at this conference — was dragged through the mud a little." I described the fangirl e-mails I'd sent to Jonah, hoping he'd have the time to chat with me about my career sometime over the weekend. Or at least, that I could score an insider interview that would help me write a great piece.

"Instead of helping me out, he told the organizer that I was stalking him." I laughed lightly, though I could still feel the searing embarrassment that followed Dustin's accusation.

"I'm sure it was the same guy. Why couldn't he just leave her alone?" Mary sniffled, and dabbed at the corner of her eye with a napkin.

My ears perked up. I handed over one of the spare tissues that Officer Torrence had pressed on me. "What guy?"

"She told me about an e-mail she received last week from one of the other writers. She was so upset. Probably the same person who was nasty to everyone, including you, right?"

I nodded quickly. "So Jonah Barrows was badgering her?"

"She never told me the name. But she did

get an e-mail earlier this week warning that he was going to raise some issue about her background during the weekend. She called me on Monday, absolutely distraught. I told her not to pay one bit of attention to him — he was trying to steal the limelight from the real stars. I told her to ignore any question she didn't like."

"Her background?" I repeated. "What kind of issues?"

Mary hesitated, cupped her fingers over her eyes as if she was thinking hard. Then she drained her drink and leaned across the table, her words slurring a little. "Are we speaking in confidence? Her reputation has been damaged enough already."

"Of course," I said, pushing my nearly empty plate aside. "Go ahead."

"What did it matter whether Yoshe's grandmother really came from the Fujian Province?"

I sat back against the bench. "That's where the tea she liked so much is grown, I remember. But her family didn't live there?"

Mary shook her head. "Six generations in San Francisco. Yoshe did a lot of traveling in China, mind you. She talked to a thousand grandmothers in provinces all over the country, including the Fujian. They just didn't happen to be her close relatives, that's all."

"But wouldn't Yoshe think this would be found out?" I asked, madly wondering whether I could use what she told me in my article in some oblique way — to support the information I'd already stolen. And concluding in the end, of course I could not.

"I think she did worry," said Mary, "though she never admitted it directly. Her other cookbooks weren't as personal as this one was going to be. Nor were the print runs this large. And I think she underestimated how easy it is to research things in this day and age — how easily people could check her bio. But she couldn't afford to backtrack."

"You wouldn't by any chance have a copy of the e-mail Jonah sent?"

"She read it to me, but I never saw it." She nibbled on a bite of sausage but then pushed the plate away, the food barely touched. No wonder she looked half my size.

"How would Jonah have known about the deception?"

"Anyone who has lunch with her former agent hears all the dirt," said Mary, dabbing her lips with the tissue. Then she extracted a lipstick from her bag and rolled on a shiny pink gloss that matched her nails. "She fired that loser last summer because she was doing a lousy job retaining e-rights and selling apps. The agent took it very personally — acted as though Yoshe's decision was a complete surprise even though Yoshe had to practically sell the new book herself."

"How would Jonah know about any of this?"

Mary shrugged, rattled the ice in her glass. "Yoshe suspected the agent got hold of the revision letter and passed it along. Just for spite."

"The revision letter?" I asked, feigning ignorance while feeling my cheeks turn pink. I didn't dare glance at my backpack, where I imagined the purloined letter might be flashing like a cop's blue light.

"Anytime an author turns a project in, the editor sends it back with suggested revisions. Yoshe and I were going to meet when she got home to figure out how she could tweak the manuscript and address the editor's concerns."

"But wouldn't the agent have known about Yoshe's background if she was the one who'd sold the project to the publisher?" I asked. "In that case, she'd be in as much hot water as your aunt."

"She would simply claim that she was

hoodwinked." Mary forked up a piece of fried potato and nibbled at the crispy skin.

I stayed quiet, hoping she'd say more.

"Among other things, the fact-checkers maintained that the new recipes weren't from our family. No one in our family cooked much except for Yoshe."

"And this would have mattered a great deal to her bottom line, right? Sales of her former cookbooks, and especially sales of the new one. Wasn't the advertising for the new cookbook going to be focused on her history?" I remembered how she'd gone on and on about the place of history and authenticity in food in the panel discussion Friday morning.

"I suppose. One of the things we talked about doing when she got home was rewriting the preface. She was seriously considering coming clean about her own family and describing her recipes as emerging from archetypal Chinese grandparents. If the food tastes great — and it will — it really shouldn't matter."

Mary tapped her forehead, and tears filled her eyes. "When my mom died a few years ago, Auntie Yoshe came through for me in a huge way. So you see, I don't care about all this — I care that someone made her unhappy. And that she's gone."

"I'm so sorry," I said again, but it sounded flat empty. "Could I ask one more question?"

She shrugged. "Why not?"

"Did she mention anything about a project she might invest in — a franchise involving a Key West–style fast food restaurant?"

"That rings a faint bell," said Mary. "Though she didn't really have a lot of cash on hand. We were both hoping the new cookbook would change that." She clucked her tongue and pulled her fur vest back on. "It's all such a damn waste."

I nodded and called for the check. After paying the bill, I added the credit card stub to the pile growing in my wallet — no way I'd be able to write this meal off. Unless I could whip up a review for the Banana Café for *Key Zest*'s next issue.

Then we headed back down the stairs and a block over on Duval Street so Mary could pick up her aunt's luggage and catch her plane. By the time I returned her to the bed-and-breakfast, she looked slightly more cheerful than when I'd first seen her — probably the anesthetizing effects of two large mimosas and not much food. She didn't yet seem to have connected the dots: that the story she'd revealed over lunch showed that Yoshe had plenty of motive to

299

murder Jonah. And take her own life after that.

Two o'clock — I had just enough time to buzz over to the tribute to Jonah, which I was certain would include remarks about Yoshe as well. I told Mary where I was headed.

"Would you like to go with me?" I asked. "I'm sure a lot of folks will want to share your grief. Your aunt was much beloved by this crowd."

Mary's eyes shuttered closed, then quickly back open. "No, thanks. The part of Auntie Yoshe I want to remember has nothing to do with her fame. I'll think of her teaching me how to use a knife properly when chopping the ingredients for a salad. Or how to choose a melon and which greens would be too bitter if they were left raw but would go perfectly in a stir-fry." Tears choked her voice again. "And the memories she shared of growing up with my mom. I'll miss those most of all."

I gave her a hug on the sidewalk, not wanting to risk another scolding from Reba. "Good luck with everything," I said, and walked away, my thoughts whirling.

Maybe it was a terrible stereotype about Asian family shame, but even stereotypes often start with a few grains of truth:

Wouldn't Yoshe have been devastated by the feedback from her editor? And despite Mary's insistence that they were working on a way to salvage the cookbook, wouldn't Yoshe have felt a terrible sense of humiliation if her family's history was about to be exposed by Jonah?

Yes, she'd been a small person, but as any petite baseball player or golfer could attest, swinging a weapon with success was all about using the levers in your arms efficiently.

20

A splash of blood from the rib eye steaks
    carved for the rich man on the hill.
A touch of green from lobsters cracked
    and cleaned for the fussy housewife,
Who will eat pink flesh but not green, no
    matter how pleasing the taste.
      — Fritz Ewing, *Death in Four Courses*

I checked my e-mail on the way back to my bike, hoping I'd finally have a message from my own mother. But nothing. I hated to think of finding myself in Mary's shoes — having lost both her mother and her aunt, the two women she felt closest to in the world. Feeling a wave of anxiety surge forward, I hopped on the scooter and drove off, winding through some of the small residential streets on the eastern side of the island. There was absolutely no reason why Mom would be over this way and not have let me know, but it allowed me to feel like I was doing *something.*

With only five minutes left before the event started, I parked across the street from the San Carlos Institute for the final session, including what Dustin had dubbed a "book-signing extravaganza." Which seemed a little more upbeat than the situation called for, but I could understand that murders or no murders, all the panelists would want those stacks of books to move.

I stood at the back of the auditorium, searching the crowd for my mother's familiar form. The seats were about half-full, none of them occupied by Mom. The red velvet curtains swept open and Dustin blundered onstage, followed by a trickle of food writers, who once again took seats at the tables of the makeshift diner. He stood at the podium, pale and unhappy.

"Ladies and gentlemen," he said, "we are devastated by the events of this weekend. We had so much to celebrate. I could not have imagined how this would turn out." He dropped his head into his hands, causing an abrasive rumble in the microphone attached to the podium.

And causing me to wonder, again, whether on that opening night he really *might* have anticipated some of what would unfold in the ensuing days. I remembered him pacing in the wings as Jonah sacrificed one after the other of the food writing world's sacred goats. Had his rage mounted as Jonah strutted and preened and made innuendos about the secrets he planned to expose, while the faces of the writers in the background tightened defensively? I wished I'd been more familiar with the panelists at the beginning of the weekend. Maybe then I could have recognized a desperate or murderous expression, suppressed for the sake of the public appearance, but perhaps incompletely.

I searched the faces of the stragglers posed onstage this afternoon. Olivia was there, perfectly coiffed and exquisitely dressed as always. Sigrid sat across the stage from her, in yet one more bright muumuu, this one resembling the dizzying patterns of a Turkish rug. Fritz, the culinary poet, the most shadowy of the possible suspects I'd considered, was seated in the back row. I pulled out my phone and typed his name into the search bar. Most of what surfaced appeared to be appalling reviews of his poetry collections, one of them penned by Jonah. Sigrid wasn't the only writer whose lifework had been panned by the featured speaker.

"As I said in my opening remarks," Dustin continued when he'd gathered his emotions, "Jonah was a bright star in our universe. He wanted the best from us — no pretense, no nonsense, no puffery. Maybe sometimes he pushed this too far, but in the end we were all better for his challenges." He paused and mopped his brow with the sleeve of his shirt. "I thought it might be appropriate at this moment, rather than ramble on with my own recollections of this brilliant man, to ask some of his colleagues to speak about their relationships with him."

Apparently Dustin hadn't prepared them for this eventuality, because no one came forward. After an impossibly awkward few minutes, Fritz stood and shambled to the mike. Dustin nodded with gratitude and stepped aside. Fritz pushed his glasses to his forehead, unfolded a half sheet of lined paper, and smoothed it on the podium. He studied his audience with pale blue eyes, then turned his attention to the paper.

" 'The Butcher,' " he said. "A poem to honor Jonah Barrows."

Morning comes, the butcher's wife hands
    him an apron, starched white.
Keep it clean, she scolds.
At night, he brings it home, layered with
    the detritus of his day.
A splash of blood from the rib eye steaks

carved for the rich man on the hill.
A touch of green from lobsters cracked
    and cleaned for the fussy housewife,
Who will eat pink flesh but not green, no
    matter how pleasing the taste.
Marrow from hacked bones,
Distributed to fancy restaurants and
    slavering dogs alike.
And as the day goes by, the hues of the
    apron morph from red to gray.
I tried, he says, handing it to the missus
    come evening. I had my work to do.

I squirmed in my seat in the silence that followed, wondering if this had anything at all to do with Jonah. Wondering if this man was a little psychotic. Up on the stage, Sigrid was rolling her eyes and muttering to the writer on her left. To my relief, and I imagined that of the rest of the people in the auditorium as well, Olivia shot out of her diner booth and moved gracefully to the podium. She touched Fritz's elbow and hovered, smiling, until he stepped aside.

"Thank you, Fritz," she said, clapping her hands as he returned to his booth. "That was most unusual. And touching." She turned back to the podium and smiled sadly. "Jonah Barrows must have had what scientists refer to as a 'supertaster' palate —

306

that is, more taste buds than ordinary humans. He could tease out the tarragon from the sage and the Tillamook from the Fontina the way few other chefs or reviewers or writers could. But he also had a sharp eye and an incisive way with words. He could cut to the bone." She folded her slender white hands on the podium and cleared her throat. "There was a tremor of loss in the landscape of technology when Steve Jobs died too young. And we in the food world feel a similar seismic upheaval with the death of Jonah Barrows. I personally am grateful to have had the pleasure of spending some precious time in his presence. Thank you." She nodded at Dustin and returned to her seat.

"That was lovely and generous," said the woman seated in front of me. "She's so right about the comparison with Steve Jobs."

I thought it was a rather major exaggeration, but I wouldn't take her on, especially at the man's memorial. After a few of the other writers took their turns extolling Jonah's talents, Dustin thanked them and moved on to speak of Yoshe's strengths and his exquisite sorrow at also losing her. Then he opened the mike for comments from the audience about both of the writers. One by one, conference attendees trooped up to the standing microphone and told stories about their love for Yoshe King's cookbooks. Few of the speakers mentioned Jonah.

Finally the session ended and I started up the aisle toward the vestibule, falling in behind Fritz Ewing. "Your poem was so unexpected," I said. "I'm amazed that you could come up with something so polished so quickly. And I couldn't help wondering if there was a message in it about the events of the weekend."

A wicked smile played across his lips. "I wondered if anyone would bother to inquire. The butcher must do his work, whether it dirties his apron at the end of the day, or not. Jonah operated that way too."

"And that means?"

"Didn't you see *All the President's Men*? Remember the scene where Deep Throat tells Bob Woodward to 'follow the money'?"

I nodded slowly.

"The same applies here."

"Okay, so have you heard anything about a franchise that several of the writers were interested in investing in?" I asked.

"Impossibly lowbrow," he said with an edge of scorn in his voice. "But all's fair. I would have invested in it myself if I'd had the dough. Or had I been asked." He doffed an imaginary hat and slipped into the stream of tourists passing by the institute.

21

So long as you have food in your mouth,
you have solved all questions for the time
being.

— Kafka

I returned to the office again, this time feeling like I had the bones of a story that
would capture the events of the weekend.
"At what price honesty?" the headline could
read.

Of course, truth was a value we'd all claim
we espoused. But Jonah took it so far that
his words became weapons. And his weapons cost him friends. I jotted some notes,
but the longer I worked, the harder it got to
concentrate. There had been two murders.
And many career and life-changing secrets
seemed to be at risk — including those
people he'd contacted before the conference. And my own mother was hot on the
trail of . . . something. And I could no

longer suppress my concern about her absence.

My phone buzzed with news of an incoming e-mail. I found a message from Mary Chen.

"Hayley, thank you for your kindness and for the wonderful though brief escape. Exactly what I needed after a horrible weekend. I'm now waiting in the Miami Airport for a delayed plane. You were so right — nothing worth eating here, though the coffee isn't bad. While I was sitting around, I tried to reconstruct what my aunt told me when she called me in so much distress. I may not have gotten it all exactly right, but here's the gist. It pains me deeply to send it on, but for Yoshe's sake, I believe it's important to let people know how destructive Jonah Barrows was.

"He told her that while he appreciated her concerns about her privacy and her career, and her intent to restore her reputation, he couldn't overlook the fact that she planned to hoodwink the very people who adored her and admired her by constructing and exaggerating a phony background. His allegiance had to be to the truth, rather than to an individual concerned about the size of her next royalty check."

Stomach churning, I saw clearly that Yoshe

had every reason to *wish* Jonah dead before Friday's panels. But had she killed him? Had she picked up that metal bird, knocked him out, and left him to drown? And if so, how and why had she died?

I read the message over again, then thought of calling Bill to see if he'd give me the password to Eric's e-mail. Because maybe Eric had received a threatening message as well. But it was one thing for her niece to invade Yoshe King's privacy — she was already dead. I doubted that Eric would ever forgive me — or Bill — for plundering his private messages when he was very much alive.

So I hurried back out to the parking lot and drove across the island to talk one more time to Reba at the bed-and-breakfast. Which by now felt a little like squeezing an old lemon, but I had no other ideas.

As I entered the lobby, Reba was checking in her latest guests, a pale young couple, both redheads, who looked like they'd blister like lobsters after one afternoon in our sun. Reba marked two *x*'s on a colored map laid out on the counter.

"Since you haven't visited our town before, Ernest Hemingway's house is a must-see. The Southernmost Point is right up the block, and you can't beat Duval Street for people-watching — right over there." She smiled, pointing outside to the intersection across the street, and then handed over the keys and the map. "We serve breakfast from seven thirty to nine thirty. Your room is on the end, third floor. We were able to upgrade you to a better view."

The young woman squealed and clapped her hands.

Yoshe's room, I thought.

As the customers mounted the stairs, Reba turned to me, her smile fading. "What now?"

"I'm sorry to be a pest, and I'm sure the police have already asked you . . . but you're certain you didn't hear anything the morning Ms. King died? No screams, no arguments? Did she have any visitors at all that day?"

"As you heard me explain" — she waved at the echoing steps of her retreating guests — "I'm busy with breakfast in the mornings. Making coffee, replenishing pastries and juice and fruit. After that, it takes me an hour or more to clean up. The kitchen does not have a water view, so thank God" — she crossed herself — "I didn't see her fall. I wasn't aware that she had any visitors. I told you about the one phone call. And I just don't know anything more. I wish

I could help — you might have more luck canvassing people in the hotel next door. Maybe someone was out on a balcony? Walking on the beach? I told your mother the very same thing. And the cops. And Ms. King's niece." She left the counter, marched back into her office, and slammed the door.

I retreated outdoors and perched on the porch swing to check my phone again. Nothing from Mom. Why not stop over next door?

I exited through the garden of the bed-and-breakfast and walked quickly through the motel entrance and out back to the pool that overlooked the ocean. The area around the pool was blanketed with chaise longues — and dozens of people reading, sleeping, and soaking up the sunshine. I hardly knew where to start — it could take days to canvass all of them. But then I saw a girl in a purple bikini and a straw hat head for the outside stairs that led to the third floor overlooking the adjoining property. A room there would have had a view of Yoshe's balcony. I trotted upstairs and rapped on the door into which she'd disappeared.

The door banged open. "We don't need our room freshened," said the girl.

I flashed a big smile. "I'm not from house-keeping. I'm looking for some information about an incident that happened next door. Maybe you heard about the woman who fell from her third-floor balcony yesterday?"

She shook her head, eyes wide. "We did hear the sirens."

"It's a long shot, but any chance you might have heard some folks arguing before that?"

"Oh my gosh," she said, covering her mouth with her hand. "I never put it together. We were trying to sleep in, so my friend got up and closed the window. Why would I want to travel all this way to hear arguments about money, when I could stay home with my boyfriend and fight for free?"

"So it was about money?" I asked. "Can you remember any details?"

"They both sounded pissed," the girl said. "And the one woman was really out of control. But I'm sorry. That's all I know."

"So the woman was angrier than the man?"

"No," she said. "It was two women."

"Two women fighting? Are you sure?"

"Of that much I'm sure."

I thanked her and headed back out to the street, my mind churning in confused spirals.

My phone buzzed. While I'd been chatting with the sunbather, Allison had left a message saying she'd helped Eric's mother sift through the boxes of stuff from his school days. Mostly they'd found high school and college yearbooks, along with a couple of textbooks on abnormal psychology from graduate school.

"But Mrs. Altman did dig out one old letter — it was so painful," Allison continued. "Eric felt his mother didn't appreciate how important it was to be open about his sexuality. She's almost certain, looking back, that he was involved with that Jonah Barrows. He was angry that she didn't want to tell his grandmother the news. The poor old woman was almost ninety and half dotty anyway. And there was a clipping about a death — a young man who'd fallen from an eighth-floor balcony in the college residence hall. None of that probably helps, but I wanted to let you know that Mrs. Altman is en route — and she's a basket case. Better have comfort food ready, because she's going to need it. And call anytime if you need us down there."

I sighed and tucked the phone into my pocket. I didn't feel much like cooking — especially with Mom missing. And Eric in jail. If it turned out he had been romantically involved with Jonah, his arrest seemed more ominous. But I'd pretty much talked to all the people I could think of.

So I drove across town to Fausto's Market and bought enough ground beef for a monster meat loaf, along with a big sack of potatoes and a bag of carrots. I packed the groceries into my scooter's basket and motored back to the marina.

The houseboat was still empty when I arrived with my loot. I put everything away and then began to pace through the small rooms, out to the end of dock, and back again. Mom's camera, I finally noticed, was sitting on the tiny driftwood coffee table, connected to her laptop with a cord. I brought the computer screen to life and began to flip through the hundreds of photos she'd taken this weekend.

I stopped when I came to the opening night party. There were three shots of Eric and Bill on the sidewalk outside the picket fence surrounding the Audubon House. In the third snapshot, taken fifteen minutes later according to the time stamp, Eric had turned to the right and appeared to be talking to a small Asian woman. Yoshe. I flipped backward and then forward. He looked fine in the first two shots — not his most cheerful and photogenic ever, but then Mom was not as skilled a photographer as she was a cook.

But in the third frame, his expression had changed to a look of distress. I studied the photo, trying to figure out what might have happened in the intervening moments. What if Yoshe had sought him out and confessed to the killing? What if she'd told him she was feeling suicidal? Would he be able to come forward with what he'd heard? It would be just like Eric to go to jail protecting someone he barely knew. But how would she ever have found his name?

I tapped my fingers furiously on the coffee table. The computer was up and running. I'd already looked through Mom's photo stream. As worried as I was feeling, it didn't seem like that much of a stretch to check her e-mail. I found the Gmail icon in her sidebar, clicked on it, and typed in her password: HayleyMills. A string of messages came up on the screen. I scrolled down until I reached the ones that she had opened earlier today, including one from the new boyfriend, Sam. *About your inquiry,* the subject line read.

Greetings from the frozen tundra of New Jersey! Sorry to hear about the trouble at your conference but delighted that you are savoring your time with your daughter. She sounds lovely and I look forward to meeting her! If she's anything like you, I know I will enjoy her.

You asked for my thoughts about what it might take to obtain financing for a fast food restaurant franchise. Does the founding chef/owner have a connection to Key West food? An impeccable reputation and hopefully name recognition, at least in the food world if not the general public? I would certainly ask those questions. But most important of all would be personal business finances. Impeccable records for any projects in progress or in the past — essential.

And I checked the status of the food foundation in my charity rating guide. They have not provided their annual report or their audited financial statements as requested and they appear to have a rather high percentage of donations spent on fund-raising versus their charitable activities.

My phone vibrated on the coffee table. Incoming call from my mother. I snatched it up and pressed *Accept.* "Mom, where the heck have you been?"

She spoke in a low, raspy voice, almost whispering so I could barely make out the words. "Followed her. . . . tall building . . . near the harbor." And then the connection went dead.

22

Leave the gun. Take the cannoli.
— Mario Puzo, *The Godfather*

I tried calling her number again but got shunted straight to her voice mail. I left a rather screechy message:

"Mom, I'm worried. Call me!"

Strands of panic unspooled as I imagined with more and more certainty that my mother had followed the killer — or someone she thought was the killer — somewhere. I gulped some air to try to calm myself down, searching for something positive to cling to. The only good news I could come up with was Lorenzo's reading. In Mom's cards, he had uncovered no devils, no death, no tower, no bad news whatsoever. And his interpretation was one hundred percent upbeat and entirely benign. She had to be okay.

Not so with my reading, in which the

tower had appeared front and center — a tumbling free fall with no safety net. My teeth began to chatter, as a gruesome run of possibilities flashed through my brain like a slide show on steroids.

Think, Hayley.

I was pretty sure she'd said "tall building." There weren't many of them in Key West. But it still could take hours to drive around aimlessly, searching their grounds for the dang pink scooter. Silly, fruitless idea, but what else did I have?

Then I thought of Cory Held. She knew the real estate on the island like her backyard. I hurtled the length of the dock, leaped onto my scooter and screeched down Southard Street, and pulled the bike up onto its stand. Then I ran into the real estate office and pounded on Cory's door, brooding over how to impress on her that my mother was in danger without revealing that my instincts were based on a seven-word phone call and a tarot card reading.

"Come in!" she called, and looked up from her computer as I burst into the office. "You're working some long hours today." Then she took a second look. "What's wrong? You don't look good."

My lips quivered, all my reasonable ideas about how to approach her evaporating.

"My mother's missing," I said. "And I'm almost sure this is related to the two murders this weekend. She called me, but she got cut off." I described the few words I'd been able to make out. "She's in danger — I know it."

"I'll call the police," Cory said firmly. "I know the chief quite well. I sold him a home on Frances Street this summer." She reached for her cell phone and began to thumb through her directory.

"The cops know," I said. "I was over at the station earlier. I hoped you might be able to help me think about the tall buildings in town. Anything near the water."

"Near the water?" she said, looking puzzled. Looking like she suspected I'd lost my marbles.

I just nodded, rather than try to explain. "Please."

She shrugged and sat back in her chair. "The lighthouse would be most obvious. I'm sure you've seen it — on Whitehead Street across from Hemingway's home."

"But on a Sunday afternoon, that would be open to the public, right?"

Cory nodded.

"So there wouldn't be anywhere to hide. What else?"

She began to scribble a list on a pad of

paper. "Here's what comes to mind. The Beach Club Condos on Atlantic Boulevard along the ocean — in fact, there are a number of multistory condos and apartments and a couple of hotels on Atlantic. Then La Concha Hotel on Duval Street — I'm sure you know that one, though it's a little ways inland. And the Steamplant Condominiums down by the ferry docks. Maybe the former Waterfront Market building? That's right on the harbor — it's painted with sea life murals. You can't miss it."

I felt a sizzle of recognition at the mention of the Waterfront Market — this would be exactly the kind of abandoned building where someone could disappear. "Is it being used for anything now?"

Cory shook her head and frowned. "They've had trouble finding a tenant. Though there's a rumor about a brewery." She ripped the paper off the pad and pushed the list across the desk. "Are you sure you don't want me to call Chief Barnes?"

"Not yet," I said. "I'm going to buzz around town just once and see if she turns up." I waved the paper. "Thanks for this."

"Call if you need me." She handed me a business card, which I stuffed into my back pocket as I hurried out of the office. I would start with the former Waterfront Market grocery store, which according to Cory had been empty for several years. Minutes later, I pulled up in front of the hulking concrete building, located in between B.O.'s Fishwagon and the harbor. The fine scent of fried fish and grilled hamburgers and onions drifted over from the restaurant, causing me a sharp pang of hunger. I zipped through the parking lot, looking for Mom's scooter, but found nothing.

The Waterfront Market had been constructed three stories high of concrete, with no windows other than the double glass doors at the entrance. But the exterior was painted with über-life-sized colorful renderings of undersea scenes — leaping porpoises, lurking sharks, slapping skates, all topped with a colorful sunset just below the flat roof. Despite its cheerful exterior, the building was abandoned and spooky — the perfect place to stash a prisoner.

I parked my bike, dashed up the steps, and peered through the glass doors. Only the ghostly bones of shelving and checkout counters remained from what I'd heard had been the best place on the island to buy organic goods, fish, meat, and produce before the store went belly-up. I dropped to a crouch, looking for new footprints in the thick coating of dust on the floor, but spotted no signs of recent activity.

Circling around to the rear of the building, I tiptoed along the alley behind the market until I reached the Dumpsters, which still smelled faintly of old fish and rotted garbage. A figure wrapped in a blue plastic tarp was tucked behind the last bin. My pulse began to pound furiously and I could hardly breathe. Should I call the cops right now? I couldn't stand to wait. My hands clammy with perspiration and my heart leaping in my chest, I edged closer. If this turned out to be my mother's body, how would I bear it? But I had to know.

Using a dried palm frond so I wouldn't contaminate the scene, I eased back a flap of the blue plastic, exposing the face of a weathered-looking man with a scruffy beard. He opened one watery gray eye and blinked. "What the hell?"

"So sorry," I said, dropping the tarp over his face and backpedaling to the parking lot. The abrupt surge and retreat of adrenaline left me weak and damp. I perched on my scooter for a few minutes to catch my breath and regroup.

The next nearest building on Cory's list would be the luxury Steamplant Condominiums near the ferry docks. I zipped up

Caroline Street, seriously tempted to refuel at the Cuban Coffee Queen. But if Mom was in danger, I couldn't afford to waste precious minutes. As I drew closer to the docks, a huge ferry disgorged a mob of passengers — day-trippers and weekend visitors from Fort Myers. I paused by the gate, searching the crowd for the familiar face of my mother. No luck. When the crowd had thinned, carried away in taxis and pedicabs, or pulling their wheeled luggage behind them, I crossed the street to the Steamplant Condominiums.

These condos had been developed in a gorgeous old art deco building tucked between the school bus depot and some new fair housing apartments. I'd seen several real estate open houses listed lately in the *Citizen,* touting big price reductions. Sales must be slumping.

Of a dozen parking spaces around the building, only two were occupied, one by a sports car wrapped in a protective tarp like the homeless man I'd disturbed earlier. And the other by a blue truck with rolls of carpet stashed in the bed. But then I spotted a glint of pink metal in the bushes at the far end of the complex. My heart drummed faster and my hands slicked up again as I trotted over to check it out. A pink scooter identical to the one my mother had rented had fallen over into the sea grapes near the back wall.

I combed my fingers through my hair, trying to formulate a story and gather myself into something presentable — something more publicly acceptable than a crazed, fortune-teller-driven madwoman with a misplaced relative. Then I circled the building, leaning hard on the doorbells to each condominium. Through the glass doors, I could see the elaborate designs in the tiled floors and enormous frescoes on the walls. But the bells echoed in each empty foyer. No one answered.

I thumbed through my iPhone for recent contacts until I found Dustin's number, which he'd given me yesterday to keep him informed as Mom and I set out in search of Yoshe. On the second ring he barked, "Who is this?"

"It's Hayley Snow," I said, my voice high and tight. "I need you to tell me if one of the speakers from the food writing conference is staying at the Steamplant Condominium complex. This is not negotiable," I added. "My mother is missing and I'm afraid she's being held hostage by the person who killed Jonah and possibly even Yoshe. I found her pink scooter in the shrubbery."

"Ridiculous," said Dustin. "She —"

I cut him dead. "Don't even start. If something happens to my mother and you failed to tell me what you know, I swear I'll make sure you never work at a literary conference again. I swear I'll e-mail every person on your board of directors and tell them you refused to help a dying woman." An empty threat if I'd ever made one, but I had no leverage other than histrionics.

After a long pause, Dustin said, "We did have some local folks offer to put a few of our guests up for the weekend. Let me think." In the background, I could hear the hum of voices in the bookstore and the clang of the cash register. "Olivia Nethercut was invited to stay in one of those apartments by a patron who has her place up for sale. The patron was besotted with Olivia's books, and also a very generous donor to Olivia's foundation. That's all I can think of."

Olivia? Of course. I'd run into her in the ladies' restroom right around the time Jonah's murder occurred. But I'd never thought of her seriously as a suspect — she acted normal enough. And Sigrid had been there at the same time. And I'd been too starstruck to question her integrity. And maybe this new theory was totally off base;

maybe my mother was just visiting with her, gathering her thoughts about the conference personalities and looking for ways to explain Jonah's murder.

"Could you phone the apartment owner for me?" I begged. "It's possible that she was involved in the murders this weekend."

"That's completely absurd," Dustin said. "What am I supposed to say to her? Did Miss Nethercut happen to hide any bodies in your condominium? Obviously, Olivia Nethercut has nothing to do with your mother's whereabouts."

"What about the pink scooter that I found abandoned in the bushes?"

"How many of those do you think there are in this town?"

He was right. In fact, the man who'd rented Mom's scooter had told her he'd had a run on pink. Dustin hung up before I could ask anything else.

Then I flashed on Cory Held's postcard lying on Miss Gloria's kitchen counter, and scrounged in my pockets until I found her business card. Chances were if I said Dustin wouldn't help me, she'd be on my side in an instant. So I called her, trying to sound calm and authoritative and not like I was in a full-blown mental-patient panic.

"I found my mother's scooter," I said

when she answered. "At the Steamplant Condos. Does the name Olivia Nethercut mean anything to you? She's supposed to be staying at one of these condos and it's on the market."

Cory put me on hold while she paged through her notes. I paced over to the pink scooter while I waited, this time noticing that the pink helmet Mom rented along with it was buried farther back in the bushes. "Let's go!" I muttered.

Finally she came back on the line. "Jean Nee has a guest from the conference staying at her place this weekend, but we were told absolutely no showings while she's here."

"It wouldn't be a showing, technically," I said. "Could you possibly get me in? If we don't see any sign of my mother, I swear I'll call the cops. Again."

23

Every card in the deck is about progress toward a happy end.

— Jane Stern

I paced the premises until Cory drove up in her ice blue BMW and hopped out, holding a large ring of keys. "This afternoon, I only, have access to one of the townhomes out of the nineteen in this complex," she said in a cheerful voice. "I can definitely make appointments for some of the others that are on the market, if you decide you like the location. I just need a little bit of notice to contact the listing agents." And then under her breath she added, "I could lose my license over this."

I grabbed the hand without the keys and squeezed. "Thank you so much for helping."

"This unit is not officially on the market," Cory said in her normal voice, "but I have a pocket listing, so I'm authorized to show it to interested buyers. If you won't need this much space, the lofts, of course, have smaller footprints. But they all have the same floor-to-ceiling windows and amazing views from the rooftop terraces. And hot tubs besides, with wiring for your future outdoor kitchen."

I started to protest that I wasn't in the market for a luxury condominium at all, but she winked and smiled, and I shut up.

"Each unit has its own elevator from the secure garage and this foyer," she said as we walked into an enormous space tiled in pale marble with a rectangular black inset.

"What is this used for?" I asked, my eyes goggling, though I was in no mood to really appreciate the grandeur.

She shrugged and said, "It makes a sumptuous entrance, doesn't it?" Her heels clacked on the shiny floor as she headed toward the elevator. "This particular condominium townhome is almost five thousand square feet with three bedrooms, three and a half baths. The owner is having her hip replaced in New York and we don't expect her back in town for several weeks at least. Although she was entertaining a few guests over this period of time, she's very eager to talk with serious prospects. Shall we start at the top and work down?"

"Do we have to take the elevator?" I asked, palms suddenly damp all over again. "I'm not good with them. A little quirk passed down in my genetic code." No need to tell her that a ride on a Macy's elevator was the setting for my mother's one and only breakdown when I was a kid. It happened just after my father moved out and I'd gone shopping with her that morning; I'd never forget her sinking to her knees and scratching at the elevator door, keening with terror.

"It's a quick trip," Cory said briskly. "Brand-new mechanicals. Each home has its own elevator."

She herded me into the compartment and as we rode to the top floor, she chatted about the cherrywood floors, the Travertine marble, the granite countertops in the laundry room, and the fourteen-foot ceilings. All of which helped distract me from the fact that I was riding in a tiny silver box, not much bigger than one of the family crypts in the local cemetery.

The elevator shuddered to a halt and the doors slid open to the rooftop — more a plaza than a deck. Spread out before us was an astonishing 360-degree view of the island, boats bobbing in the harbor on the right and a sea of palm trees and roofs to the left. One quick turnaround showed the space to be empty except for a grouping of teak lounge chairs, a covered hot tub, and an expensive-looking grill. I approached the hot tub, feeling anxious, and stood there a few minutes. Finally I lifted the lid and peeked under, terrified that I'd see my mother's body bobbed about by the pulsing jets.

But the spa contained only water. I patted my chest and took some shallow breaths.

"All set?" Cory asked, looking concerned.

"All set." I mustered a smile.

Back on the elevator, we rode down one floor, my muscles knotting with each second that passed. If my hunch was off the mark, and my mother wasn't here, we were wasting time that she might need. And I was absolutely blank about what to try next.

"Yoo-hoo. Anyone home?" Cory called as we stepped out of the car into the hallway. No answer.

"Both the master bedroom and one of the guest rooms look over Old Town Key West," she explained. "The bath has rain shower-heads and both a double shower and a marble bathtub big enough for two. Not very many homes on the island have the kind of storage space this one does."

"I don't care —"

"I know," she whispered. "Just play along with me, okay?"

I closed my eyes, feeling the tears pressing for escape, then nodded. We stopped in the doorway of the biggest bedroom, dominated by a large canvas of red-and-black modern art that hung over a heavy mahogany bed. The bed had been left unmade, sheets tangled, a thick quilt tossed carelessly to the carpet along with a peach-colored bathrobe, all suggesting a restless night. The air smelled of stale perfume. I ducked into the bathroom, where the burnished stone counters were cluttered with makeup, night cream, and an uncapped tube of toothpaste. Two plush white towels draped from the gaping drawers to the floor.

I poked my head into the walk-in closet, where a suitcase lay open, its contents spilling out onto the beige rug. I recognized the flowing purple silk pantsuit that Olivia had worn to dinner at Louie's Backyard. And the Burberry case that might have contained Yoshe's laptop.

"She did it," I whispered to Cory, my stomach suddenly queasy, and pushed ahead of her to scan the guest bedroom and bathroom, the two auxiliary closets in the hallway. Empty. I followed her back into the hall.

"Let me show you the main living area," she said, and we rode the elevator down one floor and emerged into the dining alcove. She pointed across the room. "You'll notice the copper exhaust hood and the six-burner Viking stove. Are you a chef as well as a critic?"

I nodded and, for a moment, thought longingly of what I could cook in this unbelievable kitchen. I sighed. Miss Gloria's houseboat was the only home I saw in my future. And I'd never truly belong in a place like this. And besides that, I didn't care for the black cabinets — sleek, yes. Homey, no.

I tried the door to the pantry, but it wouldn't budge.

"Sometimes the owners lock one closet where they store their private things," Cory said. "That way they can keep expensive whiskey or their best china without having to worry about guests or, heaven forbid, renters doing damage."

We circled the living and dining room areas, furnished in heavy black leather with red accent cushions and more unintelligible and frightening art on the walls. The closets were mostly empty except for a few coats and umbrellas and a pair of sneakers and there was certainly no evidence that my mother had been here.

"I guess that's it," I said. "I'm afraid I overreacted. Thanks so much for taking me around." Somehow I would have to let Detective Bransford know that I knew where Yoshe's computer might have been stashed.

We stepped back onto the elevator and Cory pushed the button for the lobby. The compartment's doors slid shut and the car lurched into silent action but then ground to a quick halt. She stabbed at the button again, and then punched the button with the arrows that closed the doors when they were moving too slowly. Nothing happened. She looked at her watch. "Drat. And I have a showing across town in fifteen minutes." She plucked her smartphone from her purse. "No service. Can you get anything?"

I pulled my phone from my pocket — no service bars on mine either.

"I've had this trouble before," Cory said. "The walls of the steam plant were super-thick and the service is horrible."

Breathing a little harder, I banged on the mirrored wall and shouted for help; then we listened. But who would possibly hear us? The nearest people I'd seen were two blocks away at the ferry dock.

Cory tried her cell again with no success, then reached for the emergency phone hanging on the wall. "There's no dial tone. Good Lord, it's hot in here." She unwound the blue scarf from her neck and fanned her face with her hand.

"I hate elevators," I said, my panic rising. "Didn't you tell me this thing was brand-new?" A drenching sweat broke out on my face and chest and I began to feel like I was choking.

"Sit down and put your head between your knees," Cory suggested, and I sank to the floor, quaking. Telling myself I was not my mother. And that we would find her. And that someone would come soon to let us out of this box. The walls pressed in closer and closer and I labored to breathe.

"It's nice that your mom could come for the conference," said Cory, still working the buttons on her phone. "Not too many daughters would care to spend three full days with their mom."

"We have our moments," I said, my face buried in my hands, not really wanting to talk about it but realizing chatting was the only thing standing between me and a full-blown claustrophobic panic attack. So I'd talk. "I got a little stressed and said something harsh this morning about her living off my father — alimony for life."

"Ouch," said Cory.

"I know. Other than that, we've had a lot of fun and it's been an interesting weekend. I realized some things."

"What kind of things?" she asked.

"It's complicated," I said. "Right out of college, my mother gave up her own ambitions to raise a family. If she really had any to begin with. She got pregnant with me in her last year of school and dropped out to be a housewife and mother. I think I've always been afraid I'd take the same path."

"You could do worse than that," Cory said.

"Yeah, but then you're at the mercy of the guy you married. Or live with. I tried that when I followed my ex down here. When that relationship blew up last fall, I felt like I'd hitched all my hopes to him. And then he lopped me off like a dead tree limb."

She nodded sympathetically. "Every woman should have a backup plan. And the money to fund it."

"It's totally creepy that I'd repeat my mother's exact mistake." Although Eric would have said it was to be expected — if I refused to explore this stuff in therapy, it was bound to haunt me.

"I can see how that would freak you out,"

Cory said, tapping furiously on her phone again and then shaking it in frustration.

I continued to jabber — all the thoughts I'd had in the back of my mind over the weekend tumbling out in their full embarrassing glory. "And that's probably part of why I feel so much pressure about my job at *Key Zest* — besides the fact that Ava Faulkner is dying to fire me. I started feeling like this would be a huge opportunity to make something of myself. It seemed absolutely critical to come out of this weekend with a big story."

The more I talked, the calmer I felt. But my nose had begun to run and beads of sweat were popping out on my forehead: I was baking in the rising heat. And it wasn't only me. Cory stripped off her blazer and rolled up her shirtsleeves. "My God, it's getting hotter and hotter."

I rolled my neck in circles, listening to the cartilage click. The third time around, I stopped to gaze at the ceiling of our cage. "What are the chances we could push one of those panels out and climb into the shaft?" I asked. "I don't think we dropped too far from the kitchen level."

"Not good," said Cory. "But we can try." She narrowed her eyes and looked me over, head to toe. "I suspect I've got a few pounds on you, so I'll be the ballast."

First we tried Cory on hands and knees as a step stool — but I was too short to reach the ceiling and too worried about cracking one of her vertebrae to put my entire weight on her. Then she crouched down and encouraged me to stand on her shoulders. After several tries, we collapsed on the floor in a panting heap.

"What if I hold my hands like so" — she demonstrated clasping them — "and boost you up onto the handrail? Maybe then you can reach."

With her help, I balanced on the railing and managed to pop out one of the mirrored ceiling panels. She hoisted me up another six inches and I grabbed a metal bar in the shaft. Wishing I'd spent more time — any time really — at the gym, I duck-walked up the wall and dragged myself into the dim space.

"What do you see?" Cory called.

"It's pretty dark. Some cables and a sort of winch. The town house kitchen's only a couple of feet up, but the outside elevator door's shut."

"You'll have to force it," she said. "But hurry up and get out of there. If this thing starts up again, you could get crushed."

"Thanks for that good news," I muttered,

and shuffled across the beam toward the sliver of light marking the exit, imploring myself to keep my mind only on what I was doing. I inched my fingers into the crack and pressed until the doors snapped open. Then I shimmied up and scrambled out onto the maple parquet floor, butt first.

Olivia Nethercut was waiting by the opening to the shaft, a bottle of red wine cocked in her fist.

"Oh my God, you scared me to death," I yelped, clutching my pounding chest.

She kicked at my knees. "One step forward and you and your mother are dead," she said.

Cory's voice floated up from the shaft. "What's going on? Get me out of here, please."

Olivia waggled the wine bottle like a baseball bat and kicked me in the side this time. "Get back in the shaft," she hissed. "Or your mother is a goner. And that nosy real estate agent too."

I curled into a hangdog ball, pretending I'd given up, but trying to figure out how to take her on. What was the point of pushing me back into the shaft? She probably hoped to crush me as Cory had warned could happen.

I took a deep breath and then sprang up

343

and lurched forward. "You've done enough damage this weekend," I shrieked as I barreled into her legs and knocked her down. I pinned her to the floor with a menacing growl. "Now what the hell did you do with my mother?"

Olivia began to thrash about like a trapped animal. I was losing control. I threw myself away from her, scrabbling to my feet and grabbing the bottle of pinot. "Where is my mother?" I said through gritted teeth, waggling the wine. "Ten seconds or I knock you cold."

She got to her feet and took off running, tearing out of the kitchen and down the hall, and then down a back stairwell I hadn't noticed on Cory's tour. I tore after her, clattering down the stairs. When she reached the bottom, she burst out into the empty garage, grabbed a metal shovel hanging on the wall, and came toward me, swinging. The shovel glanced off my shoulder and I winced and dropped the wine. The bottle shattered on the cement. With one final surge of adrenaline, I barreled into her midsection, wrestled the shovel away from her, and slammed it into her temple. She crumpled.

I punched 911 into my phone and bolted from the garage to get enough service bars so the call could go through.

Two police cars raced up moments later, sirens blaring and lights swirling. I waved them over and Officer Torrence tumbled out of the first vehicle with the female cop who'd interviewed me Thursday night, followed by two other officers I didn't know. "Olivia Nethercut is lying in that garage. I knocked her out."

"Get an ambulance," Torrence instructed one of the cops, then drew his gun and started over to the gaping door.

"I hope I didn't hurt her badly. It was me or her," I called. "I'm almost certain she was involved in the murder of Yoshe King. And Cory Held is trapped in the elevator. And my mother" — I sniffled back some tears and looked helplessly after them — "is still missing."

Then a third cruiser swerved into the parking lot and Detective Bransford and another cop leaped out. Just seeing his solid form, I felt weak with relief. "What the hell are you doing here?" he asked.

The relief drained away. Speechless, I just shook my head and pointed to the condo.

"You stay put," he told me firmly. As if I would rush in after them.

Fifteen minutes later, Olivia was loaded onto a stretcher and carried out to the ambulance, woozy and handcuffed but still spitting vitriol. One of the policemen came outside to wave me in.

I bounded through the garage, into the condominium, and up the stairs to the kitchen level of the apartment. Cory was just struggling out of the elevator compartment, red-faced and drenched with sweat, not at all her usual immaculate self.

"Thank goodness," she said. "I thought I was going to melt." She strode over to the fancy digital heat control panel on the kitchen wall and switched it off. "She had it pushed up as high as it would go. Maybe she was planning to leave us in the elevator and hope we died of hyperthermia."

A muffled banging noise came from the direction of the pantry. Bransford and Torrence drew their guns again and approached cautiously.

"Is there a key to this door?" Bransford asked Cory.

"Unfortunately, I don't have access to it."

Torrence instructed the lady cop to retrieve a pry bar from their cruiser. She returned shortly and they winched the door open. Inside, my mother lay on her side, wide-eyed, trussed like an enormous turkey, her face red and sweaty, her mouth stuffed with a red potholder.

346

While the police untied her and the detective helped her to a chair near the counter, I rushed to get her a glass of water.

"Thank God you found me," she croaked as soon as the potholder was removed and she'd taken a sip. "I had the worst choking feeling — like I'd swallowed the Sahara. But then I calmed myself down by thinking about what I'd cook if I lived here. Isn't this the most amazing apartment?"

"I had the same thoughts," I told her, ignoring the puzzled looks of the cops. "I was imagining the parties we could throw on that deck overlooking the whole island." I reached for her hands, rubbing the circulation back into her wrists.

Then she hugged me hard and took a long drink of water. "Oh, I'm so glad to see you! I heard you earlier, but I was afraid I'd make things worse with Olivia if I made noise. But then when I heard the men's voices, I figured it was safe to kick the walls so you'd know I was here."

"You're one smart cookie," I said. "I'm so sorry about the alimony —"

She put a finger to her lips, cutting me off. "Enough said. I asked him to stop paying me when you left for college — I should have told you. Anyway, I know you didn't mean it — the weekend's been a little bit stressful." And then she grinned. "But kind of fun."

I shook my head in amazement — my claustrophobic, helpless mother had come a long way. "Mom, this is Cory Held. She's a real estate agent who works in the office below mine. She got us into this condo."

Mom embraced her too. "Thank you, thank you. If my daughter decides to stay on in Key West and find her own place, we'd love to have your help. I could spot the down payment," she added. "Though you've got a sweet deal with Miss Gloria."

"Never mind that, Mrs. Snow," Bransford broke in. "Exactly what happened here?"

She fixed a stern look on him. "As you probably know, Hayley and I were trying to understand whether it could be true that that lovely Yoshe King killed herself. Not to mention why our dear friend Eric is in jail." A horrified look slid over her face. "Before I go on, how about calling the Sheriff's Department and telling those people to let him out?"

"We'll take care of that, Mrs. Snow," said Bransford. "Please go on."

"You wouldn't have any way of knowing this, but I took a lot of photos this weekend — I was so excited to be attending the conference with my daughter. While I was waiting to meet Hayley for lunch, I ran through the whole lot. Honestly, after Thursday night, no one looked like they were having much fun. But then I came across a shot of Yoshe and Olivia, who looked positively grim. And I remembered that Olivia told us she'd flown into Marathon rather than Key West. Why would she do that, unless she had use of a private plane? And she's a writer: Where in the world would she get the money to hire a jet? I started thinking about her foundation and I got a funny feeling that maybe she was using public funds in an unethical way . . . so I asked my friend Sam to look into it."

"A funny feeling," said Bransford, glowering at me. "You two are very much alike, aren't you?"

"Yes. Aren't I lucky?" Mom reached over to stroke my hair, now grinning so hard, I couldn't help smiling along with her.

"And then?" Bransford asked.

"Then I stopped in the conference bookstore. Olivia was there, holding court with her fans. When she left the building and hailed a cab, I followed all the way here on my scooter and hid it in the bushes. But she must have figured out I was onto her. A middle-aged woman wobbling down the road on a pink motorbike will tend to catch your attention."

Mom looked sheepish as she explained how Olivia had ducked into the vestibule of the Steamplant Condominiums but left the door propped open. "When I came in, she leaped out from the shadows — scared me half to death — and pretended she had a gun. Of course, if I'd called you people as I properly should have" — she pressed her hands together and bowed at Bransford and then Torrence — "this never would have happened. On the other hand, would you have listened to more theories from me?"

24

Cooking connects every hearth fire to the sun and smokes out whatever gods there be — along with the ghosts of all our kitchens past, and all the people who have fed us with love and hate and fear and comfort, and whom we in turn have fed.

— Betty Fussell

Miss Gloria had borrowed a folding table from the Renharts for our impromptu dinner party and even sweet-talked Mr. Renhart into setting it up outside on her deck. A dozen tea lights flickered on the white lace tablecloth, disguising the few stains that had collected over the years of use and showing off her antique silver flatware, which she had buffed to gleaming for the occasion.

Eric, Bill, and Mrs. Altman had arrived fifteen minutes earlier and settled onto the deck chairs with glasses of white wine. Eric had been released from the jail in time to go with Bill to the airport to pick up his mother. Mrs. Altman was doing her best to be cheerful, but she looked bleary and exhausted and wouldn't let go of Eric's hand. Every so often she reached up to stroke him from shoulder to elbow, as if he were an enormous housecat.

"Where do you keep the Ritz crackers?" my mother called from the galley.

"Be right back," I told our guests.

Mom was kneading meat loaf in a red pottery bowl in Miss Gloria's galley kitchen. I found a sleeve of crackers tucked away in one of the cabinets and put them on the counter.

She dumped them into my food processor and whirred them into crumbs. "There's no point in trying to make this dish low-fat or otherwise too healthy," she explained to Connie as she added the crumbs to the meat. "You serve it once in a while, it makes your man happy, end of story. So skip the ground turkey and the quinoa. You need ground beef, some pork if you want to be fancy, plus chopped onion, carrots, and green pepper, cracker crumbs, a few tablespoons of Lipton's Onion Soup mix, half a jar of Bone Suckin' barbecue sauce. And an egg to bind it all together." She shaped the red mass into an oval, tucked it into an oblong glass pan, slathered more sauce on top, and shunted it into the oven. "If you girls could get started on the mashed potatoes, I'll go freshen up."

Connie looked up from the notes she was taking at the kitchen table. *From Janet Snow's Kitchen* was written across the top of the note card. "This is an old family recipe, right?" Connie asked.

"Hayley discovered this one," my mother said. "I never did much care for my own mother's meat loaf." She winked and left the kitchen.

"Don't you dare tell her," I whispered. "It's my stepmother's recipe. One of the few edible things she can make."

Connie crossed out *Janet* and penciled in *Stepmom's meat loaf.* We burst into giggles and then began washing and peeling the sack of potatoes. When we were finished, I dropped them into a pot of simmering water and set the timer. We went back out to the porch to join the others. Connie's fiancé, Ray, arrived and Miss Gloria introduced him to everyone. A popping noise echoed from the galley.

"A toast to the future bride and groom!" called my mother. She bustled out from the kitchen with a fizzing bottle of champagne

353

and offered it around the table. She held up her glass. "May your life together be bursting with love, laughter, and good food!"

"Thanks so much," said Connie shyly.

Mom fingered Ray's ponytail and smiled at Connie. "With any luck, he'll get a haircut before the wedding." And then she took the seat across from Eric. "Now tell us what happened this weekend."

"Sorry I worried all of you." Eric took off his glasses and laid them on the table, slumped a little, then rubbed his face with both hands. He sat up blinking.

"From way back, Jonah loved to think about himself as a rule-breaker," he said. "Not to say he didn't start out playing by the rules — you don't land a job reviewing restaurants for the *Guide Bouchée* if you're not willing to do it their way. Or get a job as a line cook in a well-known restaurant. But once he learned their ropes, he wanted to break out and he was willing to take the risk of leaving a good job to do so."

He slid his glasses back on. "I wasn't his therapist, of course, but I think most of what he did was driven by his rage at not being accepted by his family. They would rather have pretended he didn't exist than acknowledge he was gay. But with the publication of his memoir, pretending was no longer an option. In fact, Jonah discovered last week that they had filed a lawsuit for libel against him and his publisher."

I cleared my throat. "But, Eric, something happened between you and Jonah. Your fingerprints were on that bird. And I don't believe you left the party Thursday night because you had a migraine. You've never had a migraine in your life." Then I confessed how I'd seen him on the Duval Street webcam, looking worried and guilty.

"Did you know there's a time delay on that camera?" Ray interrupted. "It doesn't show the street in real time. Did you look at who came by after Eric?"

Of course, I hadn't. I went to get my laptop, set it up so the table could see the screen, and replayed the scene I'd studied a dozen times already.

"You see what I mean?" I asked as Eric's figure hurried by in jerky slow motion. Eric nodded, wincing. Several minutes after that, Olivia Nethercut appeared on camera, walking briskly away from the scene of the crime. Determined and angry.

I groaned. "If I'd seen this and managed to convince the cops that it meant something, Cory and I could have skipped the whole elevator nightmare. And saved you," I told my mother, "a couple of hours locked in that closet."

"Probably did me some good," she said, blowing a kiss across the table. "Banished a nasty little lingering phobia." Then she turned her attention back to Eric. "So, what really happened that night?"

Eric sighed and squeezed his mother's hand. "Jonah e-mailed me last week and said he was done with secrets. Even old ones."

He told us that back in their New York City graduate school days, they'd fallen in love. Or not really, but who believes it's not real when all the hormones are raging? Jonah had pushed him to be truthful about everything, including his sexuality. "The more Jonah's parents resisted facing who he truly was, the louder he got. And the harder he pushed the people around him.

"Unfortunately, I got caught up in his fervor. My mother can tell you how bad things were."

She nodded sadly. "Not a high point in our relationship."

"But worst of all, I made a terrible novice therapist mistake. I persuaded one of my patients to tell his parents he was gay. As a budding psychologist, I should have realized it wasn't my job to persuade any patient to do anything — just help him understand himself and come to his own conclusions. This young man's parents reacted horribly to his news. They not only refused to believe it, but they refused to let him come home if he insisted on talking about it any further."

Eric took off his glasses again and polished the lenses on a napkin. Then he looked around the table. "He didn't show up for our next session. I found out later that he'd killed himself — jumped to his death from his dorm room. I've never forgiven myself for that."

"Oh, honey," said Eric's mother, squeezing his arm. "You always did take things so hard." My mother refilled the wineglasses, tousling Eric's hair as she passed behind him.

"But how is that related to this weekend?" I asked. "Why did Jonah still care?"

"Jonah wanted me to talk about that incident now — publicly. He wanted me to testify against his parents in their lawsuit and demonstrate to the world how damaging secrets and lies could be. But that would have necessitated dredging up the story about my former patient."

"The old clipping you found in Eric's belongings," I said to his mom. "But it didn't mention a suicide."

"No," said Eric, fitting his glasses back

on. "The papers referred to it as 'an unexplained death.' I couldn't bear the thought of making the suicide public. Bringing up all that old pain for this young man's parents. So I spoke with Jonah at the party that first night and begged him to let that story die. But he absolutely refused."

Eric's face reddened and he pulled his hand away from his mother. "I was furious. I gave him a little shove. He stumbled, hit his head on the metal bird in the pool, and actually broke the thing off. There he lay, soaking wet, water lilies stuck to his head, and algae running down his cheeks — and still sputtering about how he insisted I tell the truth. I picked up the damn broken bird, picturing how satisfying it would feel to hit him. Hard. He was an impossible, obstinate man."

He whistled air through his clenched teeth. "Obviously I didn't hit him. But I didn't help him out of the pool either. I dropped the bird and left him floundering." He smoothed a wisp of hair off his forehead and pushed his glasses up the bridge of his nose. "At first, I thought I had killed him by not going for help — I'd let him drown. I thought I deserved to be in jail." He looked at his mother, and then at Bill. "And I couldn't talk about it without dragging

358

that family through the muck again. And then all of you kept raising possibilities of other folks who might have killed him. So I kept quiet, hoping that the real killer would be exposed before I had to go to jail. I'm very sorry for all the worry I put you through."

"So, what really happened to Jonah?" Miss Gloria asked.

"Our lawyer said Olivia came along after Eric left," Bill said. "And Jonah called out to her to help him get out of the pool. She refused. She'd also gotten an e-mail, saying that he was going forward with her franchise idea, but taking Yoshe as his partner. He could no longer trust Olivia because of the financial irregularities he'd discovered in her charitable foundation. And he planned to address them publicly. She was furious about being cut out of the franchise when she felt it was her idea. And furious about his threats. They had a nasty exchange and she grabbed the broken bird and clocked him."

"Didn't she say she only threw it at him?" Eric asked.

"Whether she actually swung the bird or threw it, either way Jonah collapsed back into the pool and she ran to the women's bathroom," Bill said, nodding at me. "Which is when you saw her."

"No wonder she was too upset to be gracious," I said, feeling stupid. "She was an obvious suspect, but I idolized her so much I didn't see it."

"It wasn't your job to figure this out," Eric said.

"Yeah, but we were concerned about *you,*" I said.

He nodded. "I appreciate that. I do."

"Then Olivia got worried about whether Jonah was really hurt and she would be in serious trouble for letting him drown," Bill said. "So she returned to the pool after Hayley had dragged him out and run for help. But Olivia could see it was too late to save him, so she grabbed the bird with the sleeve of her sweater and dropped it over the fence. She hadn't thought one bit of this through — she obviously couldn't carry the thing out of the party without drawing attention to herself. And who knows? Maybe she intended to come back for it later. The bird had Eric's prints on it, along with those of the old man who found it, as the cops discovered."

"But why did all this come up now?" I asked again. "Why was it so important for Jonah to expose everyone else's secrets?"

"I think it had to do with the memoir,"

360

Eric said. "As I mentioned, his father is suing the publisher for libel, saying that Jonah lied about everything, starting with his childhood and right on up to the present. Jonah's reaction was the flailing we saw — digging out everyone's secrets. And some of them should have been exposed — the way Olivia was siphoning off money from the foundation, for example. He became more obsessed with honesty. And at first it might feel good to confess, but that can have terrible consequences for the people who have to hear the so-called honest truth."

The timer chirped from the kitchen. My mother popped up from her chair. "Enough of that for now. Let's eat supper."

Connie and I helped her mash the potatoes and then bring out the platters of meat loaf and the buttery potatoes and a bowl of roasted carrots. When all the plates were filled, our talk turned to Yoshe.

"I'm guessing she figured out what Jonah had planned to reveal about Olivia. After Jonah died, she told Olivia she couldn't in good conscience keep silent. Olivia went over to talk with her Saturday morning with lethal results," Mom said sadly.

"Oh my gosh," I said. "I bet it was Olivia who had lunch with Yoshe's old agent and then threatened to tell the publisher about

Yoshe's exaggerations — not Jonah. Why would he, if he was going into business with her? But by then, Yoshe had already decided to tell the truth — about herself and about Olivia."

"Which would have made Olivia crazy mad," said Eric. "Crazy enough to throw her over the balcony."

We sat in sorrowful silence for a few minutes.

"Yoshe made some mistakes too," said Mom, "but I admired so much about her."

As we finished eating dinner, the scent of warming chocolate wafted out onto the deck.

"I smell something amazing," said Eric.

"I made another one of those fudge pies," said my mother, grinning. "Since you guys weren't able to really enjoy the last one." Then her mouth made a little O of surprise. "Detective Bransford! You snuck up on us. Come down and join the party."

I swiveled my head around and saw him waiting on the dock. My heart began to beat faster.

"We'll set another place — there's plenty of food left," said Mom. She pushed her chair away from the table and started to get up.

"I only have a minute," said the detective.

"I'm on duty. But I was hoping to talk to Hayley."

Mom gave me a little nudge. I glared at her but got up anyway and followed him down the finger almost to the parking lot, where his cruiser waited, motor running, door open.

"Must not be a lot of crime around here," I cracked.

"I came by to make sure you're okay," he said, ignoring my lame joke.

"We're fine," I said, tipping my chin up. "Though it would be nice if you didn't give me the mushroom treatment every time there's a bump in the road."

"The mushroom treatment?" he asked, unable to suppress a grin.

"Keeping me in the dark," I said without smiling back.

He scratched his head and grimaced. "Civilians have no business following criminals. It's too dangerous." He sighed. "You got a little taste of that yourself today with your mother."

Time to lay it all out on the table, now or never. "I know you had an incident with your ex-wife and I'm sorry about that. But I can take care of myself."

"Figures you'd have sniffed that out." He cleared his throat and frowned. "I didn't handle that incident well. She could have been killed. I was scared and the more scared I got, the more out of control I felt. So I paid an off-duty patrolman to follow her whenever she went out alone — and I tried my best to keep her in the house. That didn't go over too well," he said, slumping against his cruiser. "She asked for a divorce. Said she felt smothered."

"Mmmm, tough," I said. "I can see both sides."

"Maybe you don't see that I'm starting to feel that way again. About you. I can't stand the idea of you getting hurt. Olivia Nethercut noticed."

"Oh," I said, completely speechless for a minute. I looked at my watch. "I guess your date with Olivia was canceled? She was really looking forward to that. She kept telling me that you were coming on to her."

"There was no date," Bransford said. "That's baloney. Maybe she thought if she made it look like I was interested in her, it would keep you from reaching out to me." Then he reached out, took both of my hands, and pulled me in close to him, close enough so I could hear his heart thumping and feel the heat of his skin. And we kissed.

"Played like a chump," I said with a sigh, pushing him away before my knees got so weak, I buckled to the pavement. In front of a gaggle of my relatives and friends, who were certain to be watching. "It worked."

"So, how about dinner at Michael's next week?" he asked, grinning again so all his dimples showed. "No offense intended, but could we make it just the two of us?"

25

We were writing about food as family history, and love, and hope, and sometimes a little splash of guilt.

— Hayley Snow

I considered not wearing the yellow shirt with the palm trees on it for the meeting with Wally and Ava Faulkner — it made me feel like a lightweight. Instead I tried on a pencil skirt with the starched white shirt my mother had insisted on giving me, along with a pair of low black heels. Ava would certainly be decked out in a stylish business suit, and at least this outfit would be in the same ballpark. But at the last minute, I changed back into my sneakers and the yellow shirt. These were my team's colors. And more than anything, I wanted to avoid being cut.

I left for work fifteen minutes early, but by the time I arrived in the office, I could see

Ava's silhouette through Wally's miniblinds, ensconced in the chair closest to him. Danielle flashed me a worried thumbs-up as I hurried past her desk and settled into a gray metal folding chair that left me sitting a couple of inches lower than Ava. Score one for the visiting enemy.

"Morning, all," I said cheerfully, refusing to sound as intimidated as I felt.

Wally nodded, but Ava barely grunted as she picked up the sheaf of papers in front of her. On top Wally had placed my restaurant review of Santiago's Bodega. Ava skimmed it without comment. Next she paged through the piece I'd written in memory of Yoshe King, including quotes from the last public meal she'd enjoyed — the lunch with my mother, Sigrid, and me. And the comments from Mary Chen, Yoshe's niece. And how there had been a groundswell of preorders for Yoshe's cookbook and how her publishers agreed that Mary could rewrite the preface and some of Yoshe's commentary so it reflected the truth about the origins of the recipes.

"Did we get this bit about the family background fact-checked?" Ava asked Wally, not even looking at me.

"I was sitting in the chair next to her when she told me," I said. "It was an exclusive interview — no one else has it. But I'd be happy to provide Ms. Chen's e-mail and phone number if you feel you need to talk with her yourself."

She flipped that page over and started on the article I'd sent Wally late last night about Jonah Barrows and honesty. I'd summed up by saying how important it was to remember that while food did mean life and death in its most elemental form, most often we in the food writing industry were talking about food as the pleasure of connections. When we wrote about simmering a stew or a sauce for hours or days, we were really talking about how much we owed to the folks who came before us and the importance of cherishing their memory. And how much we yearned to give to the people in our present who'd be gathered around our table. We were writing about food as family history, and love, and hope, and sometimes a little splash of guilt.

Finally Ava shuffled through the stack of receipts.

She slapped the papers onto Wally's desk. "That's a lot about food in this next issue. Does your staff have any plans to write something about the theater in Key West? I understand the Waterfront has an excellent season lined up, and I'd like our publication to surf the crest of that wave."

Wally turned to me and winked. "Great job. You can be excused. Go out and get something delicious to eat. It's on me."

RECIPES

RAVISHING RHUBARB CAKE
WITH STREUSEL TOPPING

1 1/4 cup brown sugar
1/2 cup butter, softened
1 egg
1 tsp. baking soda
2 cups sifted flour
1 cup milk or buttermilk
1 tsp. vanilla
2 cups rhubarb, chopped
1 cup strawberries, chopped

For the topping:
1/4 cup butter
1/3 cup brown sugar
3 tbsp. flour
4 tbsp. rolled oats

Cream the butter and sugar, and add the egg. Sift together flour and baking soda and add this to the creamed mixture with the milk and vanilla. Fold in the rhubarb and strawberries. Pour into greased 9-by-11-inch pan. Blend topping ingredients until pea-sized with a pastry blender and sprinkle on top of the cake. Bake at 350 degrees F for 30 to 35 minutes.

HOT FUDGE PIE

1 stick butter
3 squares unsweetened chocolate
1 1/4 cups sugar
4 tbsp. flour
dash of salt
3 eggs, beaten
1 tsp. vanilla

Melt the butter and the unsweetened chocolate together. (You may use the microwave — just be sure to cover the bowl, as it will splatter. I use the old-fashioned pan-on-a-stove method.) To the melted butter and chocolate, add the sugar, flour, and salt. Mix thoroughly. Then add eggs and vanilla. Pour the batter into a greased 9-inch pie plate and bake at 350 degrees F for 20 to 25 minutes.

Serve warm with ice cream.

(Author's note: My friend Linda Juliani gave me this recipe and I've made it many times. It's perfectly fast and easy and yet has all the advantages of a homemade dessert. You can bake it while you eat dinner and then eat it hot out of the oven. With ice cream.)

MK's Screw the Roux Stew
(Courtesy of Mary Kay Hyde)

1 large onion, chopped
2–3 garlic cloves, minced
1 large green pepper, chopped
2 stalks celery, chopped
1/2 cup flour
1–1 1/2 tbsp. Tony Chachere's Creole Seasoning
28-oz. box organic chicken broth
28-oz. can chopped tomatoes, with juice or crushed tomatoes
shredded meat from 1 rotisserie chicken or baked chicken
10–14 oz. smoked chicken or turkey sausage, sliced
12 oz. frozen chopped okra
3/4 lb. Key West pink shrimp if desired
rice, cooked

Sauté the vegetables in olive oil until soft. In a separate frying pan, toast the dry flour over medium-low heat until browned. Stir this almost constantly so it doesn't burn. When it is nicely brown, add the Creole seasoning. Mix well and add this mixture to the sautéed vegetables in a large pot. Stir in the broth, tomatoes, chicken, sausage, and okra. Bring to boiling and reduce to a simmer. The longer it simmers, the better. Add shrimp just before serving and cook a few minutes until pink. Serve the stew over rice.

STEPMOM'S MEAT LOAF

1 1/2 lbs. ground beef (or beef and pork, organic preferred)

1/2 sleeve Ritz crackers, ground to crumbs

1 large onion, finely chopped

1 green pepper, finely chopped

3 large carrots, peeled and chopped fine in food processor

1 egg

1/2 jar Bone Suckin' barbecue sauce, more for glaze

2 tbsp. Lipton's onion soup mix

Preheat oven to 350 degrees F. Mix meat well with all the other ingredients, reserving some sauce for topping. Shape the mixture into a loaf in a 9-by-13-inch glass baking pan. Bake for 1 1/4 to 1 1/2 hours, until meat is no longer pink. Drain grease halfway through baking; douse loaf with BBQ sauce and return to oven.

Serve meat loaf with mashed potatoes or oven-roasted potatoes and carrots and a green vegetable or salad.

NIKKI BONANNI'S GRANDMOTHER'S POTATO GNOCCHI

4–5 potatoes
4 or more cups of flour
3 to 4 eggs, depending on size
1 tsp. salt

Boil potatoes with skins. Cool. Peel. Put through ricer.

Make well with the four cups of flour. Break eggs into the middle of the well one at a time, beat, and mix them into the flour. Add salt.

Add riced potatoes a little at a time. Knead the ball of dough until not sticky, adding flour as necessary. Cut the dough into 6 pieces and roll these into long logs 1/2 inch in diameter. Cut into 1-inch pieces.

To make gnocchi, push down on each piece with two fingers, then roll them into hollow logs. Drop them into a large pot of boiling, salted water without crowding. They are done when they rise to the surface — about three minutes. Do not overcook. Serve hot with butter and grated parmesan or with the sauce of your choice.

(At Louie's Backyard, they were served with oxtail stew.)

ABOUT THE AUTHOR

Clinical psychologist Roberta Isleib, a.k.a. **Lucy Burdette**, has had nine previous mysteries published. Her books and stories have been short-listed for Agatha, Anthony, and Macavity awards. She is a past president of Sisters in Crime and blogs with seven other mystery writers at www.junglered writers.com.

CONNECT ONLINE
www.lucyburdette.com
facebook.com/lucyburdette
twitter.com/lucyburdette